MEASURE OF
STRENGTH

CAETHES FARON

ISBN-13: 978-0615718354
ISBN-10: 0615718353

MEASURE OF STRENGTH

CHAPTER ONE

"Get me another one, Terry." Jason lifted his empty glass toward the bartender. Whiskey number six hadn't done it. Maybe number seven would take away the pain.

"I think that's enough, Mr. Wadsworth."

Dammit, he was going to have to get up. The table in the back corner of Flannigan's was a long walk from the bar, and it would take some effort to make it in such a way as to convince Terry to give him number seven. Luckily, there weren't many patrons, so there were fewer obstacles in his way.

The nice thing about the corner table was that it had a handy wall to grab onto for support. Jason needed it. He lurched to his feet, steadied himself a moment, and then staggered to the bar as fast as he could in the glow of the gas lamps without the swaying floor rising up to meet his nose.

"Terry, I asked for another one." The salty smell of peanuts wafted to his nose, and he grabbed a few to munch on while he waited for his drink.

The bartender's face, wrinkled and tough like old leather, swam into Jason's view. "And I said no, Mr. Wadsworth."

"Come on, isn't my money good here?"

"Of course, but I think you've had enough for today. Why don't you go on home? I can have a cabbie pull a carriage around, and you can come back tomorrow."

1

Home. Hah. What did he know? An empty house wasn't home. That table in the corner felt more like home than the fancy townhouse ever had.

"I'll pay double. I'm a very wealthy man, Terry, one of the wealthiest in Perdana, in all of Arine. I'll buy this whole damn bar!" Jason swung his arm to make his point. The force of the swing was enough to unbalance Jason, and he landed on a barstool with a thwack. "Don't you want my money?"

"I'm wealthy enough." Terry wiped down the bar, clearly not understanding the seriousness of whiskey number seven.

"So tell me, what's the point of being wealthy if I can't drink as much as I like?"

"You may drink as much as you want at home, Mr. Wadsworth, but if you're going to drink here, you'll abide by my rules, and I say you've had enough." Another patron seated himself at the bar, and Terry moved to serve him.

Jason seized Terry's arm as it passed. Terry looked at him, and Jason sobered up as much as he could as he looked into the old bartender's eyes, needing Terry to understand. "Please, I need to stay here. Just a little longer. I need to remember."

The lines around Terry's eyes softened, and he patted Jason's hand where it rested on his arm. "I know. You're welcome to stay as long as you like, but I won't be serving you any more tonight."

Oh well, they both knew whiskey number seven wouldn't have done it anyway. Jason snatched a handful of nuts and made his way back to the table. The wood was familiar under his hands. If he closed his eyes, he could see Kale sitting across from him. The sandy blond hair, the pale green eyes, so intense, the only eyes that had ever penetrated Jason. Memory flooded him. Kale had looked good that night, even better than usual. They had laughed, and for a moment, Jason had been able to pretend that Kale wasn't his slave.

A thud startled Jason, and he opened his eyes to see a glass of water. Kale was gone, and the pain stabbed his gut.

Kale would never be there again. Jason had sold him to save him from the monster Jason was.

"Thank you." Jason looked up at Terry as he reached for the water. The cool liquid helped, probably more than a whiskey would have.

"You're welcome, lad." Terry paused, and Jason could see he wanted to say something else. Jason gave him a nod of encouragement, and Terry eased into the opposite chair. "You know you're welcome here any time, but why do you keep torturing yourself?"

Jason smirked and gave a bitter little laugh. "Torture? This isn't torture." Jason took another gulp of water and kept his eyes lowered. "I'm a monster, Terry. I kill everything I touch. You shouldn't be worried about me. It's you you should be worried for."

Terry laughed, and the sound grated on Jason's nerves. "Oh, you'd never hurt a living soul, Mr. Wadsworth."

"But I did, Terry. I hurt the people closest to me."

"I know the story, lad. It's time you be moving on from it. You can't keep doing this to yourself."

"Yes, I can." Jason looked up and met Terry's eyes, daring the man to question him.

Terry grunted and left. Jason returned to his water, finishing it. Staying here was better than going home. Here, he could at least have a little comfort from the nice memory this table held. At home there were no warm memories. It was just an empty house. Renee wasn't there—thank the gods for that. At least she had been able to escape him before he could do too much damage. He wasn't drinking for Renee.

Jason closed his eyes again and sat back, wanting to drown himself in the memory no matter how much it hurt. In his mind's eye he saw Kale sitting in the bar with him, dressed in a formal dinner suit. He looked good in it. Soon that memory morphed into another: taking off Kale's clothes, kissing him, making love to him. Jason opened his eyes with a start and clenched the empty glass in front of him so hard he thought it might break. He wished it would.

They weren't making love; Kale was a slave, and Jason had coerced him into bed. He was a rapist. A monster. Everyone he loved ended up hurt. He lowered his head to the table in despair and banged his fist against the wood, craving a physical pain to match his emotional one. When he closed his eyes, he conjured up the only picture that gave him any kind of peace: Kale looking back at him at the dealer's, just after he had been sold. It was the last picture Jason had of him, and there was sadness and a hope in Kale's eyes that was imprinted on Jason's soul. Jason shared Kale's hope for a better future. The sadness would be wiped out when he was sold to an owner who wouldn't brutalize him as Jason had. Kale had a chance at a future, and that was all the comfort Jason allowed himself.

Opening his eyes, Jason reached for a drink, only to remember that he didn't have one. He looked to the bar, gauging whether or not Terry might be persuaded to give him just one more, but his eyes stopped at the doorway.

"Damn." Even in the dim gas lighting, Jason knew that tall, thin frame could only belong to one man: Martin Grimlock.

CHAPTER TWO

Martin knew he had been spotted. As always, it was a question of whether or not Jason was going to make him go to him. The dirty tables and even dirtier patrons were familiar, though he wished they weren't. Jason owned the biggest steel business in the country. Why, when there were dozens of perfectly respectable places in Perdana for Jason to drink, was it always this one?

Martin saw the muscles clench as Jason set his jaw and looked away. It was going to be one of those nights. Martin picked his way to the corner table, practically prancing in his effort not to touch or be touched by anyone or anything that was crawling in such a place.

"Come along, sir. It's time to go."

"No, I want to stay. Terry says I can." Jason looked around Martin to Terry, and Martin followed his gaze. Terry rolled his eyes and gave him a hopeless shrug.

"I cut him off a little while ago, Mr. Grimlock."

"Thank you." Martin rested his hand on Jason's shoulder, hoping the firmness of the action would persuade Jason to be agreeable. Instead, Jason shrugged it off and glared up at him, eyes narrowed.

"Go away." It would be easy for a lesser man to leave it at that, but Martin knew he needed to get Jason home. Just the thought of the scandal it would cause if anyone discovered

Jason Wadsworth passed out at a bar sent a shudder through Martin.

"I can't do that. It's my job to take care of you, if you'll just let me." Coaxing sometimes worked.

"My wife hired you. I never wanted you here."

"Still, I'm here just the same. Now come on." Martin gestured toward the door and was relieved to see Terry supporting him.

"Why don't you listen to Martin here, and let him help you home? I'm closing up. You'd have to be leaving soon, anyway." Martin shot Terry a grateful look. If there was any way to get Jason out of there, it would take both of them.

Jason looked at Terry as if weighing his words and seeing what his options were. Martin knew Jason liked Terry, and now that he'd been cut off for a little while, he might be sober enough to want to save face. Eventually Jason nodded, and Martin released the breath he'd been holding. Tonight, he had gotten a break.

Jason stumbled to his feet, and Martin grabbed his arm and threw it over his shoulder.

"Do you need any help?" Terry asked.

"No, we'll be all right. Thank you." Martin could never bring himself to use Terry's first name—it was too informal —yet the bartender had never given his family name. He led Jason out to the waiting carriage.

"How long have you been my secretary, Martin?"

"Over two and a half years, sir."

"And when, during all that time, have I ever made it seem like I want you to stop me when I'm drinking?"

Martin helped Jason into the cab and followed him in. "Never, sir."

"Exactly." Jason stared out the window while the driver clucked to the horses, and the carriage pulled away. After a moment of silence, Jason turned to him. "It's been three years, Martin." Jason's face crumbled, and Martin felt the familiar tug on his heartstrings as he watched his boss, a titan of industry, transform into the forlorn man before him. "Three years since I proposed to her and lost everything."

Martin didn't fully understand Jason. These drunken statements were all he had. Sober, Jason never confided in Martin. These little slip-ups were the only glimpses he had. There was a deep pain in Jason, and Martin often wondered if talking about it might do him some good. He wished Jason would talk to someone, even if it wasn't him.

Back at the house, Martin helped Jason up to his room on the third floor. For the thousandth time, he thought how much more convenient it would be if Jason would keep one of the rooms on a lower floor, but his employer inhabited the third floor precisely because it was the furthest.

Once inside Jason's room, Martin began stripping off Jason's clothes. As usual, Jason fought.

"I'm quite the competent businessman, I'll have you know. I don't need a damn sitter." Jason pushed Martin away and landed on the bed. It was tempting to leave him there, but his clothes smelled of cigarettes and cheap alcohol and needed cleaning. Burning would be more appropriate, but Jason wouldn't approve of such wastefulness. Martin didn't want Jason waking up in the morning with the smell as a reminder of where he'd been and what he'd done. Starting the day fresh would make life easier for all concerned.

Jason seemed to realize this as well, because this time he didn't bat Martin away when he came to undress him. "I don't need you." Jason protested with words instead of actions this time. "If there was a way to keep my wife's family happy and not have you around, I'd fire you." The words hurt, but Martin had heard them before. To be honest, he understood Jason's stance. If their positions were switched, he'd resent him too. It couldn't be a good feeling, knowing your wife's family didn't trust you on your own. Still, after all this time, he had hoped Jason would realize that Martin worked for him, not the Arlingtons.

It never took long to get Jason into bed once he had

given up the physical fight and taken to spewing fire instead. His passionate resentment of Martin always tired him out, and Jason was snoring by the time Martin had gathered up his clothes and left.

The house was quiet as Martin descended the stairs. His room was on the second floor, but he would go to the basement first to drop off the clothes in the laundry. Sophie would see to them in the morning. He glanced at her room and saw that her light was off. No sense waking her if he didn't have to.

On the way back to his room, Martin made his usual rounds, making sure the lights were all off and everything was in its proper place. Martin always worried the newfangled electric lights would burn the house down while everyone slept. In the parlor, he spotted the decanter of scotch. He could use a drink, but Jason drank enough for the both of them, and he'd need a clear head tomorrow. Better to just go to bed.

Two and a half years Martin had worked for Jason Wadsworth, ever since Jason's father-in-law had died. Jason and his wife had agreed after less than six months of marriage that is was easier to stay married if they were separated. Two and a half years, and Jason was still as much a mystery as he had been on that first day. The urge to help him was just as strong. There was so much more to Jason than the drunk Martin had escorted home. If only Jason would let him in, confide in him. He longed for Jason's trust. Maybe tomorrow would be the day he gained it.

CHAPTER THREE

Jason tried to concentrate on his papers, but the pounding in his head drowned out his thoughts. Sometimes, he thought the pounding headache the next morning was part of why he drank so much. The pain was the least of what he deserved for what he'd done in his life.

He reached for the coffee Sophie had left on his desk for him. Thank the gods she hadn't left food. Just the thought of breakfast made him want to retch. The smell of her strong coffee, on the other hand, made him feel better even before the bitter taste had a chance to distract him from the throb.

Just when he thought he had beat back his headache enough to focus on this report on operations at an iron mine —a recent investment—a loud knocking on the door brought the pain right back to the forefront.

"Come in." Jason swore Martin did that on purpose. He knew the older man looked down on him for drinking and no doubt delighted in making his morning after headaches worse.

"Good morning, sir." Martin stopped in front of his desk and waited for Jason to wave him into a seat.

"Yes, it is a good morning, Martin." Jason waited as Martin settled in his seat and retrieved his calendar. When he was ready, he met Jason's eyes, and there was a moment where Jason wondered if the secretary would mention anything about the previous night.

"I have quite a few calendar items to go over with you, if you'd like to start there," Martin said. Good man. His sense of propriety was one thing Jason could always count on.

"Actually, I want to talk to you about this report from the Macino Mining Company. It looks as though their iron production is over twenty-five percent above what they anticipated. Seems they hit a deposit they weren't expecting."

"That's excellent news." Martin grinned as he made a note.

"Yes, it is. I want to move ahead with the plans to install another blast furnace at the north mill. This will give us the supply we need to increase production out of the new south mill, and perhaps Renee's family will stop second guessing every decision I make." When he had announced plans to build a mill near the shipyards on the southern coast, Renee's family had thrown a fit. They saw him throwing away their little girl's money. Jason was in it for the long haul, though, and he knew being able to supply the shipyards without expensive freight charges would pay off. He had just needed enough low-cost iron to produce the volume necessary to make it profitable.

"And we're going to be getting the iron for what? Ten percent below market value?" Martin lifted his pen.

"No, my investment contract says I get it for fifteen percent below for the next three years."

"Let's see…with the new supply driving the cost down," Martin scribbled some figures in his planner, "we should come in with a nice profit this year, even with the outlay you've made."

"I want you to outline this in a memo and disperse it to the interested parties. Make sure Renee's mother knows that her daughter won't be a pauper next year after all."

"You shouldn't let Mrs. Arlington bother you. She doesn't have any idea what she's talking about. I've never doubted you. Everything you've done since you inherited has

10

increased production and profit."

"I don't care whether you doubted me or not. You're my secretary. What I do care about is not getting surprise visits from my hysterical mother-in-law." Jason knew he was being unfair to Martin—the man was just trying to help—but he couldn't let himself get close to his secretary. The only reason his life worked at all was because he kept his personal and professional selves distinctly separate. Which was why they never spoke of the nights when Martin had to help him into bed.

"I understand, sir. I'll send a note to her brother and make sure he explains it to her very carefully."

"Good. Now, for the calendar."

"Yes. I've gotten quite a few invitations that need responses. The first is the Historical Preservation Society. They are having a gala the night of the sixteenth and request your presence."

"They don't want me there. Lady Grayson looks at me like I'm something that slithered in from the gutter. They just want my money. Send a note with my regrets along with a check for my yearly donation."

"Very well." Martin made a note of it. "There's also an invitation to Mrs. Carson's garden party—"

"No."

"Mr. Darby is having a—"

"No."

"Lord Masterson—"

"Definitely not."

"You really should make an effort to socialize more."

Jason raised his eyebrows at Martin. "What I don't need is my secretary telling me what I should do."

"Are you going to say yes to any of these?"

"I don't know. Give me something interesting, something that will actually benefit me, and I might." Jason stood up and paced around his office while he listened to Martin rattle off more names of people who had invited him to different affairs. All people who couldn't stand Jason and simply wanted to benefit from his presence as an influential man. He knew these social games all too well and had tired of playing them more than three years ago.

He moved to the window behind his desk and peered out to the garden below. It had not been tended since he'd moved in and was in disarray. Jason liked it. It had a kind of wild beauty. Besides, hiring a gardener was a waste when he knew he would never go outside to enjoy it.

"Wait," a name had caught Jason's ear, and he turned back to Martin, "who was that last one?"

"Lord Conrad, sir. He has given you an open invitation to visit him at his country house."

"Does it say why? Any special reason?"

Martin quickly scanned the invitation. "Just says he's interested in talking to you about how business is going."

"Accept." Jason sat back down at his desk, rummaging for his notebook. When he looked at Martin, the other man was staring at him with raised eyebrows. "He's thinking about getting into shipbuilding. He's been eyeing one of the shipyards on the southern coast for a while now."

Jason saw the realization dawn on Martin's face. "And you knew that when you decided to put a mill there."

The smile came automatically to Jason's lips. Being good at this was satisfying. "Yes, I did."

"That's a pretty big gamble. He still might not move forward."

Jason shrugged. "Even if he doesn't, it was a good move. If he does, though, he'll likely become our biggest buyer. Lord Conrad doesn't do anything half-heartedly."

"No, he doesn't. When should I say you can arrive?"

"I'm scheduled to inspect the northern mill soon, correct?"

Martin glanced at his calendar to confirm. "Yes, you are."

"Write to him, and let him know that I will be there the day before."

"It's not exactly on the way."

"No, but it will save us a trip. We can rely on his hospitality to stay the night and be to the mill in time for lunch."

"Are you sure you only want to stay for a day? The invitation is open."

"A day is all it will take. Any longer and I'm more likely to mess it up than to get his business. Don't want to wear out the welcome."

"I'll make sure to send your reply today, sir."

"Good. Is there anything else?" Jason examined the mail on his desk.

"No, sir." Martin got up and walked to the door. He turned back to Jason. "One last thing. Will you be going to the park today, sir? Sophie wants to know if she should pack a lunch or serve it to you here."

Jason's mind had already moved on to an envelope in front of him. "Oh." He glanced over his shoulder and out the window at the clear blue sky. "Yes, I think I will. Thank you."

Martin nodded and left. Once the door was shut behind him, Jason looked at the envelope that had taken his attention. Opening it, he leaned back to read the latest news from Renee.

CHAPTER FOUR

Jason had seemed fine when Martin left him, but a few hours later, Jason rang for him and told him to inform Sophie he'd be taking lunch in his office. There was no mistaking Jason's agitated look; he was going to go out drinking tonight.

Sure enough, after dinner Martin saw Jason make his way to the front door. He didn't want a repeat of the previous night. Flannigan's was a mess. Martin hated thinking about Jason getting drunk there and loathed having to fetch him when he didn't make it home at a decent hour. The thought of walking through that slimy bar pushed him to action.

"Sir?" Martin stepped toward Jason, and by the way Jason started, it was clear he had been absorbed in whatever dark thoughts led him to drink so much.

"What is it, Martin?" The words were harsh and short, and Martin knew he could be making their tenuous relationship worse.

"Why don't you stay in tonight?"

"Because I'm going out. Is there something you actually need, or are you just wasting my time?"

"Please, don't go back to that bar tonight. It's not right for a man of your standing to be seen there, and I don't want to have to come get you again."

Jason whirled on him. "No one asked you to come and get me last time, Martin. This is none of your business."

"But why go there? What draw does that place have?"

"I can talk freely there."

"You can talk freely with me."

Jason scoffed, and the bitterness in his eyes stung. "There's no way you could understand. I'm not pouring my heart out to you. You're a business associate, nothing more. Stop trying to be anything else."

"All I've ever wanted is to be your friend. You could sure use one."

There was a flash of sadness in Jason's eyes that would have been easy to miss had Martin not been so used to seeing it. "You clearly don't know me very well."

"I know you better than you think, and I'm always here if you want to talk."

"No, you don't know any of the pertinent details, Martin, and I'm not going to burden you with it."

There it was: his opening. Every once in a while, Jason let down his guard, and Martin could see just how much his employer cared about the people around him. "Fine. But please don't burden me with having to go get you tonight. You know it will just be a repeat of last night, and it's supposed to rain." Martin hated bringing up the previous night, but he didn't like seeing what that place did to Jason. Hopefully the lie about the weather would hold. If Jason was feeling ashamed enough, he would let it stand.

"Fine. I'll stay here and drink in my study." Jason turned without even looking at Martin and headed to the second floor. Martin sighed. It was better than the alternative, but not by much.

Heading down to the kitchen, he peeked into the parlor to see if it was clean. He walked to the fireplace and ran his finger along the intricately carved cherubs flanking the rosewood mantle. It came away dusty, and Martin grimaced. The first floor was rarely used—made up as it was of only formal rooms meant for entertaining. Still, it should be kept clean. There was no telling when it might be needed. A similar inspection of the rest of the floor resulted in the same. No large messes, but a general coating of dust.

"Sophie, do you need any help in here?" From the kitchen doorway, Martin could see their cook-cum-housekeeper was covered in flour, preparing bread dough for the morning.

Sophie blew a stray strand of blonde hair out of her eyes. "Aye, I can always use a hand or two."

Rolling up his sleeves, Martin came to stand next to her and sunk his hands into the lump of dough that Sophie lobbed in front of him. "The dust is starting to build up on the first floor again."

Sophie turned her rich brown eyes on him, and Martin wished he had kept his mouth shut. Sophie may have been a small woman, but she could make a man cower when she had a mind to. "Well, I'm sorry, your highness, but most houses don't rely on one woman to do all the cooking and cleaning. You can have dust in the parlor, or you can have starched clothes and warm meals. You can't have it all. I'll get around to it when I get around to it."

Martin held up his hands in surrender. "You're right, Sophie. I'm sorry. I should be a better help to you."

"I didn't mean to snap at you." Sophie turned back to the dough, and Martin followed suit. "I know you have your hands full. What is Mr. Wadsworth up to tonight?"

"Drinking in his study."

"Dear gods, I didn't realize he was that bad off."

"I'm just glad I won't have to go fetch him from that disgusting bar."

"I'm not sure the study is much better. It must drive you crazy thinking of all the dust that has to be in that room." Sophie laughed, and Martin let himself smile at her attempt at humor. There was certainly nothing funny about Jason's study. It could more aptly be named the drinking room.

"No, oddly it doesn't bother me that much. Probably because I've never seen it." Martin shrugged and went back to kneading.

"Well then, can you not look in the rooms we don't use and forget about them too?" Sophie smiled and took his ball of dough, placing it in a bread pan next to hers. "Go pour yourself a cup of tea, and we'll sit and talk some while these rise."

Tension Martin hadn't even known he had left his body as the warmth of the tea spread. When Jason got in these depressions, it was always stressful.

"Don't worry, it never lasts long." Sophie sat opposite him with her own cup of tea. Her girlish features were framed by a few loose strands of blonde hair. She was the only woman his own age he associated with. If she had been born to his class, he might have seen himself marrying her. Then again, she was a foreigner.

"How'd you know what I was thinking?" Sometimes Martin felt as if she was the only person who understood him.

"You always get tense when he's like this."

"I just wish I could help him."

"You can't help someone who doesn't want it." Sophie took a sip.

Martin tried to take comfort in the tea, but his mind raced. "I guess it would be easier if I had any idea what gets him like this."

"That man is holding on to more secrets than anyone I've ever met."

Martin considered that while he drank. "It's something to do with his wife. Only it's strange that he can seem so friendly toward her if she's the force behind his depression."

"Stop trying to figure it out. He'll either tell you or he won't; there's no sense worrying about it."

"Oh, and is that why you were kneading more dough than we'll need for a week when I walked in?" Martin smiled as Sophie's face reddened.

"Well, I worry about him too." Sophie hid her face

18

behind her tea cup until the blush passed. "How was it getting him home last night?"

"A struggle. You were asleep by the time we got back."

"You going to stay up and help him to his room when he's done?"

"No, I'll just stay here with my tea until I'm tired. If I hear him stumbling about, I'll help him up." They both knew it was a lie, but Sophie was kind enough not to comment. Martin always helped once Jason tumbled out of the study, locking it behind him. Martin knew everything about this house except what was in that room. That didn't bother him nearly so badly as not knowing what went on in Jason's mind.

Sophie washed her cup and put it away. Then she came back over and placed a hand too rough for her young age on his shoulder. "Try not to let it bother you. It'll be better tomorrow."

And that was part of the problem. Tomorrow, Jason would go back to acting like nothing was wrong.

CHAPTER FIVE

"I need you to take dictation."

Martin situated himself with his pen and paper. "I'm ready, sir."

Jason nodded. Last night in the study had felt good. It was a special torment for him, drinking alone in that room. It was where all his demons came out to play, and now they were safely tucked away for the day. There was no chance they would interrupt him in his work. If they began to hammer at him, he knew he could at least put them off until night.

"My dearest Renee." Jason smiled and began to walk around the office when Martin looked briefly up at him. He knew Martin thought Renee was the source of his late night drinking sessions. The man had been trying to put it all together for years. If he were to look in the study, though, he wouldn't find a trace of Renee there. "It was sweet of you to remember me on the anniversary of our engagement. You're a dear for worrying about me, but I assure you I am fine. The business is running better than even I could have hoped for. It's going to be an excellent year.

"It sounds as if your time at the coast has been delightful. How fortunate that you were able to find a guide to show you the ruins. I'm sure you've been busy reading up on their history." This was one of the best parts of Jason's existence.

With everything he'd been through, at least he hadn't ruined Renee's life. She was free to live out her dreams, and he took some joy in that thought.

Martin cleared his throat, indicating that he had caught up, and Jason continued. "Of course you may use the country house in Timar. Someone should, it's beautiful. I'll telephone the butler so it's prepared for your arrival."

"Will you be joining her there, sir?"

Jason gave him a baleful stare. "No." Why Martin insisted on asking questions he knew the answers to in an effort to annoy him, he would never know.

"It might do you some good to spend some time with Mrs. Wadsworth."

"Don't confuse the value I place on your penmanship with value as a confidant." Jason saw the pain flash in Martin's eyes. He didn't like hurting the man. He knew Martin ached to be a trusted advisor, but it was better for everyone if they weren't close.

"Now, back to the letter." Jason resumed his pacing. "I hope you enjoy your summer. I shall be busy with the business, but it is work I enjoy. I look forward to your next letter, no doubt detailing some of your adventures in Timar. Until then, your caring husband."

"Yes." Martin finished writing and looked over at Jason. "I'll have this sent out today."

Jason crossed back to his desk and took his seat. "What other business do we have today?"

"We have to discuss the preparations for the trip to Lord Conrad's and the mill. I'm trying to get a list of what we'll need. Which cufflinks will you be wanting to wear to dinner?"

Really? That's what Martin thought constituted business? "I don't care."

"And what about traveling clothes? I think something a little nicer than we were planning for the trip to the mill is in order."

"Martin, I don't care."

"It's important to make a good impression on Lord Conrad."

"Lord Conrad couldn't care less what cufflinks I have on at dinner, and I guarantee you he doesn't care what I show up wearing."

"There are certain rules that govern these kinds of social events."

"Dammit." Jason slammed his palm on his desk. "I'm not going to socialize, Martin. I'm going to do business. No one wants to socialize with me, and I'll not go prancing around like a peacock. Pack whatever you want. All I care is that it's tasteful and appropriate. Lord Conrad wouldn't have me in his house unless he thought he could benefit from doing business with me. Let's not pretend this is something it isn't."

"All right, I'll take care of it."

"Good. Now is there anything else?"

"No, sir."

"Fine. Make sure that letter gets out today, and tell Sophie I'll be going to the park for lunch."

"Yes, sir." Martin stood and left.

Alone in his office, Jason went to the window. It was another beautiful day. Renee was happy, and that gave him some peace. He would endure the visit to Lord Conrad's because it was his duty. Besides, he was good at this. Ever since he had stopped concerning himself with the silly social games the aristocracy played, he had begun to view them from a distance. The perspective gave him an advantage. It was easy to see which moves to make when you didn't care about the outcome, and Jason had stopped caring a long time ago.

CHAPTER SIX

The sweet taste of the wine barely registered. Jason wanted the bitter fire of something stronger, but he'd have to wait until after dinner. Lord Conrad had invited some friends and associates to join them for the evening. It was a courtesy Jason could have done without. No business could be discussed during dinner, and the other guests meant it would take longer to get through the meal and conversation.

When Lady Conrad was done speaking, he laughed automatically with the others. "That's quite the story, Lady Conrad."

"And it's all true!" Lord Conrad said from the end of the table, leading to another chorus of chuckles.

"This wine is excellent. Wherever did you get it?" Jason took another sip.

"This comes from our very own winery. My wife has quite a knack for it. I can't tell two grapes apart, but she is positively brilliant. Been overseeing the whole operation for the last twenty-some years." Of course, Jason already knew this, but the flattered, sheepish smile on Lady Conrad's face had been his goal.

"That's extraordinary, Lady Conrad. I propose a toast to our resident vintner and connoisseur." The rest of the table raised their glasses, and when Jason met Lady Conrad's eyes, he could see his work was done. She saw him as the consummate guest and would no doubt be talking about the charming Mr. Wadsworth for some time.

Dinner dragged on, and Jason did his best to endure it with a smile. Some members of parliament and even the king's nephew were present. The conversation was full of flattery and gossip, none of which interested Jason. The only people he cared about were Lord and Lady Conrad and the potential business he could do with them.

Finally the dessert was cleared away, and Lord Conrad stood, tossing his napkin onto the table. "Ladies, if you will excuse us, I believe there are cigars and brandy awaiting us in the smoking room." He nodded to the other gentleman, and they left.

Jason rose to join them, but on his way to the door, he stopped by Lady Conrad and took her hand, placing it to his lips. "Thank you for a most excellent evening, my lady. I enjoyed it immensely." Her eyes sparkled at the compliment. Beneath the graying hair and soft wrinkles, she was a handsome woman. The perfect wife for a man of Lord Conrad's standing.

Martin joined him on his way out. The feeling that his secretary looked down on him was accentuated by the fact that the man's thin frame was several inches taller than Jason's. His hair and eyes were an ordinary shade of brown, as if even they adhered to propriety by refusing to be an outlandish color. Those brown eyes were looking at him like Martin was surprised Jason knew how to behave in public. It was irritating. It seemed Martin would never understand the difference between business and pleasure.

In the smoking room, Jason accepted the cigar Lord Conrad handed him. He had never been fond of the habit; it reminded him of his father. Still, he knew how to smoke, and he wouldn't turn away the generosity. Martin on the other hand, lit up at the offer. He loved to smoke, but Jason had forbidden it when the secretary came to live with him. At least someone would enjoy the evening.

After the small talk was over, Lord Conrad turned to Jason. "I assume you know why I invited you here tonight, other than for the pleasure of your company, of course."

"Of course," Jason said.

"I'm considering becoming a shipbuilder. I've always loved ships, and I want to build great big luxury liners, the likes of which no one has ever seen."

"If there's any man who can do it, it's you."

"I have my eye on a shipyard on the southern coast."

Jason kept his expression neutral. "I had heard."

"I noticed you have a new steel mill there."

"Yes, I do."

"I'll be needing a supplier; seems logical to talk to the man next door." Conrad nodded at Jason.

"I am the closest, but that's not why you're going to do business with me."

"Really?" A smile tugged at the corner of Lord Conrad's mouth, and Jason could tell the lord found his arrogance amusing. It wasn't arrogance, though; it was the confidence of knowledge.

"Really. You're going to do business with me because I can supply you with enough steel to build a whole fleet. No one else can promise you that."

"How do you mean?"

"Well, as I'm sure you know, we don't mine a lot of iron in Arine. We rely on foreign imports, mainly from Panea."

"Panean mines account for over seventy percent of Arine's iron," Martin interjected. Jason grinned. This was why he kept the secretary around. He was always handy with the numbers and figures to support what Jason said.

"Exactly. Now, you may be aware that there's some unrest in Panea. They're on the brink of war over disputes at their northern border. The prime minister will soon be ordering that all iron stay in the country to support their own steel production. When that happens, the steel mills here in Arine are going to find themselves without an adequate

27

supply. They can try to buy locally, or they can pay inflated prices from Naiara."

"So how am I better off with you?"

"Ah, well a little over a year ago, I made an investment in an up and coming mining operation. The terms of my investment give me certain advantageous options in buying any resulting ore from the mine. They have just hit a new deposit, and production is going to far exceed their projections." Jason leaned forward in his chair and waited until Lord Conrad mirrored the motion. "And I just bought it. All of it."

The admiration in Lord Conrad's eyes was impossible to miss. "It looks as if your youth hides a cunning mind, Mr. Wadsworth."

Jason couldn't help smiling as he sat back in his chair. "Thank you."

Conrad laughed as he also leaned back, appraising Jason. "You're good, boy. You've certainly given me a lot to think about tonight. And saints know you charmed my wife. I doubt I'll hear the end of it until I invite you back."

"I'd be delighted to visit any time."

"Well, with business out of the way, what do you say we get a refill on our brandies?"

"I would love to. However, I'm afraid I must decline." Jason set his glass down on a nearby table and stood. "Martin and I must set off early tomorrow for a mill inspection." Martin rose with him.

"Quite right, I remember you telling me that. Still, what can one more hurt?"

Jason had to fight not to laugh. One more brandy wouldn't hurt him a bit. He just wanted to get back to his room so he could polish off the bottle of whiskey he had brought. "I must keep this cunning mind clear, Lord Conrad."

The older man chuckled and wagged his finger at Jason. "I admire your dedication, lad. There was a time when I was the same." Lord Conrad looked over his shoulder at one of the slaves standing against the wall, ready to serve. "You there, show Mr. Wadsworth and Mr. Grimlock to their rooms."

"Yes, master." The slave bowed and went for candles that were laid out on a side table for just this purpose. The wonders of electric lighting had yet to make it out to most country estates.

Lord Conrad stood and shook Jason's hand. "Have a good night. I won't see you in the morning, but you'll be hearing from me."

"Thank you, my lord. Please convey my thanks to your lovely wife for her hospitality."

"I will."

Jason nodded to the slave, who waited unobtrusively behind Martin with two candles, and they were led to their rooms.

CHAPTER SEVEN

"This is your room, Mr. Wadsworth." The slave opened the door and handed him one of the two candles.

"Thank you," Jason said. The small sparkle in the boy's eye gave away that he wasn't used to hearing those two words.

"I can find my own later." Martin waved a dismissive hand at the slave and took the offered candle. Jason narrowed his eyes at Martin. Why couldn't he just go to bed and let him be?

"Your room is the one next door, Mr. Grimlock," the slave said with a bow.

Another impatient wave from Martin, and the slave was gone. Martin turned his attention to Jason and spoke. "Don't give me that look. The last thing I need is you causing a scene with the slave who is undoubtedly waiting to attend you."

"I don't cause scenes with slaves. I'm more polite to them than you are."

"Hmph."

Jason pushed the door all the way open and entered the room. Standing in the middle of it was a man about his own age. Jason spoke directly to him. "Thank you, but your services are not needed tonight."

The slave looked up, and Jason could see the worry in his eyes.

31

"Sir, my master wanted me to wait on you tonight. I can draw you a bath, set out your clothes for tomorrow, help you undress."

"There's no need." The words didn't seem to reassure the slave. "You're in no trouble, I promise you. I just prefer to be alone." The slave's eyes darted to Martin, and Jason laughed. "Yes, my associate here has a hard time obeying orders. I'll be kicking him out too."

"Are you sure there's nothing I can do for you, sir?"

"I'm sure." Jason went up to the man and put a hand on his arm. "Please, I promise I'll make sure your master knows that it's not your fault you were sent away."

The slave bowed his head and left.

"It's going to be seen as a slight, you refusing Lord Conrad's hospitality." Martin spoke from just inside the doorway as Jason went about removing his waistcoat.

"What do I care? It's not something that will affect our future business relationship, and that's all you should be worried about." Jason looked around the room for his valise and found it next to a desk. Inside was his bottle of whiskey. If only Martin would leave, he could get to drinking it.

"That slave has reason to fear. You can bet he's the one who's going to suffer for it."

Jason strode to Martin, pointing a finger in his face. "No, because you're going to make sure he doesn't." Jason stayed poised with his finger mere inches from Martin's nose until Martin swallowed and nodded. Satisfied, Jason went to the bed and sat to take off his shoes.

"What is it you have against slaves?"

"I don't have anything against them. We use them in the mills. I will not take a personal slave. It's as simple as that. You're welcome to avail yourself of the one provided for you." Jason removed his shoes while Martin watched. When he was done, he made eye contact. Martin still didn't say anything. "Is there any reason you're still here, Martin?"

"Yes, I wanted to know how you knew about the Panean

prime minister."

Jason smirked as he removed one sock. "I didn't, but it sounded about right."

Martin laughed. "Aren't you worried he'll find out you were lying?"

Jason removed the other sock and laid both on top of his shoes. "No, he won't check. We'll have a deal before things get too bad in Panea. Rich people only fear one thing: not being as rich as they could be. The fear brought on by the possibility of missing out on a deal will drive him to act."

"That's an interesting opinion you have of the class to which you belong." Listening to Martin, Jason couldn't help thinking of the man who had taught him that opinion. "You don't seem to share the fear of losing wealth."

"No."

"Why?"

"I don't consider it my money. A wise man once told me that if you have nothing, you have nothing to fear." Jason wondered how true that was. Fears still lurked in dark corners of his mind. Shaking his head to clear it, he set about undoing his cufflinks.

"Well, I'm not willing to bet on fear alone. I'll have a thank you card ready to be mailed as soon as we get home. I'll also find out Lady Conrad's favorite wine and have it sent over."

Jason's mind was on the ghost who haunted him. Kale would have known Lady Conrad's favorite wine already. He would have known the right thing to say, how to get exactly what he wanted. It came naturally to him in a way it never would to Jason. "Gods, I miss him."

"Who?"

Jason whipped his head around toward Martin. Had he really spoken out loud? "Oh, no one."

Martin's eyes narrowed, and Jason knew he wouldn't let it go.

"Kale." It was peculiar hearing that name on Martin's

lips.

"What do you know about Kale?" His brow furrowed, and his voice was louder than it had been all night.

"Nothing, you won't tell me anything. But I hear you say his name. Was he a friend?"

The pressure built up behind Jason's eyes until something gave. He let out a breath, and his shoulders relaxed. "He was the best man I ever knew. He would have known exactly what to do tonight. He could read people like no one I've ever met."

"So that's where you learned it?"

The thought of comparing himself to Kale in any way was ludicrous, and Jason's eyes focused on Martin. What was he doing? He was not talking to a confidant, and he needed to remember it. "That's none of your business. Is that all, Martin?"

"Yes, sir. Remember we're leaving early tomorrow. We're scheduled to have lunch at the mill, and it's several hours from here. I'm sorry to have disturbed you."

"I'm sure you are," Jason said dryly.

Finally, Martin was gone. Jason went to his valise, fishing out the bottle of whiskey. He gave a sardonic chuckle as he unscrewed the lid. He wasn't anything like Kale. If he was, he wouldn't take such pleasure in the burn of the whiskey going down his throat. And he certainly wouldn't be planning to drink the rest of the bottle knowing the work ahead of him in the morning.

CHAPTER EIGHT

There was a tiny crease between Jason's eyes, deeper than the usual worry lines that marked his face. Martin always wondered what had caused them. Probably the same life experiences that gave his brown eyes the depth of a much older man. It was as if he had undergone a great ordeal, and these were the scars he bore. They were incongruous with his creamy skin that spoke of a privileged life.

A bump in the road caused the carriage to lurch and the crease deepened. The jostling must be wreaking havoc on his headache, Martin thought. He had become proficient in discerning the signs of a hangover in Jason. His employer kept himself together and never let on that his head was pounding, but Martin could tell. A part of him had hoped that the change of scenery would be enough to get Jason out of this latest bout of depression, but it had been a naïve hope. The man must have packed his own alcohol for the trip.

Jason was an enigma. How could a man so self-destructive be so good at his work? Martin wished to someday be as good a businessman as Mr. Wadsworth. He felt no shame in admitting that a man six years younger had a world of knowledge to teach him. If only Jason would let him in, let him learn. Who sitting at that dinner table last night would have guessed what Jason had been up to after he got to his room, or that he had to be forcibly removed from seedy bars with more frequency than Martin was comfortable with?

More mysterious than Jason's duality was his slip-up. Martin had heard the name Kale before, but only when Jason was either drunk or didn't know Martin could hear him. The little exchange last night was more personal than Jason had ever been with him. Even if it had only lasted for a moment, it was something.

Who was this Kale, and what had happened to him? The easy answer was that he was a lost lover. The thought of Jason ever having an intimate relationship tried to enter Martin's mind and failed. Perhaps Kale was a brother who had died. Martin knew nothing about Jason's family, other than that he didn't have contact with them. A dead sibling could be the reason for that.

"It's not polite to stare."

Martin hadn't noticed Jason's eyes settling on him. "I'm sorry, sir. I wasn't really. More like I was lost in thought." He didn't know where he was expected to rest his gaze. Jason's bench had windows, but Martin's didn't. He could either look at the plain black walls or at Jason.

"Hmph. Thinking about what?"

"Our agenda for the day." The truth could only make the next several hours in the small coach uncomfortable. "Wondering if we'll really be working with Lord Conrad. What it will mean if we do. Those kinds of things."

"Well, there's no sense in thinking about Conrad. He's either going to become a shipbuilder and buy from us, or he's not. I think he is, but if you don't, that's fine. It doesn't make a difference either way. If he buys from us, Arlington Steel will go from being the largest steel company in the country to the largest on the continent. Our lives won't change at all, so there's no use fretting about it."

For a man who was so good at acquiring money, Jason was certainly blasé about it. He was right. Looking at Jason's life, there was no way to tell he was one of the wealthiest men in Arine. If his lifestyle didn't reflect his current fortune, there was no reason to think that adding to his wealth would cause any significant change.

"You're right, as always. Would you like to go over today's agenda?"

"If you feel it's necessary."

Jason didn't look at all interested, but at least this way the conversation wouldn't become awkward, and Martin wouldn't go back to staring. He picked up his leather-bound planner and found the appropriate pages.

"When we arrive, we'll be having lunch with the general manager, Mr. Jones; his secretary, Mr. Walnick; and the head foreman, Mr. Pernicky, who is in charge of the floor. We will then review operational and financial reports. Next, we'll hear how they've implemented changes since our last meeting and what they feel still needs to be addressed. At that time, we will also discuss plans for future expansion."

"So we're going to be in the offices all day?"

"Yes, sir. Tomorrow we'll do the walkabout and inspect operations firsthand. You also expressed interest in surveying the surrounding properties as potential sites for expansion."

"I want to do that first thing tomorrow. We'll do the walkabout after."

"Very well, sir." Martin jotted a note to remind himself.

"I also want to meet with the shift supervisors and foremen after the walkabout. I want everyone to be on the same page with regard to how operations are to run."

Martin made another note. "I'll tell Mr. Jones as soon as we arrive."

After that, Jason turned to look out the window, effectively ending their conversation and sending Martin back into his speculations about his mysterious employer.

Maybe Jason's attitude toward Martin was a clue in itself. After all, if this Kale had been his secretary prior to Martin filling the post and things ended badly, some resentment toward the replacement would be understandable. Of course,

Kale had to have been more than just a secretary. That was it! Kale had been Jason's secretary, and they had started an affair. Then this Kale either left or died, leaving Jason a troubled man. It was the only explanation that made sense of everything: Jason's drinking, his bouts of depression, and his attitude toward Martin and people in general.

It was comforting to have solved the puzzle. Martin rested his head against the carriage wall and smiled with pride. Jason, as usual, paid him no mind.

CHAPTER NINE

"You've got the wit of a scholar and the humor of a sailor, Mr. Jones." Laughter shook Jason's body as he slapped Mr. Jones on the back.

The five men walked into the only office big enough to accommodate them all. A large, round table sat in the middle, and filing cabinets lined the walls. Everyone except Mr. Walnick took their seats, still laughing over the dirty jokes shared over lunch.

"Shall I get us all something to drink?" Mr. Walnick asked, standing by the open door.

"Just water, we'll save the harder stuff for after the work's done." Jason smirked and winked at Mr. Pernicky and Mr. Jones across the table. The other men chuckled, and the smile on Jason's face was not feigned. The dynamic with these men was so very different from the staid and proper dealings in Perdana.

Martin sat at Jason's right, fumbling through some papers. He had looked supremely uncomfortable during lunch. They had eaten at the inn where Jason and Martin were going to be staying for the night, and it wasn't the type of place Jason thought Martin would ever choose to patronize. There were nicer places in town, but Jason didn't see the point in spending more than necessary. He was there to do a job, and as long as he had a private room and bed at the end of the night, nothing else mattered.

Mr. Walnick came back in carrying a tray with a pitcher of water and five glasses right about the time Martin was done pulling out his notes and arranging himself for the meeting.

"Thank you, Mr. Walnick. Now that we're all settled, let's get started. The first thing I wanted to say is thank you. Productivity is up. Efficiency is up. Profit is up. Don't think for a minute that I take any credit for that. Compared to what you gentleman do every day, I have it easy. You make it easy. So take a moment to congratulate yourselves." Jason met the eyes of his head foreman first and then his general manager.

"Thank you, Mr. Wadsworth," Mr. Jones said. "We appreciate you noticing."

Jones was a brawny, middle aged man who had spent his whole life working first in mines and then steel mills, and he came from a long line of miners. It hadn't been a popular move when Jason came in and made him general manager. Such positions were usually reserved for men of higher social standing. Jason found that such men were out of touch with certain realities, and that led to waste and inefficient management. Jones might not have been traditionally educated, but he had a naturally quick mind and was eager to learn. His humility meant Jason could train him to run the mill the way he wanted, but his strength of character also meant he'd stand toe to toe with Jason if he thought the occasion warranted it. Jason found him to be a valuable asset.

"I do notice." Jason held his gaze a moment before turning to Mr. Pernicky. "This is your first inspection with us."

"Yes, sir. I trust you'll find we've followed your instructions adequately."

Pernicky was an entirely different creature from Jones. Pernicky was actually an employee of a labor firm—a company that hired out slave labor. Like every slave foreman Jason had known in his life, Pernicky looked as tough as the steel they milled. Jason didn't particularly like him, but as long as he did his job, Jason wouldn't complain.

"You realize your predecessor's firm was fired because of their inability to modify their procedures to fit the way I want my mills run."

"Yes, sir."

"Have you had any such difficulties?" Jason locked eyes with the man and watched as he fought an internal battle. The second Pernicky decided to speak his mind, Jason noticed. He had never been the best at reading people, but being as wealthy as he had been for the past several years, he had grown able to tell when a man was going to lie to appease him and when the man was going to speak his mind. Without knowing it, Pernicky had just risen a few notches in Jason's eyes.

"No, sir. I've made the necessary alterations to our regular procedures. I will admit it is strange, and it's a struggle. I'm used to having a free hand in my work."

"I understand. I know I'm a peculiar man."

"I could increase production and save you money if you let me have my way."

"How do you mean?"

"Every other place I've overseen, we've worked them twelve hours straight. They eat before work and after."

"And you don't approve of my methods?"

"Frankly? No. Having them stop for water breaks every hour instead of just passing a bucket ruins the momentum we build up. Breaking for lunch, again, breaks the momentum. It also makes them lazy the second half of the day."

"Hmm." Jason leaned back in his chair and surveyed Pernicky. No matter how long the silence went on, the man never fidgeted or looked away. Appearances weren't deceiving here. Pernicky really was as strong as the steel he produced. His honesty was welcome, and once again Jason's opinion of the foreman rose a few notches. "First, about the water. Did you know that, before I put that in place, we routinely lost at least one man a month to heat and thirst? It's

41

an oven down there."

"Surely that loss is acceptable. When it comes down to the lost production time and the money spent on food, I don't see how things are as good as you make them out to be."

"Well then, it's a good thing it's my money, isn't it?" Pernicky seemed to have nothing to say to that. Jason saw a man who was used to being good at his work and who took pride in his results. All Jason had to do was convince Pernicky that he was right. "Martin, why don't you show Mr. Pernicky the numbers?" Jason turned an expectant gaze on Martin.

"Of course." Martin rummaged for the appropriate papers. Once he found them, he slid them to Pernicky. "As you can see, we're producing more under Mr. Wadsworth's revised guidelines than under usual working conditions. The added cost is more than made up for by the increased output. When Mr. Wadsworth first proposed the idea, we did a study and found that the improved conditions produced an increase of over twelve percent per hour."

Pernicky pored over the numbers. In his eyes was the confusion of a man trying to accept evidence that the way he had always done things was wrong. "I hope this convinces you and makes your work easier for you," Jason said. A moment passed before he saw the confusion in the foreman's face clear.

"Aye, it does. Thank you. I admit to not understanding it, but there it is."

"You feed a man and, I swear by the gods, he'll work harder for you." It was a concept that Jason had not only tested and proved, but one he knew was innately right. Slaves were a part of life, especially in the higher classes, but they weren't subhuman. There was too much proof in Jason's experience to let him believe otherwise.

Mr. Pernicky handed the papers back to Martin, and he carefully tucked them away. Jason turned to Jones and spoke.

"We're moving ahead with the plans to install another blast furnace. There is even more reason to increase production now."

Jones quirked an eyebrow. "Oh, really?"

"Yes. I trust that you'll keep this confidential. We're going to be supplying Lord Conrad's new shipyard."

"Nothing's final yet," Martin hurried to inject.

Jason looked at Martin with narrowed eyes. "But it will be. It's just a matter of time." Turning back to Jones, he was all smiles. "We need to prepare now."

"So it's more than just a rumor that he'll be getting into the ship business?" Jones leaned forward in his chair.

"Others may think it's just a rumor, but he's going to take the plunge. I was with him yesterday, and there's no way that man doesn't close on a shipyard by the end of the year."

"But won't the southern mill be supplying him?" Jones asked.

"Of course, that's what the southern mill is there for, but you'll need to pick up the southern mill's current production load. I want them dedicated to the shipyards."

Jones's eyes widened, but he was too proud to object. Jason knew he wouldn't want to appear as if he were not up to the challenge; in fact, he counted on it. Instead, it was Mr. Walnick, Jones's fastidious secretary—the one who handled all the paperwork and tried to decrease Jones's stress level—who spoke up.

"But, sir, that's impossible!"

Jason wagged his finger at Walnick's bespectacled face. "Not impossible." Turning to the rest of the group, he added, "In addition to adding another blast furnace, we're going to add another shift. Instead of two twelve hour shifts, we're going to have three eight hour shifts."

Predictably, Pernicky couldn't stay silent. "Why cut the hours?"

"Because, Mr. Pernicky, this is the way I want it run. I think we can produce more with three shifts of fresh men

43

than with two exhausted shifts."

"But we can just use two shifts of men working eight hours back-to-back."

"We're going to be using three shifts. Eight hours between shifts is not enough, especially when transportation time is taken into consideration." The long working hours had been weighing on Jason. This change should have been made long ago.

"Please tell me we'll at least be cutting lunch now. There's no need for it with such a short shift."

"No. When you own the biggest steel company in the country, you're welcome to run your workers into the ground and get less production out of them. Until then, we'll continue to do it my way. I've already shown you proof that my methods are sound. You're going to have to trust me."

Pernicky nodded his understanding. "You're the boss."

The rest of the meeting was spent going over the finer details of operations. It was the most relaxed Jason had been in days. He knew all the nuances of this business, and Martin had all the details available when they were needed. This was Jason's element, and he felt good in it.

"Is there anything else that needs to be gone over before tomorrow, gentlemen?" Jason glanced at Pernicky, who shook his head, and then at Jones who, in turn, looked to Walnick.

"We've covered everything that was on my agenda, sir."

"Good." Jason glanced at Martin, who was making a second pass over his notes. Only when he was done did he look up.

"We're good here as well, sir."

"Excellent." Jason slapped both of his hands on the table and stood. "I will see you all tomorrow, then. Martin and I will be surveying some land nearby at nine o'clock, so I believe we should be here around ten-thirty." Jason raised his eyebrows in Martin's direction for confirmation.

"Yes, sir, around ten-thirty."

"Until then." Jason shook hands with the other three men, and he and Martin left.

Walking through the mill on his way out, Jason glanced at the floor below where slaves were hard at work. An inexplicable chill went down his spine, and he wondered what discoveries tomorrow's inspection would bring.

CHAPTER TEN

"Has the new production line been working well, Mr. Jones?" Jason had to yell to be heard above the noise in the mill. The offices were sequestered away in a quieter part of the building, but on the floor, the sound was deafening.

"Yes, sir, it has. Logistically, it all makes sense. The numbers support it, and there's no downside that I can see. It took some time for everyone to get used to, but now it's running smoothly."

"Good." Jason was obsessed with efficiency. It was the easiest and fastest way to increase profits. The business was like a game to him, one his mind loved. Spot the weak links in the operation and strengthen them, rather than build on top of the problem.

"This is the blast furnace that was down for maintenance last month," Jones said as they drew near it.

"Problems like these need to be anticipated and prevented, Mr. Jones. With another blast furnace coming, you'll need to be even more diligent in maintaining them. Don't get slack just because there's another one to oversee. That's a lot of lost production for no good reason."

"I apologize, sir," Mr. Pernicky said. Jason looked at the foreman, impressed that he was stepping forward to take responsibility. "I should have done a better job of making sure the slaves kept up with the maintenance. We've put new

47

procedures in place to make sure it doesn't happen again."

"Yes, I saw your report on it. Diligence will pay off in this, I assure you." Jason left the furnace and continued on his way. Mr. Jones pointed out different aspects of the operation that had changed or that he had concerns about. Martin followed, scribbling notes as needed, and Mr. Walnick similarly trailed Jones, making notations and reminding him of points he had wanted to bring up.

As the group walked into another section of the mill, Jason felt a familiar tingle in his spine. It was the same one he had felt the night before when he'd glanced down at the floor. What was causing it? Something caught his attention out of the corner of his eye, and his heart began to race.

No. It's impossible. It can't be true.

Slowly, he turned to the right to get a better view, to prove that he was just seeing things. Every nerve in his body was on edge. How could his blood feel cold at the same time his skin was so hot? When his eyes focused on the scene before him, he still couldn't believe it. Twenty yards in front of him, a row of slaves shoveled ore. One shirtless figure stood out. The shape was unfamiliar, all muscle and bone, the skin tone too red, hair too short and dark, face covered with too much stubble. All pathetic excuses. Jason's eyes and his very soul were telling him the same thing. Still, he made a last ditch attempt to explain it away, for no other reason than to try and preserve his sanity. But then the slave moved his lowered head to the side and there was no mistaking it; the profile was his.

This man was Kale.

Jason's world narrowed to hold only himself and Kale. Everything else was peripheral. There was no sound other than the rushing of blood in Jason's ears. How could this be? Kale was a gentleman's valet, not a mere labor slave. Suddenly Jason was aware of how dry his mouth was, and his hand started to shake, keen to curl around a bottle.

"Is everything all right, sir?" It was Martin asking, and

Jason could hear the concern in his voice. The men around him stopped and stared at him. Jason was acutely aware of his surroundings. The blazing heat, the thick air, the acrid smell of sweat and smoke, and the sound of a whip cracking caused him to flinch. This was hell, and he needed to get Kale out of it. The thought of him being here was too much for Jason to handle. The only way he could function was if Kale was somewhere else.

"Yes, I'm fine. Must be the heat getting to me." Jason smiled at the others, and they accepted it as proof that nothing was amiss. Looking at Martin, though, he could tell the secretary wasn't entirely convinced. "That slave over there," Jason pointed to Kale, and he couldn't help his breath catching, resulting in an unnatural pause. "I want you to take him up to the office and have him wait for me there. I want to ask him some questions about working conditions."

Martin searched Jason's face with narrowed eyes. "Are you sure you're fine? You look drawn."

"I promise you, I'm all right." Jason not only smiled, but reached out and touched Martin's arm in a comforting gesture. It was more than Jason was accustomed to doing, but he wanted badly for Martin to give up his line of questioning. "Go get the slave, have him wait for me, and then you may rejoin us."

"Very well." Martin nodded and started off, but Jason stopped him after a few steps.

"Martin." The secretary paused and looked at him again. "Make sure he understands he's not in trouble."

Another nod and Martin continued on his way. Jason knew he should turn back to the other men and continue the walkabout, but he couldn't help watching. Inside, a war was being fought with one part of him wanting desperately for Kale to look up and see him and the other praying he wouldn't.

When Martin reached Kale, Jason wished he had continued on his way. What he saw made his stomach turn.

Kale shuffled to a halt, his head resolutely bowed. The foreman for the area approached, hand on his whip, and Martin stilled him with a raised hand. Words were exchanged. The foreman went about his work. Martin talked to Kale—there was no sign that Kale even heard him—and at the end of it, he walked off the floor with Martin following. Shoulders hunched, head down. He was different.

No, not different. Broken.

Martin looked back to Jason and nodded on his way out. There was nothing more Jason could do.

"Let's continue on our way. What were you saying before my interruption, Mr. Jones?" The words poured out of Jason's mouth as if they were spoken by someone else. The last three years of feigning interest in others for business were paying off. He could now appear engaged when his mind was up in an office with a slave he had thought never to see again.

What would he say to Kale? What could he say? Clearly, he had failed in the one thing he thought he had done well for Kale: getting him to a better life. While he could keep up a conversation with his manager and foreman while he was thinking about other things, he wouldn't be able to do that with Kale. There would never be any faking with him. Kale had been able to see through him even before Jason knew there was a façade to see through.

How would Kale react to seeing him? Anger was the only emotion Jason could imagine. Jason had raped him and then apparently sold him into hard labor; he could expect nothing else. From the looks of it, though, there might not even be enough left in Kale to stir up anger, and the thought sickened Jason. Perhaps he shouldn't even talk to him.

No. That was the coward's way out. Or at least that was the excuse Jason gave himself. Any excuse was much easier than admitting the fact that three years had passed and his heart still raced for Kale.

CHAPTER ELEVEN

"Sir, can I get you anything?" Martin's voice was soft and concerned. Jason couldn't help feeling grateful for his secretary at that moment. There was a good chance he had just saved Jason from appearing a fool.

How long had he been standing outside the office door? Jason could have closed his eyes and reproduced that door with the tarnished doorknob and chipped wood at the bottom in perfect detail. He had stared at it long enough. On the other side of that door was Kale. The thought was incomprehensible. It had been so long since Jason had last seen him. Yet, in some ways, it seemed like hardly a day had passed since he had watched another door close and separate him from Kale, seemingly forever.

"Sir?"

This time, Jason turned and looked at Martin. His secretary's furrowed brow reminded him of what a sight he must be. The amount of effort it took to focus his eyes on Martin was evidence of the vacant look that must have been on his face. As he closed his parted lips, he tasted the sweat trickling down his face. For the first time, he noticed his hand flexing, his fingers dancing for a bottle. If there was ever a time that Jason needed a drink, it was now. Even at his lowest, in the dark, drunk nights, the one hope that had kept him from going over the edge was that he had saved Kale.

Jason cleared his throat and spoke. "Could you get me a glass of water, Martin? The air on the floor has dried out my throat."

"Of course, sir." While his tone was businesslike, Jason didn't miss the look in Martin's eyes that clearly said he wasn't buying Jason's attempt at normalcy.

The cool glass of water in his hand made Jason realize how hot he was. Was this normal? The mill was always hot, but there was more to the red flush on his skin and the sweat at his brow. The racing of his heart hadn't slowed for a moment since he'd seen Kale. Surely, this couldn't be healthy.

As he drank, he tried to concentrate on the feeling of the water going through his body, willing it to calm him. Everything was going to be all right. This was Kale. Any anger he had toward Jason was deserved. He would take it, and then he would move on.

Finally, there came the moment when the need to see Kale overrode every fear and anxiety. Only then did Jason set the glass down and reach for the door. His body was drawn forward of its own accord, and Jason knew that no matter what happened, he was going to see Kale, and that made it all worthwhile.

One moment he was watching the door open, and the next he was looking at Kale. There he was, standing in the middle of the room, facing the entry with his head bowed so low Jason couldn't see his face. It was naïve to suppose that Kale would lift his head and look at Jason the way he used to.

He doesn't know it's me.

The thought hit Jason with such force that it momentarily took his breath away. No one had used his name, and Kale hadn't seen him. Did he not feel the same electricity Jason did? Of course not. While Jason's heart was full of love, Kale's held no such emotion.

It was tempting to speak and make himself known, but years of cunning led him to think before he spoke. There was a momentary advantage to keeping his identity secret. This was a unique opportunity to simply gaze at Kale. Once he knew he was standing with Jason, there would be issues to address. For now, Jason could look at him in relative peace.

It was hard to find much familiarity in Kale's appearance. How much of that was due to his physicality and how much to his mannerisms? Jason walked around him, eyeing him up and down. There was not an ounce of fat on him. Kale's diet was lacking, that was apparent. Toned muscles covered his bones, but just barely. With the work he was doing, he should have had more bulk. All these changes were catalogued and filed away in Jason's mind. Later, when he was alone, Jason would pull them up again and wallow in his guilt over having done this to Kale.

The gasp that escaped Jason's mouth when he came to Kale's back was unnaturally loud in the quiet room. In front of him was a tangled mess of flesh. Scar tissue marred the beautiful skin Jason remembered. These were not the faint, thin lines that had striped Kale's back when Jason first acquired him. These were deep, wide, and in such a pattern that led Jason to believe it was from several beatings.

Jason's eye was drawn to the first movement Kale had made since Jason entered. At the sound of Jason's gasp, Kale's right hand had started to fidget, rubbing his thigh.

In an odd way, it was the most disturbing thing Jason had seen all day. The nervous gesture was out of character for the calm and assured man Jason had known. The physical differences could be healed, but this was indicative of a much more vexing change. In that one action, Jason saw the depths of the damage he had done.

When Jason moved back in front of Kale, he started to fidget himself. His fingers were itching to caress Kale's face, to lift his head and look into the eyes he saw every time he closed his own. But it wasn't his place; Kale wasn't his lover. That lesson had been well learned, Kale had made sure of it during their last days together. But what could Jason say? The only thing he had been thinking when he called Kale here was to get him off the work floor. Kale wouldn't want to see him or talk to him, but Jason liked to think that he was a better option than the work Kale had been doing.

"You shouldn't be here." It was the only thought Jason could articulate. It summed up everything he had been thinking and feeling.

"I'm sor—" There was nothing familiar about the dry, raspy voice. The apology came to Kale's lips like a reflex, but when his brain caught up to the sound of Jason's voice, he looked up for the first time. Those beloved green eyes widened before quickly looking back down at the same time as his hand began to rub more furiously at his leg. Kale's eyes had shown shock, anger, and—did Jason imagine—longing?

"No, Kale. Don't. I only meant that you shouldn't be doing this type of work. This isn't the life you were meant to have."

Silence answered Jason. Kale didn't move other than that damned nervous tic with his hand.

"Please, sit down. I'm sure you could use the rest." Again there was nothing. Only more fidgeting. It was clear that Jason was making Kale uncomfortable.

"Sit down, Kale. I own this mill. I hired the company that owns you now. You're not going to get in trouble." It made Jason ill to see how hesitant Kale was to take a seat. Finally, he complied, balancing on the edge of the plainest chair in the room. His frame was so rigid that there was no rest in his posture.

Just as he had been overcome with the need to see Kale, Jason was now overcome with the need to leave. It wasn't because of the difficulty in seeing Kale like this, in seeing this empty shell of the man he had loved so fiercely that his chest hurt. It was because, in that room, he couldn't do anything to fix it, and he needed to fix it. "Stay here for a moment. I'm going to have my secretary bring you a glass of water. You're to drink all of it. He won't hurt you." Hopefully leaving Kale would also allow him to relax some.

In the outer office, he found Martin waiting for him, far enough from the door for Jason to know he hadn't been eavesdropping.

"Martin, bring him some water and leave him alone to drink it." Jason didn't make eye contact as he spoke. His mind was moving too fast for his eyes to focus on any one thing.

"Where are you going, sir?" Martin's guarded expression made Jason stop and think. He must look a mess to others, and where was he going? Nothing good would come from storming around the mill ranting, although it was tempting. And then it came to him. His course unfolded in front of him.

"I'm going to talk to Pernicky."

CHAPTER TWELVE

When the door closed behind Jason, Kale looked up. What had just happened? For a moment, he gazed at the spot where Jason had stood. Had he really been there? Ever since Kale was assigned to work at the mill, he'd known Jason owned it, but it had never crossed his mind that he might actually see Jason. Why would he? He had just taken it as one of the ironies of his life—a sick joke the gods saw fit to play —and left it at that.

Outside, there were footsteps, and Kale snapped to his feet, automatically lowering his head again. The same man who had brought him to the office entered and held out a glass of water.

"Here, sit and drink this."

Kale reached for the glass. Water was one thing he would never turn away. Thirst was a constant companion, and it was hot as hell in the mill. As soon as Kale had the glass firmly in his hands, Jason's secretary left.

He had a secretary. That man was part of Jason's life. It was strange to think of the people who must populate Jason's life who Kale didn't know anything about.

After he was done with the water, he sat and rolled the glass in his hands. It felt good to be off his feet, but it wasn't entirely restful. He was poised on the edge of his seat, ready to jump up as soon as anyone else entered the room. In an odd twist, his mind was blank. There were too many things to think about, too many emotions to feel, and instead of delving into the abyss, his mind simply stayed out of it. In all likelihood, he would be sent back down to the floor in a little while, and life would go on. It could be dangerous to start down a line of thought that would prove distracting.

The minutes ticked by, and Kale began to wonder if he had been forgotten. While the thought of staying quietly in the office was appealing, there would be consequences that Kale shuddered to think about if he was being missed somewhere. There wasn't much he could do about it, though. He had been ordered to stay, so he would.

More footsteps outside the door sent Kale scrambling to his feet, barely remembering to hold on to the empty glass. The same secretary entered again and threw a shirt at him. Kale caught it without understanding its purpose.

"Mr. Wadsworth has purchased you. You're to travel to Perdana with us straightaway."

The world was spinning. The floor had opened up, yet refused to swallow him. A hand took the glass, and he was led to the front of the mill.

Once out of the office, Kale's thoughts caught up with his body. What was wrong with that son of a bitch? Couldn't Jason just let him be? The anger built in him until he was outside the mill standing in front of a carriage. With Jason and his secretary.

Kale's throat began to constrict, and his chest tightened. How long was the ride to Perdana? It didn't matter. Any amount of time in such close quarters with Jason was enough to leave Kale gasping for air. Nothing Jason could do would make him travel in there with them.

"You may ride on the rear luggage rack." It was the secretary speaking. Of course, they wouldn't want Kale riding in the carriage with them. It wasn't his place.

A movement to the side drew Kale's eye. Jason was getting ready to speak, and Kale could guess his intention.

Raising his head under the pretense of nodding his understanding of the secretary's order, Kale suffused his face with as much gratitude as he knew how to show. Thankfully, Jason decided not to comment and instead climbed into the carriage, followed by his secretary. As soon as Kale shrugged his shirt on and sat in his place, they were off.

It was a hot day, but the wind felt cool against Kale's skin, and his body reflexively relaxed even as his mind whirled. Watching the mill fade into the distance, he knew that his days of hard labor were over, at least for the moment. In Perdana, he would face a different battle than the one he had fought and grown accustomed to over the past three years. There would no longer be a struggle to make his body keep going when he felt he was being pushed past endurance. It would be his mind that would be pushed once they reached Perdana, and he didn't know if it was up for the challenge. Ever since Jason had sold him, Kale had tried to lock his mind away—it was the easiest way to get through each day. He had never been entirely successful, but as his body had grown strong under the constant labor, his mind had grown weak from neglect.

Riding through the countryside with nothing for his body to do, his mind was set free and questions tumbled in. How would Renee react to seeing him? She and Jason had planned to marry shortly after Kale was sold, which meant it was likely they had a baby or two. The thought of Jason as a father was strange. He was probably good at it.

Those were exactly the kind of thoughts he needed to control. He didn't know Jason. Not anymore.

Besides, Kale hated Jason Wadsworth. Now more than ever.

It had been hard enough the first time, convincing Jason that Kale didn't have feelings for him, convincing Jason that Kale viewed him as nothing more than a master to be serviced. He had never gone so far as to call Jason a rapist, but he hadn't done anything to disavow Jason of that notion once he got it in his head.

It had been the hardest thing Kale had ever done. He knew what he was getting into, and he had prepared himself for it. Then Jason came back and, once again, tipped his world upside down. Why couldn't he just let Kale be? Let him move on? Let him live out his miserable life? Instead, Jason insisted on playing with him. How long would Jason keep him in Perdana? How long until he was sold again? What was Jason going to do to him?

These were all questions he couldn't answer. He had no control over what would happen to him. There was no point thinking about it. That concession was all his mind needed in order to join his body in relaxing. Perhaps he would just close his eyes for a minute. He had no idea how long it would take to reach Perdana, but it was surely long enough to get a little sleep. As Kale closed his eyes, his mind wandered to inside the carriage. What were Jason and his secretary doing now? Were they sleeping too? Probably. Was Jason snoring like he used to? Kale smirked. Probably.

Chapter Thirteen

Silence was not a new thing between Martin and Jason, but in the confines of the carriage after the odd scene that had just played out, it was unsettling. Watching Jason gaze out the window with a faraway look in his eyes, Martin could almost see the cogs working in his employer's brain. Was Jason really just going to stay silent, pretend as if it was customary to bring home a labor slave every time they went to the mill, like a souvenir?

Martin opened his mouth to speak, but Jason beat him to it. "You didn't have to make him sit on the luggage rack."

Was that what was under Jason's skin? "He looked grateful. It's probably cooler out there anyway, with the breeze. When he saw you standing at the door of the carriage like you expected him to join us, he looked terrified that he would dirty it up."

"Yes, terrified is exactly how he looked." A pained grimace flashed across Jason's face. "I had hoped after all these years, he wouldn't be so afraid."

The last part surprised Martin, but he was already beginning to ask a question by the time Jason's words registered. "Why did you buy a labor slave in the first place? And one from the mill?"

Jason looked at Martin for the first time since they'd left. "He's not a labor slave. He used to be a personal valet."

"How do you know that? Do you have a history with this slave?" As Martin leaned forward, waiting for an answer, Jason looked away. The shame in his eyes piqued Martin's curiosity even more.

"Yes, Kale and I definitely have a history."

The words knocked the wind out of Martin, and he sank back in his seat. "That's Kale?"

Jason was not forthcoming with an answer, but it didn't matter, Martin probably wouldn't have heard him anyway. In his head, pieces were beginning to fall into place. The drunken nights, the anguished mutterings of Kale's name, the shame he saw on Jason's face. This latest bit of information provided a crucial piece of the puzzle, but it didn't come anywhere close to revealing the full picture. Once this new tidbit was filed away, Martin was flooded with questions.

"When did you own him?" Jason was looking out the window again and didn't even acknowledge that he heard Martin. "When did you sell him?" Still nothing. "Why does he have this effect on you? He's only a slave."

"It's none of your business."

No, of course it wasn't. Martin was merely the person tasked with cleaning up the mess after this Kale had gone. He was the one who had to deal with Jason's moods, depressions, drinking. Just as Martin was about to retort that Jason had made it his business, Jason turned back to him.

"And Kale is more than a slave. I don't want him treated as one. You're to give him the red guest bedroom on the second floor with the en suite bathroom so he can have some privacy. And he has free run of the house. I want him to rest and get better. He shouldn't look like that." Jason's eyes got a faraway look again, and Martin wondered how he remembered Kale. When Jason began to speak again, his voice was softer and more timid. "I did terrible things to him, Martin. Things I can never atone for. But I can do this. I can save him from working hard labor, and I'm going to do it."

It was more of an admission than Martin had expected,

but it still left him wanting. Treat a slave as a guest? It was absurd, even for his often eccentric employer. Even though Jason could be callous and uncaring at times, Martin had a hard time imagining him doing anything terrible. It wasn't in him.

"The guest bedroom, sir? We have quite comfortable slave quarters in the basement. I'm sure after what he's used to it will be luxurious." Having a slave living in the main part of the house was a breech in decorum that Martin had a hard time stomaching.

"No, Martin." Jason's temper flared. "He's a guest in my home. You're to treat him as one."

"But it's not appropriate."

"Fuck it, Martin. I don't give a damn about what is appropriate. If you feel you can't follow my orders, then you are welcome to leave."

Never before had Jason been so hostile while sober. Why should he care so much for a slave? Even one he felt he had abused in some way? Surely getting him away from the mill and putting him to work in an upper class home was more than adequate.

Perhaps, once Kale was settled in, Martin could coax more of the story out of him. Martin tried to think about this new addition to their household, but he had a hard time conjuring up a picture of him in his mind. Before he'd known who Kale was, he had paid him the same mind as he did any other slave—which wasn't much.

How would Kale's presence affect Jason's already volatile moods? Would Kale be the key to locking the depressive episodes away? One look at Jason brooding told Martin that the answer was no. If anything, it seemed Kale would act as a catalyst, and Martin worried that the worst was yet to come.

Chapter Fourteen

The excitement stirred in Kale's belly the moment they entered the city. The best memories of his life were in Perdana—and the worst. Over the tops of buildings, he spotted the grand library on the university grounds. There was a time when he'd thought it the most magical place in the world. Was he even capable of such feelings anymore?

They rode past the park, and Kale had to turn away. That particular spot held too many memories that were now painful to examine. There was the opera house and art gallery, and then there was Flannigan's. The memories there weren't quite as painful as the rest, but now was not the time to entertain them. Kale watched people fluttering around him as they made their way through the city. Not much had changed since he had last been here. People in fancy clothes still twittered about, and the streets were still filthy with both trash and the poor.

They passed the homes of the aristocracy, some of which Kale had visited with Jason. Somewhere in the dark recesses of his mind, locked in a back room, were the names of all the people who lived here, their tastes, preferences, and scandals. He was comforted in a way to know that the knowledge was all there in his mind, that he hadn't lost it, even if he never accessed it again.

It was in this section of town that the carriage stopped,

and Kale glanced up at a townhouse he didn't recognize. For some reason, he had supposed they would pull up to the same townhouse he had left three years ago. It was a silly thought. Logically, he knew that Jason had moved. When he thought about it, he was surprised that Jason was even living in Perdana. It would have been more probable for Jason to move into one of Renee's family estates for the coming summer. Then again, Jason had always loved Perdana.

Renee. Family. Kids. Who exactly would be inside that house? Kale's pulse raced. He got off the carriage and bowed his head as much as he could while still being able to lift his eyes and see any gestures that might be directed his way. Would Renee be mad at Jason for buying him or indifferent? Kale almost snorted. Indifferent was a futile hope. Renee would be furious.

Jason got out of the carriage, shot Kale a quick glance on his way to the entrance, and nothing more. He disappeared inside the house, and Kale found himself resenting Jason for leaving him to face this alone. The secretary made a gesture for Kale to follow him and then walked to the front door. It was an unexpected twist. He had struck Kale as the type of man who put a lot of stock in propriety and wouldn't abide a labor slave coming through the front door. When he proceeded to lead Kale to a fancy guest room, Kale thought he was batty.

"This is the room your master wishes you to use, against my strong objection. There is an en suite bathroom to ensure your privacy, about which the master seems concerned. Mr. Wadsworth instructs that you are to spend the rest of the day here resting. Sophie, the cook, will bring you something to eat."

During this little speech, Kale stood with his head down. He hadn't looked at much of anything on the way in—he was too scared of who he might see—but he could tell that this was a much finer home than the one where he had lived with Jason before. Even back then he hadn't warranted his own room, and especially not one outside the slave quarters. This was a foreign and unsettling situation. No matter what he did, he felt sure it would lead to trouble.

"Do you have any questions?"

Yes, Kale had questions, but none that he would give voice to. Especially not to a stranger whose name he didn't even know. And he wasn't about to ask for it as though he had any right to use a free man's name.

"And you don't have to bow your head like that, especially to me."

Kale raised his head to look at him, though not straight on. He knew the secretary's kind. The man didn't like the bowed head of a broken laborer in his fancy house, but Kale didn't doubt that he'd still slap a slave silly for not showing the appropriate amount of deference.

"No questions?"

That damned right hand began to fidget again. All Kale wanted was for this man to leave. As if the situation wasn't awkward enough, he didn't want to be standing alone with a free man who clearly despised him. Kale needed time to think everything through, and time was a luxury he was not being granted.

In the face of Kale's silence and nervous twitching, the secretary softened. "Please, rest. You don't have to fear anything here. No one has the authority to punish you other than the master, and seeing as he's given you this room, I don't think you need to worry about him. He will be upset if you don't take advantage of his hospitality. I'm going to get you some clothes. Lay down. Sophie will be in shortly with some dinner."

He stood still, looking at Kale as if for some confirmation. Kale wasn't about to go lay down on the bed with him standing there, so if that was what he was waiting for, the secretary was sorely mistaken. As a general rule, Kale tried to speak as little as possible to free people—he found it drastically reduced his chances of saying the wrong thing—

but it seemed like Martin wasn't going to leave without some kind of response. So Kale murmured, "Yes, sir. Thank you, sir."

Satisfied, the man nodded and walked out. Once the door was shut and Kale could hear footsteps retreating, he finally took a proper look at the room. What he saw made his mouth hang open. From the looks of it, this guest room was where a visiting noble might be placed. Against the wall, the bed called to him with its red and gold down comforter that would be too hot for this time of year, but still invited him with its fluffiness. It would be so easy to collapse onto it, but Kale knew he was a mess, and he didn't want to soil such beautiful bedding.

The en suite bathroom was fully equipped with a tub, but Kale wasn't bold enough to draw himself a bath. Instead, he stripped down and took a wet washcloth to clean the grime from his skin. It took several sinks full of water to get the washcloth to rinse clear, but eventually he achieved a state that resembled cleanliness.

Further examination revealed a razor and shaving soap. Kale scratched at the itchy stubble he had been forced to wear much of the last three years. The urge to sleep didn't stand a chance against the need to shave. The labor firm had a barber shave the slaves every couple of weeks, but it was to prevent lice and was done with perfunctory efficiency.

Kale took his time lathering the cream, enjoying its cool touch on his skin. When he took up the razor, he slid it over taut skin carefully, achieving the closest shave he'd ever had. Just as he was patting his face dry with a towel and enjoying the new sensation of air on his jaw, a woman walked in carrying a tray. She set it down on a table in the bedroom and came to the bathroom.

"You're supposed to be resting."

A familiar fear entered Kale. Had it been presumptuous to make use of the bathroom when he had been ordered to lie down? If he had dirtied the bed, then surely he would be in more trouble than whatever was headed his way. As he scurried backward into the corner of the bathroom, covering himself with the towel, he tried to make himself as small as possible. "I'm sorry, ma'am."

"Martin was right. You are skittish. I thought maybe it was just him. It's all right, honey, you haven't done anything wrong. I was teasing you."

The thought that he wasn't in trouble when everything about this situation was wrong didn't make sense. At least now he knew the secretary's name. "I'm sorry, ma'am."

"There's no need to apologize. You're fine. I just thought you'd be fast asleep in that nice bed when I got up here is all. It's very thoughtful of you to wash first, but trust me, this room could use some dirtying up. We never have guests, and we could use the chance to do some cleaning."

For a few seconds they stood there, Kale stark naked, looking at the ground and holding a towel before him. Then the woman snatched his tattered pants from the floor. Icy fear gripped him and compelled him to speak. "Please, ma'am."

"That's a start, except you can drop the ma'am. My name's Sophie."

Kale could hear the smile in her voice and peeked up at her. She was short and slight, with the lightest blonde hair Kale had ever seen knotted high on her head. The smile on her face widened when she caught him looking at her.

"You don't need to be so shy. We're not brutes. You can lift your head." Kale obeyed. There was nothing threatening about this woman. "Now what was it you were wanting to ask me?"

"Please," Kale couldn't bring himself to use her name. There had been a time when he used the names of free people, but it was so long ago that he was out of practice. "My pants. They're the only ones I have."

"I know. Martin is getting you some clothes, and I'm going to take these out and burn them."

The grip of fear tightened. Kale didn't want to ask her for a favor or contradict her, but he couldn't let her take them. Instead, he relied on his eyes to do the talking. He tried to look as miserable as possible.

"You scared of being without them? I guess you don't have any reason to trust us, although we would never leave a man naked. Fine, I'll leave them. Once you get new ones, I'll take these away. Don't put them on now, though, after you've just cleaned. Wrap the towel around your waist and come get your food."

The fear slowly left his body and was replaced with relief. "Thank you."

"Sophie."

"Sophie." Kale nodded. It would take a while to remember how to be around people who didn't view him as an animal.

In the bedroom, she gestured for Kale to take a seat at the table with the tray. Sitting in front of a free person was more than uncomfortable, it was fear inducing. He wanted to nod to her to sit first, but that felt dangerously close to issuing orders. There was a solution tucked away in a part of his brain he hadn't used in years, the part that knew how to function in polite society. He figured she wouldn't get mad at him for observing good manners.

"After you," Kale gestured to the other chair at the table and swallowed. "Sophie."

Sophie looked pleased and took a seat, after which Kale followed suit.

"I brought you some soup and bread. It's not much, but I was worried your stomach might not be able to handle more. I know how scarce you must have been fed, and with all the excitement of the day, I didn't want you heaving it right back up."

Sophie discarded the tray's cover, and Kale thought he must have died and gone to heaven. The smell of warm, freshly baked bread with a healthy slab of butter on it actually brought the pinprick of tears to his eyes. The bread rested against a bowl of simple tomato soup with steam still wafting off it. He was determined not to give in to the urge to lift the bowl to his lips and gulp it down. He wouldn't eat like an animal in front of this lady. The spoon felt awkward in his hand, but he managed to fill it with soup and raise it to his lips. As soon as the warm, creamy smoothness hit his tongue —so different from the watery stock he had been subsisting on—he couldn't help himself. He shoveled it into his mouth. It tasted so fresh, and he was so hungry. His body hunched over the bowl while his free arm encircled it. He couldn't risk losing this meal now that he had tasted it.

Once the bowl was empty, he eyes lighted on the slice of bread. It was light, fluffy, and soft enough to sop up the thin film of soup remaining in the bowl. He had forgotten that bread was supposed to be soft. The last time he had lived under the same roof as Jason, he had eaten better than this, but Kale couldn't remember food ever tasting so good. The rest of the world faded into the background as he focused on eating while he had the chance.

When he was done, he became aware of Sophie's eyes resting on him, concern and pity evident in their brown depths. Kale didn't like being pitied, but he was too content to care. Let her think what she wanted. For the first time in three years, his belly was sated.

"I take it you liked it?"

"It was the best meal of my life, miss." Kale's body was limp with warmth.

"See, all it takes is some food in you to loosen your tongue." Kale looked away, remembering his place. "No, now don't go clamming up on me again. I need someone to talk to. It's much too lonely in this house."

Kale's eyes darted up and then back away. Sophie's words tickled at an observation Kale had made on the way to this room, but he kept quiet.

"What is it? Do you have a question?" Sophie reached

71

over and turned Kale's face so it met hers. "Go ahead and ask. You can speak freely around me. I won't bite, I promise."

Her smile was so disarming that Kale found himself believing her. "You said it was lonely, miss. Where is everyone?"

"Everyone?" Sophie didn't seem to understand.

"Yes, miss. The rest of the slaves and staff? Re—The family?" Kale corrected quickly. The mistress of the house had always been Renee or Miss Arlington to him. Now she was neither.

"There is no one else. It's just me, Martin, and Mr. Wadsworth."

"But I thought…" Kale let the question die on his lips. It was too presumptuous.

"Thought what, dear?" Sophie wrapped her hand around his in encouragement.

"Nothing. I just thought it would take more people to keep a house like this running."

Sophie removed her hand. "Oh, it does, but Mr. Wadsworth doesn't like having slaves. You're the first he's had since I've worked for him. He's also a bit of a recluse and can pinch pennies tighter than any man I've known. He doesn't want more people in the house, and he refuses to spend money on the upkeep."

That wasn't right. Jason wasn't a recluse. And since when did he shy away from spending money? He had enough of it.

"By the way, now that we're on speaking terms, what's your name?"

"It's Kale, miss." The name sounded foreign on his lips. He hadn't had much reason to use it. The past three years had been about survival. He didn't talk to the other slaves he worked with, and they didn't talk to him. Even if they had had the energy for it, there was no point in developing friendships that couldn't last in the uncertainty of their lives.

"Kale?" Sophie's voice was hollow and unbelieving.

"Yes, miss." It was clear from her facial expression that she had heard his name before.

"Well then, I'd guess you have more questions."

"Why? What do you know about me?"

"Oh, I have plenty of questions myself. I know hardly anything about you. I've only heard your name a couple of times, always when Mr. Wadsworth thought I couldn't hear. But you've been like a ghost in this house for as long as I can remember."

Did Renee and Jason still fight about him? Why couldn't that boy just let go and move on? He had done everything he could.

"Go on. Ask me what you want, dear."

Kale was hesitant, but he needed to know. "Where's Renee? I mean, Mrs. Wadsworth."

Sophie's eyebrows rose at the use of Renee's name, but other than that, she seemed nonplussed. "I don't know. I've never met her. From what I understand, she and Mr. Wadsworth separated not long after her father died. They were only married for around six months when it happened."

Then why was Jason at the Arlington Steel Mill? "So he's divorced?"

"Gracious, no. I believe they simply found it easier to be married if they weren't around each other. Martin knows more about it than me. I was hired on after all that business was done."

After all that, after everything Kale had done, Jason still couldn't manage to be happy. And now he had drug Kale back into his miserable life. "What questions do you have for me, miss?"

"How long will it take for you to stop calling me miss, for starters?"

Kale shook his head. "That may take a while, but I'll try. Sophie."

"That's all I ask." Sophie rose and gathered the tray. Kale stood with her, not wanting to sit in her presence if she wasn't.

"I thought you had questions."

"I do, but they can wait. Frankly, they're none of my business. You get some rest. I'll be back later with more food." The sparkle in her eye brought a smile out of him.

Kale went to the door and held it open for her. As she swept by, he built up the courage to speak again. "Thank you, Sophie."

"You're welcome, dear. Now go get some sleep."

When the door was shut again, Kale stared at the bed. It was huge, ornate, and entirely inappropriate for him. Instead of sleeping, he went around the room examining the furnishings. There was a large wardrobe with intricate floral carvings. A bookshelf against the wall caught his attention. Turning his head to look at the spines, his eyes scrambled to make sense of the letters. A back room in his mind slowly opened to provide him with the information he needed. None of the books looked terribly interesting. It would have been slow going if he had dared to pull one out and tried to read, but the knowledge was still there, safely tucked away. Kale was satisfied that if he wanted to, he'd be able to read again.

As he lazily made his way around the room, he kept stealing glances at the bed. It was enticing, but he was terrified of falling asleep and waking up in trouble. His orders had been clear, but his brain rebelled, asserting that the comfort of the bed was not meant for him. The floor would do. Then again, would he appear ungrateful if he was discovered rejecting the bed?

Oh, screw it. After three years, his body was ready to take the offered rest, no matter the risk. Kale disposed of his towel and folded down the comforter. The sheets were cool on his bare skin as he lay down. Muscles relaxed, and he was pulled back to the memory of the last time he had been in such a nice bed. It was so similar, only this time there wasn't a warm body next to him. That reminded him; he needed to retrieve something from his pants before he surrendered to sleep. It wasn't likely they'd be there when he woke.

His body protested the movement as he rose and picked up his pants. There was a pocket on the right side, behind the fabric Kale had worn thin with his fidgeting. He fished out its contents, discarded the pants, and went back to bed. When he was situated, he opened his fist to reveal a lock of brown hair. Kale twirled it in his hands and then lifted it to his nose. It still smelled of him after all these years. Common sense told Kale it had to be his imagination, but any time he smelled it, the scent of Jason consumed him. The dream Jason—the one Kale could handle—comforted him. The real Jason was a different matter, and Kale was still so upset at his master—gods, he still couldn't believe that this man was his master again—that he didn't want to spare him a single thought.

This little lock of hair, tied with string, had made it with him the last three years. It had been hard to keep it hidden so it wouldn't be taken, but it had been worth the effort. There were times when the brown lock had been all that stood between him and madness. He couldn't let it go now. If anything, he needed it now more than ever. How could he face Jason again without the comfort of what they had once been? Inside himself he felt a dark knot of hatred in the pit of his stomach. Kale had resigned himself to his life long ago. He didn't need to be toyed with to assuage Jason's guilt, or whatever it was that inspired this turn of events. How much worse would it be when Jason sold him this time? Kale had barely survived the last time. He didn't know if he could again.

Somewhere among the beatings and starvation, he had changed. At the root of that change had been a growing hatred of Jason Wadsworth. The man he had loved more than his own life hadn't cared enough about him to make sure he was safe. Jason had just dropped him with a dealer to handle his sale. But that wasn't what really fueled the hatred.

The real issue was that Jason had sold him at all. After all they had shared, Jason simply turned his back on him. Kale didn't care that it was his idea, that he'd had to fight Jason to make him accept that it was best to sell him when Renee had demanded it as a condition of marriage. That was irrelevant now. Jason had done it. When Kale had told Jason that he never loved him, Jason had believed Kale's blasphemous lie as if they had never been more to each other than master and slave. Kale's lies had stemmed from his love for Jason. Jason's betrayal stemmed from selfishness, and Kale couldn't forgive it.

Clutching the hair in his fist, the memento tempered his anger. These weren't thoughts he should give energy to; there was nothing he could do about them. He needed to rest up to face whatever would come when he woke. Putting his hand under the pillow where it would be safe from prying eyes, Kale breathed out as his eyelids lowered, willing the darkness inside to recede.

CHAPTER FIFTEEN

"The slave is awake, sir."

Jason was staring at the back garden, thinking about nothing and everything. "Kale."

"Yes, sir."

Jason turned from the window to Martin. "No, I wasn't asking for confirmation, Martin. Did you think I thought you meant one of the other slaves in this house? I meant, 'Kale is awake, sir.' You can call him by his name."

"Yes, sir."

"Martin, this is a lonely house by design. I've shut out the world and only granted you and Sophie entrance. I did that to myself, but I don't want Kale to suffer for it. He's always been a social creature. Try to befriend him. He's a good man, better than any I've ever known. Give him a chance, and he'll surprise you."

"Yes, sir."

Jason sighed. Martin was just the type of man Jason used to think he wanted to be. He knew that it would be nothing short of a miracle if Martin ever viewed Kale as anything other than a slave. If only the secretary knew he was the one losing out. "Has he eaten?"

"I saw Sophie taking a tray to his room a moment ago."

"Thank you. You're dismissed."

When Martin was gone, Jason slumped in his chair, relief

pouring through him. He had been worried when Sophie had reported that Kale was still asleep when she went in with breakfast yesterday morning, and then again with lunch and dinner. When he hadn't been awake this morning, Jason had vowed to call a doctor if lunchtime yielded the same report. That vow had been made less than two hours ago.

Jason was antsy to see Kale again, although he didn't know what he would say or do. He would wait though, and give Kale time to eat. No sense disrupting his breakfast when he had more than a day of eating to make up for. Besides, it wouldn't hurt Jason to freshen up a little. He'd been drinking last night, and he felt a mess. A comb through his hair, some cold water on his face, and a spritz of cologne would do wonders.

Half an hour later, he stood outside Kale's door. Should he knock or just walk in? He didn't want to barge in on Kale and violate his privacy, but if he knocked, he wouldn't blame Kale for not answering. If he entered after being refused permission, he would feel like an ass.

This was silly, damn it. It was his house, and he'd go where he pleased. He rapped his knuckles a few times on the door in preamble and then entered.

Kale stood in front of the table with his head bowed, the chair behind him askew. "You can look at me, you know." Jason was surprised to hear the vulnerability in his own voice.

Kale raised his head, but kept his eyes averted.

"You know what I mean."

Kale's eyes snapped up, and Jason's lips parted, drawing in a badly needed breath. Those pale green eyes were just as he remembered, except they were more vivid in the flesh. A dark shadow hovered behind them that was absent in Jason's imaginings.

"I never meant for you to end up like this."

Silence.

"I thought with you knowing how to read, and your experience, that you'd be sold to an aristocrat."

Still nothing. The man before him could very well be made of stone if it weren't for the heat of his gaze.

"Please, Kale. Speak to me."

The only movement was the clenching of Kale's jaw muscles.

"I know you must be mad at me. I expect it. Say what you like, I deserve it. Just, please, speak to me." Jason yearned to hear the voice he used to drown in, even if it was raised in anger.

"What do you want me to say?"

That was a start. It was something. "Anything you want. I need to know what you're thinking."

"What I'm thinking? No, you don't want to know that."

"Yes, I do. Please, Kale, talk to me."

There was a twitch along Kale's jawline, but nothing came of it.

"The Kale I knew never shied away from speaking his mind."

There was a grunt and a pause. "The Kale you knew doesn't exist anymore."

The softness of Kale's voice hit Jason. There was an aching truth in Kale's words that Jason didn't want to acknowledge. "Yes, he does. He's standing right before me. I can see your emotions spelled out on your face. You have the same mind. You just need to speak it. Please, tell me what you're thinking."

Kale tensed, as if it took increased effort to hold his tongue.

"Unless you're scared, which I completely understand." It was cheap, but Kale never used to let a jibe at his pride go unanswered. Jason was taking a gamble, hoping a sliver of that pride still existed. If it didn't, he would be defeated.

Kale's tension increased until the pressure erupted out of his mouth. "I think you're a damn naïve fool, that's what I think. You thought knowing how to read was going to save me? You think the dealer you sold me to even cared about that? Did you really think that your rich, snooty friends would go to the likes of him to buy their valets? The truth is you didn't give a shit what happened to me as long as I wasn't your problem anymore."

"That's not true." Jason felt like he had been punched in the gut. Any delight in convincing Kale to speak vanished. Kale had never lost his composure like this. He had always been the calm voice of reason. To see him so impassioned, especially after viewing him as a broken man a couple days ago, was a shock.

"You didn't even bother to see who I was sold to. And now you come traipsing back into my life? I hate you. I hate that you keep toying with me. Why can't you let me be? I'd rather be shoveling ore right now. At least there I knew what was expected of me. I knew that I was a dead man, and I made peace with it. How much more difficult is it going to be now, when you get tired of this little game and shove me aside again?"

"I won't let you go back there. You're not a dead man, Kale. Everything is going to be all right."

"Like it is now? Where's your wife? Your kids? I gave up everything for you, and you still couldn't be happy."

"Selling you wasn't about making me happy. It was about getting you away from your rapist."

"So you thought a death sentence was better?"

"What?" Jason was taken aback.

"Did you see any gray hairs on my crew? No one lasts long."

Is that really what Kale's life had been like? True, Jason had never seen an old man on the floor, but he hadn't thought about it. How many nights had Kale stayed awake wondering how much longer he had left to live? Did Kale know what his future held when he pushed to be sold? Jason's breakfast stirred in his stomach.

"I'm sorry, Kale. I didn't know."

"Damn right you didn't know, and you didn't care."

"I do care." How could Jason convince Kale?

"All you've ever cared about is yourself. All you wanted was to be rich and popular. Well, how does it feel?"

Jason couldn't say anything. The vitriol in the voice he had so loved tore him to shreds.

"Now that your life didn't turn out the way you wanted, you thought you'd come mess with mine. You couldn't make it work with Renee, so now you're going to try and make it work with me. And when it doesn't, I'll be thrown in the gutter again. No more soft bed, no more good food, and it won't mean anything to you."

"You're wrong, Kale. I didn't bring you here to try and have a relationship with you. I brought you here to make things right. That's all. I swear."

Kale's beautiful face twisted in a sneer. "No, you didn't. You may think you did, but I know you. I know the way you work. You're carrying around some romantic notion that if only you can make things right, you can be with me the way you wanted to before. You think if you do this, you can be happy."

"No, Kale. Happiness is something I know I can never have again." Jason's resigned voice appeared to bring Kale up short. Instead of continuing his ranting, he gazed back at Jason, perfectly still.

Everything about Kale called to him. Even in the midst of Kale's anger, Jason wanted to be with him. If given the opportunity, he would suffer any penance, make any restitution, to earn his forgiveness. In the face of all this bitterness, Jason still loved Kale. However, he knew this time that the only way for him to give voice to his love was to leave Kale alone and let him heal and find peace without intrusion.

"I know it does nothing to fix the past, but I am sorry. All these years I thought the one thing I did right in this whole affair was to get you out. Now I see how wrong I was. It looks like it's just one more thing to add to my long list of sins. You won't have to worry about me making advances toward you while you're here. I'm under no illusions about our relationship this time. But I do want to make it up to you, to try and set things right. You have free rein of the house. Rest and eat as much as you like of whatever you like. If there's something you want and we don't have it, ask Sophie to get it, or have her give you some money so you can go to the market. Please, try to be happy."

Facing Jason was the man he had loved, the man he still loved. But all that stared back at him was hatred and pain. It was unbearable. "I have no doubt you'll fit in well with Sophie and Martin. You were always good with people."

"Time changes a man."

"Not in as many ways as you'd think." As much as he loathed himself for what he'd done to Kale three years ago, Jason still wanted him. He had been kidding himself when he thought he could move Kale to the back of his mind and move on. He thought he had been managing it well. Whenever the memory of Kale assaulted him, he simply drowned it. Perhaps Jason secretly wished he'd drown as well.

"I won't bother you in your room again. It's yours, and I shouldn't have come in here. Have a nice day." Jason closed the door behind him and cursed himself for ever thinking things could get better.

Chapter Sixteen

A warm, spicy scent wafted to Kale's nose, and before his mind could even register it, a loud and embarrassing growl erupted from his stomach.

As soon as Jason left, Kale wanted to flee, and the only place he felt he could escape to was the kitchen. The air in his room was thick with his emotional outpouring. He still didn't know where his outburst had come from, but it had been three years in the making, and it had felt good.

"You can go anywhere in the house you like; you don't have to be down here in this heat. I'll bring your meals to you." Sophie ladled the source of the tantalizing scent into a bowl.

"I'm sorry, ma'am. I'll go."

"No, now stop right there. We're all the way back to ma'am, are we? Come in here and sit down. I just don't understand why you'd want to be in this heat when you could be upstairs."

"It's not as hot as what I'm used to." Kale took a seat, and Sophie placed a thick stew in front of him. "Thank you."

"You're welcome."

Kale shoveled the stew into his mouth. There was a part of his brain that refused to accept that food would be readily available for the foreseeable future.

"That was delicious."

"I'm glad to hear it. There's always more where it came from. You'll make yourself sick if you keep eating that fast." Sophie cleared his bowl away, and Kale sat back, his stomach distended. The ache that resulted from inhaling his food was a welcome change from the ache of hunger.

"Do you mind if I stay down here?"

"Not at all, I'm happy for the company."

"I've always felt safest in the kitchen."

"No owners in the kitchen to cause problems, huh?"

Kale felt his lips twitch in the beginnings of a smile. It had been so long that the muscles felt strange. "That's about right. How do you know so much about the way slaves think?"

Sophie grabbed a basket of mending and sat at the table with him, taking up a needle and thread. "I've been in service a long time."

"You're not from around here."

She looked up from a button she was sewing onto a white shirt. "No, I'm not. How'd you know?"

Kale shrugged. "You have a slight accent on some words. I'd guess you're from Naiara."

"Yes, I am. I grew up in a little town outside Calea."

"How did you end up here?"

"My father died, and then my mother fell in love with a man from Perdana who was doing some work in Calea. When his work was done and he left, my mother followed him. We were poor, and so I went into service and have been working with slaves since we moved here."

"That must be a shock, coming from a country without slavery."

Sophie chuckled. "Yes, it was at first. Slaves scared me to begin with. In Naiara, we hear about them, and I grew up thinking they must be different somehow. When I came here, I was surprised to find that they're just people, like everyone else, just with different problems." She moved on to darn a sock. "Look at me, sitting here talking about myself. Surely

84

there's other things you'd be wanting to know about?"

"Last I remember, the Arlingtons had more money than the gods. Why doesn't the master hire more help or buy some slaves?"

"Well, he's never liked the idea of owning slaves. To be honest, I thought you'd know more about that than me. As for staff, Mr. Wadsworth is adamant that he doesn't need more help. He never has people over, and it's just him. He thinks it's a waste to spend as much money as he does."

Kale took note. He didn't quite understand why Jason would have an aversion to slaves. He certainly didn't mind working them in his mill. "What is it you want to know? What do you already know?"

"Like I told you, not much. I've heard your name muttered here and there. Didn't expect for you to turn out to be a slave."

"I used to belong to him. When he met Miss Arlington, she wanted me gone before they were engaged, so he sold me."

"That doesn't sound like him. Why sell you for a woman he didn't even end up staying with?"

"Well, it's the truth." Kale was not willing to delve deeper into the matter. "What's the story with this Martin fellow?"

"Oh, he's Mr. Wadsworth's secretary. Last name's Grimlock. He's big on decorum, so it may take him a while to warm up to you. Don't worry, though, his bark is worse than his bite. He's a good man and does the best he can."

"How long has he been with the master?"

"Since Mr. Arlington died."

Kale didn't know what made him ask his next question, but he needed to know. "Does he take good care of him?" It came out as barely more than a whisper.

Sophie put down her mending and reached across to pat Kale's hand. He knew she didn't understand, but her eyes said she would try. "Yes, he does. We both do. He doesn't make it easy on us, but we both worry about him and take care of him as if he were family."

The hand on Kale's seemed to touch deeper than skin. He didn't know how he felt about all the recent developments in his life, or about his newfound knowledge about Jason, but for the first time in a long time, he didn't feel alone.

"Why don't you go lay down, Kale?"

"It's the middle of the day."

"So? Your body is making up for lost time. Go relax, and we can talk more later."

In truth, Kale was tired. Only it wasn't the kind of tired that led him to sleep for more than a day. This was a weariness that went much deeper. Nodding, he stood and dragged himself up the stairs to his room.

On his way to collapsing in bed, his eye caught on the table where he had eaten. Stacked on top of it were some books, a sketchpad with plenty of paper, charcoal pencils, and some pastels. Stepping closer, he read the spines of the books. From the titles, it was evident that Jason had hand selected these for him. Something stirred in his chest. With a tentative hand, he reached out to touch the drawing supplies. The feel of the paper and pastels was as foreign to him as the thought of drawing. That was a part of his past he'd thought would never return.

The gesture touched him, but it also aggravated him. Did Jason really think he could just pick up where he had left off? Was he so naïve to think that Kale would just slip into the life of drawing and carefree reading that he had given up three years ago? It didn't take long for the black knot in his gut to consume any trace of feeling in his heart. Kale had known that he was hurting Jason earlier, but he didn't care. Fuck him. Kale had been hurting for three years.

While he wouldn't even consider drawing, he did concede that reading might be a good idea. He needed to get back in practice, seeing as he was going to have a lot of time on his hands, and reading in his room was a great way to avoid

Jason. He grabbed the book at the top of the stack and went to bed. The sight of Jason's gifts had stirred up enough feelings that Kale was sufficiently awake to begin working to regain the fluency he had lost.

Chapter Seventeen

Jason turned the page of his newspaper. The rustling of newsprint was the only sound besides the tick-tock of the office clock. As he focused on the headlines, he realized that he hadn't finished reading the last story. Turning back, he scanned the page, but couldn't find anything familiar. He resolutely shut the paper and discarded it.

This wasn't working. Jason went to the window overlooking the garden. It was a depressing sight. Eventually, the sound of his finger tapping on the glass began to annoy him enough that he moved. He stayed locked away in his office to avoid seeing Kale, but all he could think about was Kale. Where was Kale now? What was he doing? These were pointless questions, but Jason couldn't seem to focus on anything important.

At his desk, he saw his plate from tea time. There were crumbs from a blueberry scone. Thinking back to how delicious it had tasted, Jason checked in with his stomach. Yes, he was hungry. Well, maybe not hungry, but some food wouldn't hurt.

The entire way down to the kitchen, he tried to convince himself that he really was hungry for more than just a glimpse of Kale. The sight that greeted him reminded him why he was staying in his office. Sitting at the table was Kale, hunched over a plate of food as if guarding it. It reminded him of beggars he had seen eating old bread in the street.

"Is there something I can get you, Mr. Wadsworth?"

Sophie's voice pierced his musings, but did nothing to Kale. He stayed frozen. "Yes, I was wondering if you could bring me something to eat in my office." His throat was unusually dry.

"Yes, sir, of course."

Jason couldn't take his eyes off Kale. The tense line of the slave's shoulders didn't so much as twitch under his gaze. The man was as still as stone.

Sophie appeared in his line of sight. "Is there anything else, sir?"

Jason's eyes focused on her. "Uh, no. Thanks, Sophie."

"No problem, sir. I'll be right up with some food." She held her arm out to the door, ushering him away.

Ten minutes later, Sophie stood before his desk with a tray.

"The way Kale was eating earlier, is that normal?"

Jason stood, and Sophie arranged his meal on the desk. "For him it is. He's been eating like that since he got here."

"But why? Do you think he'll ever eat normally?"

"Of course he will, once his body realizes that it's not going to go hungry here. Once he trusts us, he'll relax some more."

"You don't think he trusts us? Do you think he's scared? Has Martin mistreated him?" Jason's volume increased with the speed of his speech.

"No, sir. Martin's been fine. I think Kale's mind trusts us, sir, but his body isn't going to give up the instincts that have helped him survive."

Jason sank into his chair. "Oh. I suppose that makes sense."

"Don't worry, Mr. Wadsworth. Kale is in good hands."

"He didn't even look at me. Is he that way around you?"

"No, sir. He's been surprisingly open with me."

"Well, I won't encroach on his space anymore. You may

pass along to him that I won't be going to the kitchen again."

"I'm sure he'll appreciate that, sir. He likes having a space where he knows he can't get into trouble. It's common enough in slaves."

Jason didn't think anything could hurt more than knowing that Kale feared him. Kale, who Jason loved more than he had ever loved anyone, feared him. "Thank you, Sophie. I appreciate the help you've been with him."

"It's my pleasure, sir. He's quite charming when he forgets to be scared."

Jason smirked. "Yes, he is." Jason knew better than anyone just how charming, witty, and insightful Kale could be. "You may go now."

◆ ◆ ◆

A few days later, Jason sat reading a report from one of his men on the southern coast. He had paid to be kept in the know about the goings on with the shipyard there. Apparently, Lord Conrad had taken the next big step. He hadn't yet begun the process of purchasing the property, but he had purchased the option to buy it. Jason didn't know why the man didn't just go ahead and do it. They both knew he would.

This was potentially the biggest deal Jason would ever make. He wasn't going to lose out on it by not being informed. Jason decided to put some time into studying the process of shipbuilding and went down to the library to retrieve a book that would suffice. When he got downstairs, he was brought up short by the sound of laughter in the library.

"—and he just kept jumping up and down, squealing, 'Get it off! Get it off!'" That voice. It wasn't dry or hoarse. It wasn't weighed down by vitriol. It was Kale's voice, sweet and smooth, solid and assured. How he had missed that voice. Jason could close his eyes and remember lazy days spent listening to that voice. He positioned himself so he could see into the library without being obvious.

"And did this Charlie ever pay you back?" Sophie's light voice was trying to overcome her laughter. The two of them were dusting.

"No. To tell you the truth, he kind of took the fun out of it. He was always much too nice to play pranks, but he was such an easy target that it wasn't long before Simon or Jacob —"

"Or you."

Kale grinned at her. "Yes, or me, decided to have another go at him."

Kale appeared more relaxed than Jason had seen him. The tension was gone from his shoulders. His face lit up, and his mouth was quick to quirk into a smile. Jason felt like an intruder, spying on this carefree moment. Gods knew Kale deserved the unmolested time to regain some happiness. Jason moved to leave, but at the exact moment that his foot creaked on a floorboard, Kale and Sophie's conversation entered a lull. The sound reverberated in the silence, and they both looked at him.

The reaction was instantaneous. Kale appeared stricken and immediately bowed his head and backed away, making himself as small as possible. Tension filled every line of his body where mirth had been only a moment before.

"Sorry to disturb you. I just came to get a book." Jason stepped forward and grabbed the book from its shelf.

"Oh, it's no bother, sir. We were just in here getting caught up on some dusting." Sophie was as jovial as ever. It seemed she hoped Kale would follow her lead, but he didn't move a muscle. Jason would have seen: he kept his eyes riveted on him.

"I appreciate that, Sophie. It looks like you and Kale are doing a great job. I barely recognize the place." Jason desperately wanted to restore the comfortable atmosphere he had intruded on.

"Thank you, sir."

Jason was mesmerized by the change in Kale. Was he really that scared of him? Jason stared at him, hoping for any sign that the Kale he knew was still in there. When he didn't find any, he felt awkward. "Right, well, I'll leave you to it." Jason left, ignoring the urge to look behind him to see if Kale had moved. At the end of the hallway, he stopped and listened. The voices had resumed, albeit more subdued.

Once in his room, Jason tossed the book on his bed and strode to the cabinet that held his whiskey. Wherever he went he brought sadness, even to the one man whose happiness was Jason's top priority. Lying on his bed, he didn't even spare a glance for the book as he took his first drink directly from the bottle. At least he knew how to numb the guilt.

CHAPTER EIGHTEEN

"Is there anything else I can get you, sir?" Sophie was running errands, so Martin was helping out by delivering Jason a sandwich made from leftover roast beef for lunch.

"No, that's all." Of course it was. In the weeks since Kale's arrival, Jason had become more distant than ever.

Kale, on the other hand, was becoming less reserved. He no longer acted afraid of Martin, but Sophie was always with them. They hadn't been alone since that first day. Without her presence, Martin wondered how Kale would react to him.

When Martin entered the kitchen with the empty tray, Kale stood up from the table.

"I'm sorry, sir. I'll just get out of your way."

"Nonsense. Sit back down. I wouldn't mind company for lunch." Since Jason insisted on Kale not being treated like a slave, Martin tried not to think of him as one. It made it much easier to converse with him. Right now, Kale was the best source for the answers Martin wanted. Jason had revealed nothing further about his new slave, and Martin was eaten up with curiosity about their shared past. The only way he could help Jason was by learning what was bothering him.

Martin fixed a sandwich and joined Kale at the table. The slave still wasn't comfortable around him. His right leg bounced, and his right hand was fidgeting on top of it. "You're not scared of me, are you?"

That got the fidgeting to stop. "No, sir."

"Good. I'm not the violent type. I won't hurt you. Besides, if I so much as said something cross to you, Mr. Wadsworth would skin me alive. He's made that perfectly clear."

There was a hint of a smile on Kale's lips. "He always did have a flare for dramatics."

"Hmmm. I wouldn't say that. It's more like he's really intense."

"I guess that's another way to put it."

"Is he the same as he was when you knew him?" Martin took a bite of his sandwich, trying not to appear too interested in Kale's answer.

"Yes and no. In some ways he's so much the same that I could swear no time has passed at all. It's scary, quite frankly."

"How long has it been since he owned you?" Martin knew Kale had opened up somewhat to Sophie, but she was keeping her lips sealed. She insisted he hadn't told her anything at all about Jason, but Martin knew if Kale had told her something in confidence, she wouldn't divulge it.

"I don't think we should be talking about this."

"Well, I do." Martin felt his temper rising, and it was tempting to treat Kale like any other slave and demand the information from him. "I'm responsible for taking care of him, and I can't do it if I don't know what he needs."

"Sophie says you do a fine job."

"Sophie likes to pretend it's not as bad as it is. She's not the one who's had to deal with his drinking. With you to distract her, I doubt she's even noticed that he goes to bed drunk every night."

"He never did hold his liquor well."

"That man can down more alcohol in a night than I do in a year and go on the next morning like nothing is wrong."

Kale's eyebrows rose. "Really?"

"He didn't drink like that when you knew him?"

"No. He was a lightweight."

Martin snorted. "You know, I used to think that his wife was the reason he went to that wretched bar and drank. The anniversary of his proposal, their wedding anniversary, she's the common thread. But she's not. You are."

"The master I knew never stepped foot in a bar."

"Well, now he spends enough at Flannigan's to keep the place afloat."

"Oh." A flicker of recognition passed Kale's face.

"I've gathered you were sold around the time he got married. I tried to get Sophie to tell me more, but she refused. She didn't even tell me that tidbit, she just didn't deny it."

"Maybe you should ask the master if you're wanting to know more. It's not my business."

Martin couldn't help the bit of nastiness that crept into his voice. "Oh, but it is your business. You see, he only used to get into these depressive bouts on special occasions. They may last for weeks, even months sometimes, but they were always predictable. Now he's withdrawing even more when it's time for him to be returning to normal."

"I haven't heard him leave to go anywhere, much less out drinking."

"He doesn't always go to Flannigan's. Sometimes he drinks right here at home, locked away in that study of his."

"Sophie said no one uses the study."

"That's why. He keeps it locked, only goes in there when he wants to get so drunk that he knows he won't be able to make it home from the bar. What drives a man to drink that much?" Martin watched Kale closely, looking for any hint that might help.

"Like I told you, he didn't drink before. I have no idea why he does now. Ask him."

Martin let his exasperation drive his next words. "You don't think I've tried? You don't think I've spent the last two and a half years praying to the saints that he would tell me? All I get are fragments when he's too drunk to know what he's saying. The only sober thing he's ever said on the matter was that he did terrible things to you that he needs to atone for."

Kale's leg began to shake again, and his hand resumed its nervous tic. "He did do terrible things, just not the ones he thinks he did." It came out barely louder than a murmur. Kale's eyes were vacant, like he was looking past Martin.

"Well, whatever happened, he's been drinking to forget. Perhaps if I knew what it was, I could help him through it without him resorting to the bottle."

Kale lowered his head and looked around, as if looking for an escape. "I'm sorry. I can't help you." The frenzied fidgeting of his right hand against his pants crescendoed until the nervous energy erupted, and Kale shot to his feet and hurried away.

Martin sighed and leaned back in his chair. It was evident Kale was at the center of all this. Martin hated ceding control, but he was beginning to believe that this time it was going to have to be Kale who intervened and put a stop to Jason's self-destructive behavior. He only hoped it wouldn't have to get much worse before it got better.

CHAPTER NINETEEN

Martin was right. When Kale paid attention to more than just himself, he noticed that Jason did retreat to the study quite often. Whenever Kale thought about Jason and what Martin had said about him atoning, he felt a thawing in his chest. Part of him wanted so badly to give in to it. How easy would it be to surrender to that warmth? Why couldn't he put the past behind him and love Jason the way he used to, the way his frozen heart still did?

Kale was on his way to the library to fetch a book he had spied while helping Sophie clean. To keep the boredom at bay, he had taken to reading voraciously. The escape was a welcome distraction. During the day, he spent much of his time talking with Sophie and helping her, but she continuously insisted that he rest. Rest was the last thing he needed. When he tried to rest, his mind wandered to places he didn't want it to go. Boredom was the enemy. Most days, he longed for a hard, long day's work so he could collapse into bed at the end of it, too tired to entertain any thoughts.

On his way back to his room, book in hand, a crash brought him up short. Kale cocked his head to the right, in the direction of the sound. A garbled string of curses followed. It was coming from the study.

Kale went to the door, holding his breath as he listened. The venomous voice was barely recognizable as Jason's. It sounded like he was fighting with someone. A quick test of the doorknob revealed that Jason hadn't locked it. Curiosity warred with Kale's common sense. He wasn't welcome here; this was none of his business. But it was. He knew that one way or another, this had to do with him. His hand hovered over the doorknob. Did he dare take this step? Did he want to know? His hand tensed into a fist as he thought it through. If he walked away, he could continue on in the same pattern of existence. It wasn't perfect, not compared to the idyllic days he had spent with Jason years ago, but it also wasn't bad. If he opened this door though, he knew he would be committed.

In the end, curiosity won. A part of him still couldn't believe Martin's description of Jason, even though the evidence supported it. He had to see for himself. Kale grasped the doorknob and carefully opened the door.

Jason's voice stopped. The clatter that rang out was Kale's own book crashing to the floor. The contents of his stomach swirled, threatening to come up.

"What are you doing in here? It's not enough that I give you free rein in the house? You have to intrude on this room where I come to escape you?" Jason slurred.

The irony of Jason's words was like a blow. All around him, on every possible surface of wall and ceiling, were the pictures Kale had drawn when he lived with Jason. The room was literally covered in them. Across the floor were sketches that had fluttered out of their piles at the force of Kale's entry.

"You happy now? You can tell Martin and Sophie how disturbed I am." Jason lounged askew on an armchair in the center of the room, swinging a nearly empty bottle of whiskey. Next to him was an upturned table—probably the source of the crash—and empty bottles littered the floor.

Kale moved to speak, but the acrid taste of vomit in his throat stopped him. The sense of violation Kale felt was strange. He'd always assumed his drawings had been lost or destroyed. At best, they had been packed away somewhere. Kale should have known better. Such practical courses of action lacked the dramatic flair with which Jason insisted on imbuing everything.

"This is who I am, Kale. Do you like what you see?" Jason spread his arms. "I'm a pitiful excuse for a human being. Welcome," Jason wobbled to his feet and turned in a slow circle, gesturing with his bottle, "to my confessional."

Kale was too stunned to maintain his slavish behavior. He met Jason's stare straight on. He wouldn't have been able to tear his eyes away if he'd wanted to. The brown eyes that had always been so soft and quick to light up were now nearly black. Kale thought he could almost see Jason's demons clawing their way out through those dark orbs.

"Don't you have anything to say?" In a strange mix of belligerence and vulnerability, Jason's face begged for words from Kale.

Kale couldn't look at that face anymore. It tore at something inside him. Given a chance, it would tear at him until it untangled the twisted hate in his gut, and that could not be allowed. Instead, he eyed the bottle. "I thought you didn't like whiskey."

The vulnerability drained from Jason's face to be replaced by a hard mask. "Tastes change." Jason shrugged and downed the last swallow.

"Yes, so I'm learning." Jason had changed. This wasn't the man whose lock of hair he held in his pocket. Everything changes, that was the only thing Kale could hold to. Why had he expected this to be different?

"What's that supposed to mean?" Jason walked toward a table holding fresh whiskey bottles.

"It means, I never thought you'd violate me this way."

"Why not? I've violated you every other way. Surely this can't be any worse." Jason was back in his chair, nursing a new bottle.

Kale shook his head. "It is." Kale found it hard to speak

past the bile in his throat. "I know they're yours and you can do anything you like with them, but I didn't expect this."

"They're not mine, Kale. They're part of you. That's why I have them here."

Jason always liked to pretend Kale was free, and it was damned annoying. He wasn't free, and he never would be. Why couldn't Jason accept that? "But you owned me when I did them."

"Yes, I owned you, but not in any of the ways that matter. Not in the one way I wanted to."

"I'm a slave and you're my owner, why have you never been able to wrap your head around that? That's the way it's always been and the way it's always going to be. Stop mourning—or whatever the hell it is you're doing—for something that has never existed and never will."

"Oh, I am mourning, Kale. I'm mourning for you." Jason walked to the sketch Kale had drawn of a flowering weed in the park. "This was you, Kale." Jason's voice had lost its hard edge and was just a whisper as he stared transfixed at the picture. A second later, he closed his eyes. When he reopened them, he was back to his distressed self. He pointed to the drawing of the library rotunda Kale had done after his first visit to campus with Jason. "All this beauty. And now look what I've done to you." Jason sneered at him.

These were some of the happiest memories of Kale's life, and Jason was using them as some grotesque decoration for his own pit of despair. If he hadn't been so angry, Kale might have felt pity. But he was mad, because a part of him saw the truth in Jason's words. Kale was a completely different man from the one who had drawn these pictures. All that was inside him now was bleak darkness.

Jason strolled around the room, stopping to admire certain drawings as he went, as if in a museum. Kale didn't know what to do. He could barely hold himself together. He couldn't take on Jason's problems as well. It wasn't his place. Still, there was a part of him that wanted to try. He started toward Jason, and his foot stubbed against something. Looking down, he saw his forgotten book. It would be so much easier to retire to his room and indulge in the escape he had sought.

Scooping up the book, he resolved to do just that. This wasn't his problem to fix, he didn't know how, and he shouldn't even want to try. Jason was still gazing at the drawings, and Kale left without saying a word.

CHAPTER TWENTY

The throbbing was constant. Jason rolled over and cracked his eyelids open. The dim light in his room sliced into his eyes. There was a glass of whiskey on his bedside table, but he wouldn't drink it. Not yet. Not until he was sure he remembered everything that had happened and had a plan to deal with it.

Last night had been worse than a nightmare. For years he had kept the contents of his study a secret, and then the one person he didn't want knowing about it came traipsing in. The horrified look on Kale's face had mirrored Jason's self-loathing. Even after the humiliating revelation of his secret, Jason didn't have any plans to surrender it. He couldn't. The memories were too important.

What must Kale think of him? Nothing good. Gods, he must appear like some sort of predator keeping all those drawings and then seeking Kale out and buying him again. The thought made Jason sit up. If Kale had any fears about Jason's intentions, Jason needed to alleviate them right away.

Jason reached for the drink on his side table and downed it in one gulp. There was no point in waiting. It wasn't fair to Kale to put off the inevitable conversation, no matter how awkward it made Jason feel.

Once he was dressed, he felt marginally better, but Jason was cognizant enough to know that if he avoided talking to

Kale until he felt fine, it would never happen. Before he left, he took a minute to look out his window over the back garden. It was a beautiful day. Jason remembered lying in the grass with Kale in a much smaller garden. Those days were gone, and they were never coming back, but perhaps Jason could improve Kale's future.

When Jason reached Kale's door, he still didn't know what he was going to say. If he thought about it too much, he was afraid he would lose his nerve and not say anything at all. Jason rapped his knuckles against the door three times and held his breath. For a moment, he wondered if Kale was going to answer. He didn't know if he wanted him to be there or not, but before Jason could decide, the door opened to reveal Kale. The pale green eyes flitted to Jason and then quickly away.

"Yes, master? Is there something I can do for you?" It broke his heart to see Kale behave this way.

"No. Actually, I came to talk to you, Kale." Jason caught the nervous glance Kale threw behind him into the room. "It doesn't have to be here. We could go to the parlor?" Jason had no desire to intrude into Kale's space.

Kale nodded and stepped out into the hallway, closing the door behind him. If there was anything good about last night, it was that Jason had seen a glimpse of the old Kale, without the slavish affectations. Except they weren't affectations; they were learned behaviors designed to keep Kale alive. The reasoning behind Kale's attitude was even more bothersome than the attitude itself.

It shouldn't have come as a surprise that Kale didn't sit when Jason did after they reached the parlor, but it annoyed Jason just the same. He knew they could never be to one another what he had hoped they would, but certainly there could be a degree of civility between them.

"Take a seat, Kale." The hesitant shuffling as Kale moved to sit stirred a thought. "I'm not mad at you, if that's what you're thinking. What happened last night was not your fault." Jason cursed himself for not reassuring Kale earlier. Clearly last night had been embarrassing for Jason, but he hadn't stopped to think about how his response might impact Kale. An eternity ago, before he had fallen in love, Jason would have reacted to that kind of embarrassment by lashing out at his slave. Not anymore.

Kale sat back in his seat. His head wasn't bowed, but he kept his eyes averted. It was clear that was as relaxed as he was going to get. It was magnitudes better than the resolute stiffness that was Kale's usual posture when Jason was in the room.

"The first thing I wanted to do was let you know that, despite what you saw last night, I still have no intention of pursuing any kind of relationship with you." Jason was hoping for some kind of reaction, but the only indication that Kale had even heard him was the slave's right hand tapping at the same spot he had fidgeted with the day Jason found him in the mill. "I was also hoping for a chance to explain myself."

This time Jason waited for a response. This speech was purely to assuage his own guilty feelings. He wasn't going to force Kale to sit through it. They endured a strained moment of awkwardness as Jason waited.

"An explanation would be..." Kale pursed his lips, and Jason couldn't deny the attraction he felt. Those lips held pleasurable memories. "...interesting," Kale finished. Still, he didn't look at Jason.

"I know what I did in the past was unforgivable, but I can't help remembering the time we shared together. I can't help being in love with those memories. And then I remember how spectacularly I screwed it all up and how much I damaged you in the process. It hurts. It hurts so badly sometimes that I think I'll never be rid of the pain. So I drink."

"Does it help?"

Jason stopped to think about Kale's question. He had

never really thought about it. The habit was so deeply ingrained that it was beyond questioning. "No, I don't suppose it does. Not really. But I need it. It dulls the pain for a moment. I keep hoping if I drink enough, I'll forget."

"If you want so badly to forget, then why the hell are you keeping all those damn pictures in that room? Why do you go to Flannigan's, for gods' sakes?" Kale's eyes finally met Jason's, and Jason was stunned by how wrong he had been. Kale hadn't been keeping his eyes averted in a submissive gesture. He had kept them averted to hide his anger. Rage flared in his eyes that his voice only hinted at.

Here was the great paradox of his life. How could Jason explain it to Kale when he didn't fully understand it himself? "I don't know. I guess not remembering is more painful. Pretending you never existed, acting like what I felt for you wasn't real, that is unbearable. If I don't have those memories, it means I let my marriage fall apart for no good reason. My study is my own particularly bittersweet torture."

Kale just sat and listened, his arms crossed. He had gone back to not looking at Jason. Jason didn't know which was worse: thinking Kale was looking away out of an ingrained fear, or knowing that he looked away to hide his hatred. In the end, hatred won out—hatred he could abide, but it would pain him to believe Kale was still afraid of him.

When it was clear Kale was not going to say anything, Jason continued. "The back garden is yours. I know you enjoy being outside. It's bigger than the garden at the old townhouse. It isn't in great shape, but I thought you might find some pleasure there. You can do whatever you want with it." Kale's expression changed almost imperceptibly, but Jason couldn't decipher if it was because Kale liked Jason's gesture or not. "Don't feel like you have to do something with it," Jason hurried to add. "I just thought you would like it."

"Thank you."

"I know I wronged you—"

Kale snorted and shook his head, muttering, "You still don't get it."

Jason didn't doubt that he didn't fully comprehend the hurt he had caused Kale. "I'm trying, though. That's the best I can do, Kale. I know it's not enough, but it's all I have."

"It's not enough. It will never be enough." Kale met his eyes again for a brief moment, and the hurt and anger in them stabbed at Jason.

"I know. We're two broken people, Kale. I deserve my lot, but you didn't deserve any of this. I ruined you, and I'll never forgive myself."

There were probably a million things Jason should have said, but he couldn't come up with any more words. He stayed for a moment longer, giving Kale a chance to say something. The silence thickened with each passing second. It was almost impossible to believe that they used to talk entire nights away, neither one aware of the passage of time. Once the oppressive tension grew so tight that Jason thought it would snap, he rose. In the doorway before he left, he turned back to see Kale hunch over and drop his head into his hands.

CHAPTER TWENTY-ONE

All this time Jason was torturing himself for the wrong sins. Kale had wanted to set him straight, but he couldn't. Was Jason really so blind? After all that time, he still failed to see through Kale's lie. Jason shouldn't have been agonizing over his sexual relationship with Kale. Hell, that was one of the few things in Kale's life that he didn't regret. It was Jason's very insistence at remaining blind to the lie that Kale couldn't forgive him for.

Jason should have made sure he was sold somewhere decent.

He should have insisted that Kale stay.

That was what Kale really couldn't overcome. Jason should have seen through him. He should have told Renee to go fuck herself. He should have chosen Kale. Instead, Jason had believed the lie because he wanted to. He wanted Renee, and when he finally got her, he ruined that relationship too.

Back in his room, Kale saw the sketchpad on the table where he'd first found it. He hadn't touched it. Was Jason right? Was Kale broken? He knew he was different. A person didn't survive three years of hell and not come out the other side without some callouses to show for it. But was he dead inside?

He felt dead. He hadn't felt the urge to draw since he arrived, but that was something that would come back, wasn't it? Part of the reason he had avoided drawing was Jason. Kale resented Jason and his gift. But this wasn't about Jason, not really. He needed to know if Jason was right. All those pictures in the study had been created by Kale. He needed to know if he was still capable of creating anything, beautiful or not.

Before he entirely knew what he was doing, Kale strode to the garden, sketchpad and charcoal pencil in hand. Jason was right. This garden was bigger than the old one, but it was untended. There was overgrowth, and despite the season, no flowers bloomed. Kale didn't much care what it looked like. He only cared that he was outside, and it felt nice. If anything had ever inspired him to draw, it was nature.

There was no bench, so Kale sat on the ground. It suited him better, anyway. He put his hand in the grass and reveled in the cool feeling of earth beneath his fingers. It contrasted nicely with the steady warmth of the sun on his shoulders and back. Since going to work at the mill, he hadn't been outside much, and before that, being outside had meant baking under the sun or freezing in the cold as he laid railroad track.

Things were different now. He had to change the way he looked at the world, see it the way he had a lifetime ago. He closed his eyes and tried to conjure up a pleasant memory. His mind immediately went through an extensive catalogue of moments with Jason, and he quickly dismissed them. The feelings between Kale and Jason right now had no place in this garden. Instead, he focused on an image from his childhood in Malar County. He remembered sneaking out with his younger brother and going to a nearby pond to listen to the bullfrogs and skip stones. It was easy to see the beauty in that memory. If only he could find beauty here.

He opened his eyes and surveyed the scene. The grass was thick, vividly green. The ivy had grown unchecked, consuming the fence and the wall of the house. The weeds were the only things flowering. It was tempting to be sucked into the memory of a time when he had been able to capture the beauty of a weed on paper, but Kale pushed the memory away. This was about the here and now. Was he capable of seeing beauty?

Yes, he could. His eyes pricked with tears he wouldn't allow to fall. The garden was wild, but it was also beautiful. A quick pass of his sleeve over his eyes ensured that no wetness touched his cheeks. He picked up his pad and pencil and waited for inspiration. His hand hovered, poised over the paper, but the only urge in his hand was to scribble a black mess over the perfect parchment. None of the beautiful, flowing lines around him were making their way to his hand.

He refused to give in to the urge, if for no other reason than doing so would make it real. If he didn't act, it was just a problem he thought he had. As soon as he unleashed his darkness on that piece of paper, it would become real. While it was easier than he thought it would have been to see the beauty around him, there was nothing beautiful inside him anymore. And whose fault was that?

Kale grabbed the blank sheet of paper and tore it up, releasing his frustrations and preventing his tears from falling. What on earth could he do with a garden? How could he possibly make it better when he was such a wreck?

Chapter Twenty-Two

The metal on metal sound of the knife sweeping across the sharpener was hypnotic, satisfying. Good.

The kitchen was empty, but he needed to occupy his hands, so he had taken it upon himself to sharpen all of Sophie's knives. She had mentioned on more than one occasion that they were getting dull.

"You don't need to do that." Sophie's voice startled him out of his precarious reverie.

"I don't mind." His words were quick and clipped. Hopefully Sophie would overlook his tone, but Kale knew it was a vain hope.

Sophie gave him the entire time it took her to put away the purchases from her shopping trip before questioning him.

"What has you worked up?" Sophie sat at the table and looked at him with a pointed stare, making it clear he was not going to sidestep her question.

That wouldn't stop him from trying, though.

"Kale." The pointed stare transformed to baleful, and her tone brooked no argument.

"He gave me the back garden to do with as I please."

Sophie's surprise showed on her face. "That's nice. I'd thought you'd be happy. That garden needs tending."

Kale stopped sharpening and sat down, but retained his hold on the knife and sharpener. He knew if he put them down, his hand would begin to fidget. That damned habit was proving hard to break. "What am I going to do with a garden, Sophie? I feel ruined. I can't even draw anymore. It was a part of who I was, and now it's not there anymore, like it just disappeared."

"You've been through a lot, dear. Give it time. It'll come back."

"But how do you know?" There was no hiding the desperation in his voice.

"Because I do." Sophie reached across the table and rested her hand on Kale's forearm. "Look, I don't know the details of what happened between you and the master. I haven't pushed because it's none of my business, but I think the sooner you work through your issues there, the sooner things will begin to look rosy again."

"I don't know if I can." It was a whisper. Even talking about letting go of the darkness inside him was difficult.

"You can. You just have to make the choice that something else is more important than holding onto the past."

Was it really that simple? Could he really act like nothing had happened? No. How does someone brush aside that kind of betrayal? Maybe Sophie could, she was always so happy and full of light, or maybe she had never really been hurt. Could a free person even understand what he was going through?

"Now, as far as that garden's concerned, I've always thought it would be nice to have a vegetable and herb garden. When I was a little girl, we had one, and there's nothing quite like cooking with ingredients from your very own garden. I just never got around to it. There's always been other work that's come first."

Sophie's voice distracted Kale from his thoughts, and he latched on to what she was saying. That's what he needed for the backyard: a purpose. If he could help Sophie by cultivating the garden, then that would not only give him direction, but it would also give him purpose. He still felt awkward being a slave with no official duties. While he helped out wherever and whenever he was asked or saw an opportunity, this garden could be his project, his way of contributing.

"Where do I start? I don't know much about growing."

"Talk to Martin; he has all the catalogues. He'll get everything you need ordered." Sophie stood and started to pull down the pots she would need to fix dinner. "I think there's also a book around here somewhere about gardening. If not, have Martin order you one."

Kale wished Sophie would just take care of it. He knew she could, but she wanted him to get along better with Martin. It wasn't that he couldn't be friendly with the other man, more that he tried to avoid him. Sophie was easy. The small woman was open and welcoming. Martin, on the other hand, was austere and off-putting. Plus, Kale knew Martin didn't approve of him—a slave being treated so un-slavelike —on principle. Not to mention the fact that Martin was closest to Jason, a position Kale had once occupied.

So it was with great reluctance that Kale stood in front of Martin's desk an hour later.

"What can I do for you, Kale?"

Don't fidget. This man has no power over you. "The master gave me use of the back garden."

"Yes, I heard. I think it's a marvelous idea."

Kale was taken aback by the genuine smile on Martin's face. He felt some of his nervous tension melting. "Thank you. I'm glad. The thing is, I don't know too much about gardening."

Martin waved his hand. "Don't worry about it. You'll be fine. Besides, it's not like you can make things worse out there." Martin stood, began walking out of his office, and gestured for Kale to follow. "We have a couple of books on gardening. Don't ask me why. That's one thing Mr. Wadsworth doesn't skimp on: books. I've gathered from him that you know how to read."

"Yes, sir."

"Good, then you'll find these helpful." Martin stopped in the library and handed him two books on gardening. One seemed to be composed mainly of pictures, while the other was a dense text. "Now, do you know what you want to plant?"

"I was thinking vegetables and herbs for Sophie."

"Good. I think Mr. Wadsworth would like that very much."

"Sophie also said I should talk to you about ordering supplies."

"Ah, yes. I'm afraid we don't have much here. I'll put in an order for everything you'll need and have it couriered over. Give me a couple of days to compile a list of supplies."

"That's fine. There's no hurry. There's plenty of work to be done before I can even get around to planting anyway."

"Excellent. If you think of anything else you want to plant, just let me know and I'll order it."

"Thank you, sir."

"You're welcome, Kale."

"And thanks for being so kind to me. I know you don't approve of my presence here."

"It's not that, Kale." Martin hesitated. "Maybe a little. I just want Mr. Wadsworth to be happy, and it's hard for me not knowing how to help him. When he told me about giving you the back garden, I was pleased. It will give you something to do so maybe you won't feel so awkward. And Mr. Wadsworth spends a lot of time looking out his window over that garden. Maybe seeing it tended to will cheer him up some."

◆ ◆ ◆

Kale spent much of the next two days outside, clearing away

118

the overgrowth and doing his best to get ready for the arrival of the supplies. When he wasn't outside, he read the books Martin had given him. There was a lot to learn. He had no knowledge of planting seasons or watering or soil. Any time he came across something else he needed, he went to Martin, and Martin assured Kale it was already on his list. Apparently Martin's mother had a garden, and he had helped her as a child.

The thought of being watched by Jason was a little disconcerting, but Kale had to come to terms with the fact that Jason owned him again. After the yard was cleared, Kale sat in his room leafing through a book Martin had given him: the one with all the illustrations. There were pictures of all kinds of different plants, many Kale had never seen. Flipping through the flower section, he stopped on a picture of calla lilies. Kale knew they were one of Jason's favorites. He'd always loved to see them on display at parties.

A plan formed in Kale's head. He wasn't over the past. He wasn't even anywhere near wanting to be over it, but he did need to try and move on to a better place. A quick check showed that calla lilies were able to be planted at this time of year. Kale knew Jason would be looking out at the garden. There was no reason not to give him something he would enjoy looking at. Besides, Kale was grateful for Jason's gift of the garden, and this was a way to show his appreciation.

"Martin, could you place an order for some calla lilies in a variety of colors?" Kale popped his head around the doorway to Martin's office. The last few days, Kale had become more at ease with Martin. It was necessary with how much they talked about the garden.

"Yes, but you do realize that flowers are more delicate than vegetables. It will take a lot more care to get them to stay beautiful."

"I understand."

"Why the sudden interest in calla lilies? I thought you wanted a kitchen garden?"

"They're the master's favorite. I thought it'd be nice when they bloom to put some around the house. Brighten it up a bit."

Martin's face softened. "Yes, that would be nice. I forget sometimes that you know him better than I do."

"Well, he's different now than he was then. I doubt you'd have the opportunity to learn his favorite flower." Kale's feelings toward Martin were complicated. In a way he was jealous, but mostly he felt sorry for the man. It was apparent Martin wanted nothing more than to help Jason, to be taken into his confidence, but Jason was beyond the kind of help Martin could give him. Kale didn't think anyone could get through to him.

"No, he doesn't exactly talk about such things."

"I spent a lot of time watching him be happy. It was easy to pick up on what he liked back then."

"If you think there's a chance seeing fresh calla lilies will make him the least bit happy, I'll order you every one in Arine."

"Let's make sure I don't kill one order first." Kale grinned, and Martin's smile met it. Already Jason's gift was improving Kale's life.

CHAPTER TWENTY-THREE

Kale stopped and pulled a handkerchief from his back pocket to wipe the sweat off his brow. His tongue darted out to moisten his lips, and he tasted salt. The sun was at its peak, but Kale wasn't about to stop. He was almost done.

When he pulled the handkerchief back from his face, he saw that his hands had made a mess of it. Dirt was caked under his fingernails, and his skin was covered in a fine layer of grime, making it appear a shade darker than it actually was. He had foregone gloves in favor of the cool feel of soil against his sunbaked hands.

His face wasn't the only part of him covered in sweat. Yet, the heat wasn't oppressive as it had been when he was laying rail. It was odd that the same sensation could feel so different just by virtue of doing the work freely. Grabbing the packet of seeds from the ground near his leg, he poured out a few more and placed them in the earth. How something could grow out of a seed so small was beyond him. He still half doubted whether anything would come from this at all. He covered the seeds and patted the soil on top. That was it.

Sitting back on his haunches, Kale surveyed his work. The seed had all arrived two days ago. Yesterday morning, he started early, but hadn't been able to finish. Martin had offered to help, but Kale needed to do this on his own, and Martin had seemed to understand. Today, he had been up with the sun, determined to finish. With the planting complete, he felt an overwhelming sense of satisfaction. Before him were rows of dark brown mounds, each containing the seeds that his books assured him would grow into actual, edible plants.

Martin had also ordered some lawn furniture as a surprise. He said there wasn't much sense in planting a garden if there was no way to sit back and enjoy the fruits of one's labor. And that was another surprise: Martin had ordered some small apple trees and berry bushes. Kale had completely forgotten about fruit in his plans.

Grabbing a book he had brought out with him in anticipation of this moment, Kale sat back in one of the lawn chairs and began to read. Relaxing was easier for him when he felt he had accomplished something.

It didn't take long for a tingling feeling to settle over him. Someone was watching. Kale could feel eyes on his back. He took a deep breath of air heavy with the scent of freshly turned earth, and then slowly released it, willing the breath to take away his irritation. There was nothing to be worried about. Jason watched him from an upstairs window. After all these years, Kale could still distinguish Jason's presence from anyone else's. He marveled that he hadn't known it was Jason back in the office of the steel mill. Of course, he had been too scared to pay attention.

Kale continued reading, pretending he wasn't unsettled and trying hard to not actually be unsettled. He was following orders, so he knew he couldn't be in trouble. If Jason was going to get mad for no reason, then it didn't matter what Kale did. Besides, this wasn't as bad as actually being inside with Jason. Out here, there was too much distance—not to mention a brick wall—between them for Kale to give anything away. Kale didn't need Jason knowing the extent of his confusion, which was why he still tensed every time Jason came near.

Kale slipped his right hand down to his leg and felt the

lock of hair through the material of his pocket. He might as well get used to Jason staring. He would never be able to escape. Jason had made sure of that. Maybe a part of him didn't want to escape. He didn't know.

All Kale knew was that he felt more content in the garden than he had since coming to Jason's house. And no amount of being watched was going to change that. As long as he kept his distance, nothing bad could happen.

Chapter Twenty-Four

Jason was being indulgent. Below him in the garden, he didn't see his slave. He saw his former lover, lounging on a chair and reading after a day of gardening. Jason held out a ridiculous hope that Kale would look up at him and smile, but he never did. Kale never gave any indication that he knew Jason was watching.

Over the last couple of weeks, a new routine had been established. Kale would work in the garden in the morning when it was cool, and then sit and read. Jason always watched. It was the only time Jason could picture Kale the way he wanted him to be.

"Sir? You wanted to see me?"

"Yes." Jason didn't face Martin. He needed to soak up just a little more of Kale. By the time he was done talking with Martin, Kale would have retreated back indoors, and Jason wouldn't see him again until tomorrow.

"He's doing well." Martin's voice was closer, and Jason broke away from the window.

"That's what I wanted to talk to you about." Jason seated himself at his desk and motioned for Martin to sit across from him.

"Oh?"

"As you know, I keep my distance, so I don't know how he's doing, how he's settling in, or if there are any problems."

"Problems? No, none at all. He seems to be settling in quite nicely, especially now that he has the garden to keep him occupied. He's even begun to relax around me."

"Good. I was serious when I told you I wanted you to be congenial toward him."

"If we're not friends, I'd say we're awfully close to it."

"What about his nervous tic?"

"The fidgeting with his right hand?"

"Yes."

"It's calmed down recently. In fact, the only time I see it now is when you're brought up, if you don't mind me saying."

"Not at all. It's to be expected. It doesn't surprise me in the least." Surprising? No, but very disheartening.

"Other than that, he seems to be happy, or at least content. Sophie gets along well with him."

"Sophie gets along with everyone." Jason smiled when he thought of his cook-cum-housekeeper.

"Yes, but she's sort of adopted him in a way. She's good for him, being a friend when he needs one, but also pushing him. She got him to finally warm up around me."

"How'd she manage that?"

"She told him he had to come to me to order the supplies for the garden. She's too busy to help with it anyway, but I know she wanted us to have to talk."

"So it worked out well?"

"Surprisingly so. We had spoken before, but this project required enough back and forth that he eventually realized he could relax. I think he had it in his head that I didn't like him before."

The thought of anyone not liking Kale seemed absurd to Jason. "How is everything else in the house?"

"In general, I'd say things are better than ever. It's nice having Kale around. I know Sophie likes the company."

"What about you?"

"I like having him here too."

"Any particular reason?"

Martin looked decidedly uncomfortable at the question. Did Martin hold romantic feelings toward Kale? The thought made heat flare in Jason's stomach. The urge to make it clear to Martin that Kale was his was overwhelming. Only Kale wasn't his that way. He never really had been. Any relationship of a personal nature between Martin and Kale was none of Jason's business.

"In a way, he understands me better than I thought he would."

"Well, I think it's only fair to tell you that I've been looking for a buyer for him."

"What?" Martin sprang to the edge of his chair. Jason didn't think he'd ever seen this much emotion from his secretary.

"Nothing's going to happen right away. I won't repeat the mistake I made last time. I won't sell him until he's ready, but I've been quietly looking for someone who would be a good fit."

"When he's ready? How can you do this to him? He's finally settled, we've all grown attached to him, and now you're going to sell him? I'm sorry, sir, but what you're suggesting is cruel. Why let him become accustomed here when you're just going to pull it all away from him? He's never going to be ready to leave. That's asking the impossible. What slave would want to leave this life?" Martin rose to his feet, his face red from the passion of his speech. Jason had not expected this reaction.

"He will want to leave, Martin. Trust me."

"How can you be so sure?"

"He hates me. You said it yourself. The only time his nervous tic comes out is when someone mentions me. Whenever I'm around, he's tense and stiff."

"I disagree."

"I'm only keeping him so he has a safe place to heal, to see if I can undo some of the damage I've done. Once he's over the trauma of the last few years, he'll be much happier as far away from me as possible."

"You're wrong."

"No, I'm not." He heard the steel in his voice. "Anyway, you're not to mention it to him. I don't want him worrying that he's going to end up sold back into hard labor. I won't allow that to happen, but he has no reason to believe me. I just wanted you to know so you don't become too attached."

"I can't believe you can be this blind. This isn't right. You're being a damned fool. It's one thing to watch you self-destruct, but I wouldn't have believed you could be this destructive to the people closest to you."

Martin's words smarted. Didn't he realize Jason was trying?

"That's enough, Martin. You're dismissed." Jason was more stern than he could ever remember being.

It was clear that Martin wanted nothing more than to remain and give Jason more of his thoughts on the matter, but after a few breaths, he turned and left.

Jason knew the truth, and if Martin knew it too, he would understand. Jason wouldn't tell him, not out of any self-preservation instinct—he doubted anyone had a lower opinion of him than Martin—but because he couldn't violate Kale's privacy that way. But Jason was sure that if Martin had all the facts, he would agree with him.

There was no hope that Kale would ever be comfortable around him. All Jason was trying to do was get Kale back to his old self. And that alone might be an impossible task, but Jason was going to try. If he failed, he would let Kale stay for the rest of his life, and Jason would keep out of his way. But if he succeeded, then he wouldn't force Kale to tolerate belonging to him any longer than he had to.

Chapter Twenty-Five

The sun was only just beginning to peak around the buildings, and the air was still cool when Kale stepped out into the garden. His early hours were spent here, weeding and watering. It was his only responsibility, and he performed it with care.

He set his book down on the patio table and patrolled the rows of plants. Except, they weren't plants yet. Kale was still waiting for the first seed to sprout. If he was honest, this gardening stuff was kind of boring, and he was losing faith that anything would come of it.

Then he saw it. Straight ahead was a patch of green. Sure enough, after he dusted off some dirt, he could see rows of green sprouts. Before he knew it, a whoop of excitement had left his mouth. An inexplicable joy filled him at seeing these little plants, this little bit of life that had sprung from nothing.

Pride swelled in his heart. He had created something out of seed and earth and water. Kale's mind went back to the time when he had told Jason that if he were free, he would like to cultivate his own bit of land. Had Jason been thinking of that when he gave the garden to Kale? The thought irritated him, and he pushed it aside. He didn't want to get sentimental where Jason was concerned. He was grateful, and he could just leave it at that.

Kale lay down on his stomach to closely examine one of

the sprouts. It was a simple green stem with two branching leaves. The contrast of the bright green—so vibrant and full of life—against the dull brown of the earth was remarkable. One day, this sprout would grow into a carrot, and all around it would be a lush garden. In his mind's eye, he saw the picture clearly.

Kale found his inspiration.

He scrambled to his feet and ran inside to his room. He didn't even wipe off his hands before grabbing his sketchpad and a charcoal pencil from the table. Back outside, he took up position on his stomach again and began to draw. He tried not to think too hard, worried that he might scare the image away. He sketched, trance-like, until the inspiration ran its course.

When he was done, Kale focused his eyes on the paper. There was a single sprout in the foreground. Behind it was a rendering of the garden, ripe and in full bloom. Kale sat up and stared at the picture. He had done this. He had drawn this. Not only had he depicted what was before him, but he had been able to conjure up in his own mind a beautiful imagining of what the garden could be. It was the first beautiful thing he had produced in more than three years.

Taking a deep breath, he looked up and closed his eyes, letting silent tears fall and dry in the rising sun. This was a good day.

When he knew no more tears would fall, he dug the lock of hair from his pocket and looked at it. The Kale who had clipped this hair was a different man. Kale had always thought Jason was the naïve, idealistic one. Looking back, Kale could see that he was more idealistic than he would have admitted.

Could he ever regain his sense of life? Could he get that spark back? As he looked down at the picture he had drawn, Kale began to think he could. A day ago, he would have never believed he was capable of producing any type of art again. The drawing was a token of hope. If he could do that, then maybe he could salvage some part of himself.

The night he had clipped that hair, he had finally been able to admit the truth to himself: he loved Jason, and Jason loved him. After the last few years, Kale didn't know if he could even comprehend the love he had felt back then. So much had happened. Now that old life, that old love, was like a mythical fairytale. He held to it for the strength it gave him, but he didn't really believe in it. The person he had been was a stranger. He would never be able to be him again, but maybe he could simply be happy.

CHAPTER TWENTY-SIX

The contract in front of Jason was a mind-numbing mess. Plans for the northern mill expansion moved forward, and that meant reams of papers to look through, amend, sign, approve, decline, and pass along. It was early, too early to be messing with this sort of thing. That was the justification Jason gave himself for gazing out the window before he started on the day.

Kale sprawled on his stomach in the garden. It was a familiar position. If Jason closed his eyes, he could picture Kale just like that in a myriad of settings: on Jason's bed, in the park, on the sofa, on the floor once, drawing from the perspective of a cricket that had found its way inside.

That last memory must have bled over into reality. Jason could swear he saw Kale drawing. It was wishful thinking. Jason hadn't seen Kale draw since he brought him home, and from what he gathered from Martin, no one else had either. It was all part of the healing process. Eventually, Kale's gift would come back. Jason had to believe it would.

Wait. There was movement below. Kale shifted, and Jason gasped. There was, indeed, a sketchpad in Kale's hands. Not only that, but it was full. From this distance, Jason couldn't make out what it was, but there was no mistaking that there was a picture. Jason yearned to get a closer look. This was the first drawing Kale had done since his return, and

Jason needed to see it, if only to convince himself that Kale was healing.

Rushing down the stairs, Jason couldn't help the excitement building in his stomach. For three years he had studied every picture Kale had left him. He knew them all in excruciating detail. Now he was going to see something new. What would it be? He knew he would love it by virtue of it being Kale's, but would he like what it revealed? Drawing had always been his window into Kale's soul, and Jason's stomach fluttered at the thought of what he might see.

Before opening the door to the garden, Jason stopped to compose himself. A few deep breaths helped him gather his wits. If he wasn't careful, he would scare Kale off. The only way he would get a peek at that drawing was to be covert. Slowly, Jason turned the doorknob and pushed open the door. Kale was still there—thank the gods—only he wasn't drawing anymore. Jason held his breath as he closed the door behind him, willing it to not make a sound.

Kale sat, his face lifted to the sky. Tiptoeing forward, Jason craned his neck to view the picture in Kale's lap. From what Jason could see, it was breathtaking. After all this time, it was surreal to be near a new creation of Kale's. He couldn't make out the details yet, but it appeared to be a drawing of the garden in bloom. It was a happy drawing. Jason found none of the anger or sadness he'd feared in Kale's art.

Just a little closer and Jason could get a perfect view. Movement from Kale stilled Jason in mid-stride. Jason watched with bated breath as Kale reached into his right hand pocket and pulled out…what was that? Kale's hand moved, and Jason got a clear view. It was a lock of hair. Brown hair. A familiar chill went down Jason's back, and his eyes darted to Kale's face. It looked dry now, but he could make out tear tracks in the dirt speckling his cheeks.

A hand flew to Jason's head. Of course not, that lock of hair was clearly old. But yet, Jason couldn't deny it. That was a lock of his hair. He didn't know how he knew, only that he did.

Why would Kale have that? He must have clipped it before Jason sold him. But why would he? Why take a token of your rapist with you into your future? Why hold onto it all these years? It didn't make any sense.

Kale twirled the hair in his right hand and a piece of the puzzle shifted into place. The tic, that relentless fidgeting any time Jason was near or mentioned. It was always the right hand over Kale's right pant leg. Always the same. Furiously rubbing at something. Not something, this lock of hair. Jason's hair. What did it mean?

And why did Kale look at it the way he did? In Kale's face, Jason saw happiness, hope, longing, and—did Jason dare believe it?—love. In light of the drawing Kale had just created, Jason could understand those feelings for his art, but not toward that lock of hair that Jason knew to the core of his being was his.

This didn't make sense. Jason's mind ran in circles, tangling itself more and more as it tried to figure out the riddle. Jason closed his eyes and ordered his mind to cease its frantic searching. There was a simple and logical explanation for all of this.

Kale loves you.

No. There was a sensible, pragmatic explanation.

Kale loves you.

That was impossible. Kale didn't love Jason. Kale hated him. It was obvious in every line of his body. If Kale loved him, why would he have said what he did all those years ago? Why would he have all but begged to be sold?

Because he loves you.

Jason was transported back in time. To the bed he and Kale had shared. The look on Kale's face as they made love. The crushing disappointment of Renee's refusal to marry him. The night they had shared, mending wounds and comforting one another. Those were acts of love. But they could not overcome what happened next.

Kale had so deftly pointed out that he never loved Jason, had never said the words. He had called him a rapist.

No.

A frantic search through Jason's memory proved that Kale had never spoken that word. Jason had been the one to use the label. Kale had merely not disagreed with him. But why had he pushed until Jason came to that conclusion?

It was a lie.

Of course it was a lie. Jason had even called Kale on it. Only, the next day when Kale had confirmed all the worst things Jason secretly thought of himself, he had forgotten everything else. In the harsh light of the reality of what Jason was, everything else washed out.

But it was a lie.

No. Jason had been cruel to Kale. He had humiliated him. Beat him. If it was a lie, then why would Kale let himself be sold? A single word from Kale would have stopped the sale. Jason would have kept Kale and forgotten about Renee. It only made sense if Kale had been telling the truth. The last three years of his life only made sense if Kale had been honest. Why would he lie? Why would he put himself through the agony of these last years?

Because he loves you.

It was a lie.

The last three years of Jason's life were built on a lie. It was a blow to the gut, and Jason sucked in a ragged breath.

Kale turned at the sound and jumped to his feet as he saw Jason.

"Is that my hair?" Jason pointed a shaky hand toward Kale. He didn't know why he was asking. He already knew the answer. There was no evidence other than his gut feeling, but he knew. He knew it all now.

Kale's only answer was to stuff the lock of hair back in his pocket. Even with new clothes, Jason could make out the faint signs of wear on Kale's pants.

"Why did you keep it?" Jason was unsteady on his feet

136

under the weight of his new worldview. He took a step toward Kale. "You have feelings for me?" And another. Kale stayed resolutely still, neither confirming nor denying what Jason was saying. It didn't matter. All the confirmation Jason needed was in Kale's face. "Why do you have a lock of my hair, Kale?" Jason's voice grew progressively louder and came out as a demand for information that even Kale couldn't ignore.

"How do you know it's your hair?"

"How did you know the only way to get me to sell you would be to convince me that I was a rapist?"

Kale blanched and took a step back. Hoorah for Jason. After all these years, he'd finally unnerved Kale.

"This isn't what you think."

"What is it then, Kale?"

Kale visibly gathered himself and leaned forward. "Why can't it just be about me holding on to something, like you and those damn drawings? Not everything is about you."

"I hold on to the drawings, Kale, because I still love you."

Kale clamped his mouth shut and looked away.

"You lied to me all those years ago. You made me think I had been raping you."

Kale's head whirled back around. "I never said that. You put that on yourself."

Jason laughed bitterly. "Yes, I know. A search through my recollections shows that you didn't use those exact words, just like you didn't say 'I love you.' It was all plausible deniability."

"What?"

"Don't act stupid. You may not know the term, but you know what I'm talking about."

"It doesn't matter. That was then."

"It matters to me. The truth matters a great deal, Kale."

"Fine. Yes. I did it. I lied to you to protect you and ensure your happiness. Much good it did. You still managed to screw it all up."

Jason had made a mess of everything. He knew that. Even before today, he was aware of what a failure he had been. "But the way you were looking at my hair. There was love in your eyes, Kale."

"So?"

"So, you love me."

"No. Loved. Past tense." Kale did the thing with his lips that Jason loved, pursing them as he thought about what to say. "I was crazy in love with you back then, so crazy that I thought it would be better if I was sold so you could live out your dream with Renee. That was a long time ago. I no longer love you. Not the reality. Not the drunk estranged from his wife, holding on to ghosts of the past. Not the man who abandoned me and turned me into this pitiful shell of a person. I hold on to the hair because that's the fantasy, the dream. I hold to it to help me get through each day. It has nothing to do with you."

It was so strange to hear those words from Kale. Hearing that Kale had loved him was a bright ray of light in Jason's life, and he wanted nothing more than to bathe in it forever. There was a hope in Kale's words, and Jason clung to it. "If you loved me before, you can love me again."

Kale merely grunted. His expression gave no encouragement.

"You told me once that a man can change."

"I was stupid."

"No, you weren't, Kale. You were never stupid. I can change. I can be the man you loved again."

"We can't go back in time. You've changed too much. And even if you hadn't, I have."

"All right, then maybe I can become the kind of man you can love now."

"It's time you start living for yourself."

"I can do this, Kale. I promise. I can. I can be a better man."

Kale met Jason's eyes. The swirl of emotion was still in

138

his face, but Jason was shocked by an addition. Now there was fear in his expression as well. "I know you can." Kale's voice wavered, and he looked down, his eyes despairing.

Jason couldn't stay and decipher Kale's demeanor. He couldn't help Kale at all. Not like this. He needed to help himself before he could be of any use to Kale. Jason strode indoors to his office, bellowing for Martin as he went.

CHAPTER TWENTY-SEVEN

"What's wrong?" Martin burst, breathless, through Jason's office door only seconds after Jason arrived.

"Nothing's wrong, Martin. Here, you want a drink?" Jason went to the decanter and began to pour, but then thought better of it. His body called out for a drink, but giving in would not bring him closer to his objective. "Never mind." Jason tipped the contents of the glass back into the decanter.

"If nothing's wrong, then why were you yelling for me when you could have rung just as easily?" Martin never was one for spontaneity.

"I couldn't wait. Nothing's wrong, but we have a lot of work to do." Jason couldn't help grinning like a fool. It had only been a glimmer of hope, but in the wake of the last three years, a glimmer seemed like a damned flood. Kale had loved him. If he had once, he could again. Jason only had to become the kind of man who was worthy of such love.

Even in the excitement of his newfound knowledge, Jason had to check himself. Love might be too lofty a goal at the moment. First, he needed Kale's respect. He knew he could earn at least that much. From there, he would see where their feelings took them.

"First things first. As of this moment, I'm giving up alcohol. I want it gone. All of it. I don't want so much as a drop left in this house for cooking." Jason paced the room as he talked, his hands gesturing as quickly as his mouth. Too many thoughts and emotions coursed through him for him to have any hope of staying still.

Jason looked at Martin to see if he was taking all this in and was unsurprised to see him sitting quite calmly at the desk, his planner open on his lap. "Are you getting all of this?"

"You're giving up alcohol?" The hint of disbelief in Martin's voice was not welcome.

"Yes. What? You don't think I can? You don't think I'm serious?" Jason stood over him, meeting Martin's gaze with a firm stare.

The beginnings of a smile tugged at Martin's lips. "Yes, I think you can do it. I know you can. I guess I'm just wondering what brought all this about."

It was a fair question. He knew Martin disapproved of his drinking, but Jason had never done anything to curtail it. The enormity of the journey he was embarking on caught up with him, and he collapsed into his chair, winded. It all came down to one simple truth. "He loved me."

"Wha—"

"Kale. He loved me. Before. I never knew."

"Oh." The tenderness in Martin's voice surprised Jason. Martin seemed happy for him. This man who Jason had always viewed as an inconvenience at best and an adversary at worst.

"I know you've been wanting me to quit, but I never realized I could until today. Right now, I feel I could do anything. I have so much work to do."

"I'll make sure all the alcohol is out of the house within the hour."

Nerves crept back into Jason. Could he really do this? Maybe just one more drink.

He felt a warm hand on top of his. "You won't have to do this alone."

The warmth of Martin's hand was echoed in his eyes. "Thank you, Martin."

"Is there anything else you need?"

"Yes." Jason gathered himself and resumed walking. "I want you to look through all the invitations I get for charities. Bring me the ones that seem most worthwhile, where you think I can make a real contribution. And I'm talking about more than money here, Martin. It's time I start doing more with myself. Also, I want to see all the latest reports about production and work conditions at the mills. I know we're better than most places, but we can improve. Be better. That's going to be the new motto around here, so be prepared."

"I will be, sir. It will be an honor." Martin stood and gave a quick bow of his head.

"Oh, and don't say anything to Kale. I don't want to burden him with my life."

"I'm sure he would like to help you, sir."

"My problems aren't his to fix."

"Very well, sir. Would you like me to start right away?"

"Yes, you're dismissed. Don't forget the decanter on your way out."

Alone in his office, Jason contemplated the huge undertaking he had just shouldered. The sheer magnitude of the information he had taken in during the last hour was overwhelming. After all these years of being miserable, of believing he was the monster he had painted himself to be, everything had shattered in a single morning.

All that wasted time. All the pain he had put Kale through. The way Kale looked when Jason found him at the steel mill. Oh gods, he couldn't think about that. It would be too easy to plunge back into the abyss. At least now there was an anchor to hold to. At the moment, the best way for him to help Kale was to help himself. Jason only hoped that on the other side of this journey Kale would be there, willing to give him a second chance.

CHAPTER TWENTY-EIGHT

Kale's stomach dropped. The blood rushed in his ears. He felt like he was falling, but that was impossible: he was already on the ground. How, he didn't know, but his knees were hollow, empty of the strength needed to support him.

Had that really just happened? How was it that every time Kale felt like he was beginning to get comfortable, to settle into life, Jason had to come and turn it all upside down again?

Somewhere, birds chirped. That was good. Kale listened to the springtime melody. He needed proof that the world continued around him. He ventured a peek at the sky. Fluffy white clouds rolled in the wind. On the ground, Kale felt only the faintest of breezes.

Kale closed his eyes. He needed to find the calm center that used to come so easily to him. Instead, all he saw was Jason as he appeared right before he went inside. Kale's eyes snapped open. The image did nothing to help his fear.

Most terrifying of all was the look of hope on Jason's face. Kale knew what to expect. With Jason's stubborn streak, he would make a concerted effort to wear down Kale's defenses. Jason never let go of an idea once it took hold, especially when it concerned his feelings. Could Kale hold up against the kind of assault Jason would mount on his heart?

He didn't think so. He had already played that game and lost. He couldn't let his emotions get involved. Emotions meant one thing for a slave: pain. There was no escaping it.

Kale lay down. Deep in his bones was a need to be close to the earth, as if it offered the security he craved. Above him, the clouds continued to morph, the fluffy masses breaking off into little wisps.

How had Jason not known? After all this time, it still hurt that he had believed the lie. There had been a moment when Kale had thought Jason would put a stop to it all. Those last few days, he had expected Jason to realize the truth and demand with tenacious insistence that Kale cease the foolishness. But that was naïve. Kale had gotten exactly what he wanted. So many memories, so many emotions. Kale couldn't untangle them all.

The singing birds flew across his view. He envied them their simple lives. Kale had thought his life would be simple. It should have been.

Why couldn't Jason just accept that he had loved him once, but wouldn't ever again? Was that the truth, or just another lie Kale had told himself? He didn't know. Where did the lie end and the truth begin? Had Kale forgotten what the truth was? Which lies had he told to protect Jason and which to protect himself? After his first lie to Jason, Kale had lost track. There had been so many since then.

Kale was honest about one thing: he was scared. Fear crept through his skin, because he knew if there was one man who could pull this off, it was Jason. It would be a fight. Jason had a host of his own demons to battle before he could even set his sights on Kale. But once Jason had succeeded—and Kale knew he would, he hadn't been lying to him about that—he would work to reestablish a relationship with Kale.

Deep breaths of the fresh air worked to calm his racing heart. At least his fear the last few years had been somewhat manageable. He knew what it was he feared: the whip and—for some reason passing understanding—death. This fear was much more abstract, like the clouds he was trying to make pictures out of. He didn't know what was going to happen.

There was no way to prepare himself.

Kale didn't have the strength to fight. He was too tired. But Jason wasn't. In some ways, he was the same boy Kale had known. Jason worked in only two modes: apathetic and passionate. Kale didn't want Jason apathetic. He had enough caring in him to want Jason to mend, but there was no chance the healing passion Jason would need would stop once the job was done. That passion was going to pour over straight to Kale as soon as it was able. Jason was always surprising Kale, and Kale knew this would be no different.

The breeze stilled, and the birds quieted. Above him, the clouds barely moved. Kale hadn't achieved the calm he sought. Tranquility hadn't been a part of his world for quite a while. But he had gathered himself enough to look at the situation clearly.

Jason could pull this off. Jason could change. He was the one person who could get Kale to release his bitterness. And it scared him. It scared him because, deep down, Kale desperately wanted Jason to win.

◆ ◆ ◆

There was no point in staying outside any longer. What would happen would happen. Kale didn't really have any control over it, just like the rest of his life. Shaking the dirt from his pants and shirt, Kale went inside. He dropped his sketch off in his room. It seemed like an eternity since he had drawn it. As he looked at it on the table, he felt the pride swell in his chest once again. This was a victory. He needed to relish it and ignore what else had happened. Kale was taking care of himself now.

Down in the kitchen, he was ready to help Sophie and put away his other thoughts for later.

"Oh good, just what I needed. Can you hand me all the wine up there?"

Sophie teetered on tiptoe, reaching for bottles that were just out of her grasp. A strong draft could have toppled her. Kale rushed to help.

"What do you need all these for?"

"And the ones on the top shelf, dear."

Kale retrieved the wine and then looked around in amazement. Sophie was surrounded by dozens of bottles. "What is all this?"

"Mr. Wadsworth's orders. He wants all the alcohol out of the house. Looks like he's finally giving it up—and it's about time—but why he couldn't make an exception for cooking alcohol is beyond me. So many dishes will be wanting now."

Kale shouldn't have been surprised, but he was. Of course, Jason always went at things full tilt. It looked like he had wasted no time. Kale cursed himself for giving Jason hope by letting him know that he believed he could change. No, that was wrong. If Jason could sober up his life, then Kale would support him.

"How has your day been?" Sophie's innocent question was almost funny. How did one answer such a mundane question when the day had been anything but?

"Good." Kale couldn't elaborate further. Besides, it was the truth. Good, if a little frightening. "I drew some."

"Really? That's excellent, Kale." Sophie's genuine delight over his little victory brought a smile to his face.

"Do you want to see it?"

"I'd love to."

"Just a minute." Kale didn't know why he offered to show it to her—he had never been the type to enjoy others looking at his work—but he needed to focus back on what he had accomplished. Besides, showing Sophie would make it more real. Especially after seeing what Jason had done with his pictures, Kale needed more people than just himself and Jason to see this drawing.

When he returned, he handed Sophie the sketchpad.

"Kale, this is extraordinary. When you told me you used

to draw, I had no idea you meant like this."

"It's nothing, I'm just glad I can draw at all. For a while there, I didn't think I'd be able to."

"Well, I don't agree with your evaluation. And of course you can still do it. I was never in any doubt of that. It's a part of you. We never lose parts of ourselves. We just forget how to use them. Are you going to keep it up now?" Sophie handed the sketchpad back to Kale.

"I hope so."

"Don't just hope for it, do it. Don't get rusty again."

"All right, Sophie."

"Promise?"

Kale laughed. "I promise."

"Good. It looks like it's been a big day all around so far. I'd say we should drink to it, but I hate to go against Mr. Wadsworth's orders."

"Don't worry about it. We don't need drinks when we have your fine cooking."

"That's a good point. I'll get started on something special for tonight. We could all use it. Why don't you go tell Martin we have all the liquor rounded up down here?"

Kale gave her a peck on the cheek and went in search of Martin. Today had been a good day, all things considered. Kale was still worried about the future, but today he had drawn. He had seen beauty. Nothing else mattered.

Chapter Twenty-Nine

Dinner was delicious and blessedly peaceful. Kale didn't know what he expected, perhaps Jason insisting on eating dinner together like they used to, but there wasn't sight or sound of him. It was a relief.

The next day, Kale didn't see Jason either. Not that they spent a lot of time around each other, but Kale had grown used to peeking up at the window and seeing Jason in his office or feeling Jason watch him. Even when Kale didn't see Jason, his presence was usually felt somehow, whether in Martin or Sophie's running to bring him something or the muted cursing and thumping that indicated he was drinking in the study. Kale didn't so much as hear a whisper about Jason for two days.

On the third day, Kale was in the garden trying to capture the image of an ant carrying a leaf. It was a fascinating subject. The ant soldiered on, as if the burden it carried wasn't absurdly large for its small stature. This was the type of subject matter Kale loved, but his heart wasn't in it. He had stayed true to his word to Sophie and kept drawing. It was surprising how easily it came back to him, almost like second nature.

Except it wasn't coming to him now. Another peek at the window showed what Kale already knew: Jason wasn't there. It was disconcerting. There was no way Kale could focus with so much unease in the house. Martin and Sophie hadn't said anything; they were tiptoeing around him. He barely even saw Martin. And that was exactly what was so unsettling. The distinct absence of anything to do with Jason left Kale feeling his presence more than ever, and not in a good way.

The sketch in front of him was enough to work from later. He packed it up and dropped it off in his room before heading to the kitchen. This had gone on long enough. He was going to get some answers from Sophie.

"Do you want another cup?"

"No, it's about time for me to get back up there."

"You'll be no use to him if you're about to collapse yourself."

Kale heard Sophie and Martin talking as he approached the kitchen door. Usually, he was still outside at this time. No doubt they thought this was a private moment.

"Fine, one more cup." Martin's voice was weary.

"And a biscuit."

"No."

"Come now, what kind of gentleman doesn't take tea and biscuits?" Sophie was insistent. Martin would be foolish to try and refuse her.

"Fine."

There was movement as Kale assumed Sophie served the tea, and then there was the clank of silverware. Kale couldn't let this opportunity pass him by. He needed to know.

He opened the door and marched in with far more assertiveness than he had intended. Martin started, and Sophie looked up from the mound of silverware she was polishing. Martin appeared as worn down as he had sounded. Dark circles framed his light brown eyes. His usual stiff posture was broken over his cup of tea.

"It's time I got back." Martin spoke before Kale had a chance and began to rise from his seat. Kale stopped him with a hand on Martin's shoulder, pushing him back down. For a moment, a twinge of fear flashed through Kale. Martin was a free man, and Kale had no right to treat him this way, much less be this forceful. The feeling passed. Some things were more important than propriety, and from the resignation in his eyes, Martin was aware of that.

"What is going on?" Kale looked between the two.

"What are you talking about, Kale?" It was Sophie, and Kale felt betrayed. How could she treat him like this?

"I haven't heard the master leave his room in three days. Something is going on, and you two know what it is. I want to know."

Martin looked at Sophie. "Don't look at me. This is all on you, Martin."

Martin released a heavy sigh. If Kale wasn't so agitated, he would have felt sorry for the secretary. "He didn't want you to know."

"Know what?"

"He's in a bad way, Kale."

"What does that mean? Is he sick? Is his life in danger?" His eyebrows knit in confusion as his voice gained speed.

"Have a seat. I'll get you a cup." Sophie maneuvered Kale into a chair and placed a warm cup of tea in front of him. Sophie apparently thought tea was the cure for all the world's ills. It wasn't working; Kale wouldn't drink it until he had some answers.

"Mr. Wadsworth's drinking was worse than any of us knew. I guess we were fooling ourselves. We knew it was bad, but we liked to convince ourselves that he had it under control. He's always so much in control." Martin's face showed just how deeply he blamed himself. "All the alcohol leaving his system is making him sick."

"Then fetch a doctor. Get the man some help. You can't just let him be!" The anger in his voice was a diversion from the cold lump of worry in Kale's gut.

"I went to the doctor, Kale." Sophie placed a hand on his arm to calm him. It was about as effectual as the tea. "He said we just have to wait it out."

"So, if this is all normal, why are you so worried?" Kale looked from Sophie to Martin and back again. Neither of them seemed to have an answer for him.

"You don't know what it's like, Kale." Martin shook his head as he spoke, like a man who had lost all direction. "At this point, I almost want him to take a drink just to lessen it. The doctor even said it's madness for a man to give up alcohol all at once. But Mr. Wadsworth won't hear it."

That sounded like Jason. He would kill himself with his stupid stubborn streak. Kale shot to his feet, intent on storming to Jason's room and ending this foolishness. This was all because of him, and he was the only one who could put a stop to it.

Martin's hand latched onto Kale's arm. He may have looked look tired, but his grip was firm.

"You're gravely mistaken if you think you can stop me." Kale stared him down, hoping his face looked as menacing as he felt.

"You know I can't, Kale. I don't know the full story of what happened between you and the master, and it's none of my business, but it's clear he loves you. If you have one ounce of love for him in return, you won't go to his room."

"Why not?" What did this man know? Kale certainly wasn't going to sit by and do nothing.

"For one, he's finally sleeping. Second, his one request was that you not see him. He has his pride, Kale. He doesn't want you to worry about him."

"But you're allowed in." Kale felt the jealousy surge within him. It should be him at Jason's side, not this man who didn't really know him.

"Yes, because he doesn't much care what I think. Like you said, I can't stop you if you want to see him, but realize you'll be taking the last shred of pride he has. You'll leave him broken, and you won't help anything."

Kale stared into Martin's eyes, wanting the other man to fight him, craving that outlet, but all he saw was resignation.

Martin wasn't going to fight. He was going to make Kale come to this decision on his own.

Slowly, Kale lowered himself back to his chair.

"It'll be fine, Kale." Sophie patted his back. "You made the right choice."

"It doesn't feel right."

"That's only because you want to be doing, but there's nothing we can do."

"It's time I get back up there." Martin heaved himself to his feet, but Kale caught his hand before he could get away. Martin's brow lifted in question.

"Will you at least ask him if I can see him? Let him know I miss him and was asking after him?" The thought of Jason all alone, going through this pain, hit something in Kale. It superseded all other feelings. He didn't know how he felt toward Jason, but Kale knew the idea of Jason suffering hurt him in a way he couldn't bear.

Martin appeared to consider Kale's request and then nodded. Kale released his hand and began nursing his cup of tea. It would take all the tea in this house to soothe his nerves.

CHAPTER THIRTY

Martin dragged himself up the stairs, trying to steel himself for what awaited him in Jason's room. With any luck, he'd still be sleeping. Martin knew he had Sophie's—and now Kale's—support, but he was the one who had to face this alone. At least he had some experience with these matters.

"Who are you? Get out. Leave me alone. Don't hurt me." It took a moment for Martin's eyes to adjust to the dimness of the room. The drapes were drawn, and the only light came from an oil lamp turned low. Jason crouched in the corner of the room, waving a fire poker. It had been asking too much to hope Jason would sleep for any appreciable length of time.

Martin spread his hands out to his sides, palms up, and advanced slowly toward Jason. "It's me, Mr. Wadsworth, Martin Grimlock. I'm not going to hurt you. I had to go down to the kitchen, but I'm back now."

"I know you?" The confusion in Jason's voice was heartbreaking. These delusions were the most difficult part. To see Jason so confused was disconcerting compared to his usual surety.

"Yes, I'm your secretary. You're sick. This is all going to pass." Martin was now mere inches from the poker. He lowered himself to his knees and tried to capture Jason's gaze with his own.

"Martin?" There it was. Jason's voice cracked, and his

grip loosened, sending the poker clattering to the floor.

"Yes, it's me." Martin gathered Jason in his arms and held him as a mix of sobs and tremors ran through his body. Martin brushed Jason's matted hair back from his forehead. His hand came away covered in sweat. Jason's skin was clammy, and his eyes darted frantically round the room, wide and frightened.

"Here, let's get you back into bed. Try to sleep."

"All right, if you think that's best."

"I do."

Martin helped Jason up and untangled the sheets enough to get him ensconced between them. The room smelled of stale sweat, and Martin yearned to change the sheets, but he didn't want to leave Jason alone long enough to do it, and Jason wouldn't allow Sophie inside.

Once Jason was situated in bed, Martin saw comprehension come back into his eyes. "Thank you, Martin. I'm sorry about that."

"It's no problem. I understand."

"How? How'd you know it would be like this?"

"My father. He was a drunk. He sobered up when my mom went to live with her parents." The words came with surprising ease. His family wasn't something Martin was fond of speaking about. His father's problems had always been a source of shame.

"Did he succeed?"

"No, he went back to the bottle when she told him she didn't love him." Martin wasn't going to soften the realities for Jason. "For what it's worth, though, I think you'll beat it."

"Really?" Jason seemed almost scared to hope.

"Yes. You have a lot of people who support you." Martin chose his next words carefully. He had made a promise to Kale, and he would fulfill it. "In fact, I saw Kale this morning in the kitchen. He's worried about you. He says he misses you."

"You didn't tell him what condition I'm in, did you?"

There was genuine alarm on Jason's face.

"No. I told him you're sick." It was the truth. No matter what Martin had said, there was no way Kale could have fully understood the extent of Jason's condition.

"Good."

"He wants to see you, though. When I told him you were sick, I had to physically restrain him from coming up here."

"No."

"But—"

"No, Martin. Don't let him. You can't let him. He can't see me like this. Not like this. He deserves so much better. He can't see what a mess I've made of everything."

"He won't mind. He cares about you."

"No. Keep him out. Please, Martin. Please, you have to make sure he doesn't see me like this." Jason's hands were clasped in front of him in supplication, and his eyes were wild with fear. The lines of tension in his face were deep and pronounced.

"All right, I won't let him come."

"Promise me."

"I promise. Now calm down, lie back, and just try to rest."

Jason settled back down. "Thank you."

"I think it's the wrong choice, but it's yours to make, and I'll honor it. He's the one who caused all this. He should at least be here to see it."

"It's not his fault, Martin. You don't understand."

"If you say so, but if you don't improve soon, I'm going to have to send for the doctor again."

Jason's hands dug into Martin's arms in desperation. "No, Martin. I can't stand for anyone to see me like this. I'm too ashamed."

"Ashamed or not, this may be beyond our capabilities."

"It's not. I'm getting better. I promise."

"This is the longest you've been lucid in a while."

"See." Jason said it with the conviction of a child proving

to his mother that he could have what he wanted.

"If you keep improving, I see no need to involve the doctor. But, if you don't show significant improvement tomorrow, I'll have Sophie fetch him."

"Fine." Jason sulked into his pillow, but Martin could see the worry in his eyes.

When Martin had gone through this with his father, it hadn't been nearly so bad. Looking back, though, he wasn't entirely convinced his father had quit so completely. This was out of Martin's depth, but he could understand Jason's feelings. If a man didn't have his pride, what did he have?

Martin went to the bathroom and brought back a dampened washcloth. Perched next to Jason on the bed, he gently removed the sweat, first from Jason's face, and then his arms. A bath would do him wonders, but Martin worried that he might become disoriented. Mixed with a slick floor, that could lead to disaster. This would have to do until he was convinced Jason was lucid for good.

"Get these sheets off me." Jason violently attacked the sheets, succeeding only in tangling himself further. "Get them off!"

It was starting again. Foregoing the bath had been the correct choice. "Here, let me help you. Calm down." In a few seconds, Martin had deftly released Jason from his web.

"Make it stop." Jason's eyes were riveted on his shaking right hand. "Make it stop."

Martin reached over and clasped the hand in both of his, forcing it to still as much as was possible.

"No, the other one. Dear gods, what's going on?" Jason's left hand had started to tremble too, and he lifted it to his head, pulling fiercely at his hair.

"Shh. Let me help." Martin released the hand and grabbed both of Jason's wrists while simultaneously standing on the bed and lowering himself behind Jason. Maintaining his grip, he enveloped Jason with his arms and legs. Pulling Jason's back flush against his chest, he began to rock.

"It's going to be all right. You're just having a bad spell is all. It'll pass."

"What's happening to me, Martin? I feel like I'm losing my mind."

"You're not. You're getting it back."

Miraculously, after a few minutes of rocking, Martin felt Jason's body slacken. A minute later, he heard the snoring that signaled Jason had finally succumbed to sleep. Martin carefully scooted out from under him and situated Jason comfortably in the bed.

These were rare moments for Martin to do a little straightening up and get some washcloths ready, should he need them. Martin was happy to do it, but he knew he wasn't the one who should be there. Martin cared for Jason, but it was clear Jason and Kale had some special bond. Kale could be a comfort to him in a way that Martin never would. Despite what Jason said, Martin knew Kale was the reason behind this. The least the slave could do was be there to see what Jason was suffering through, to witness the price Jason was paying for his sobriety.

If things weren't better tomorrow, he would have Sophie bring the doctor. And, whether Jason liked it or not, he would bring Kale in. There was only so much Martin could do, and he was quickly losing his footing. Martin prayed to the saints that it wouldn't come to having to break his word.

CHAPTER THIRTY-ONE

Jason cracked one eye open. The room was flooded with light. It was harsh after the darkness of sleep, but no more than was normal. His tongue swiped across his lips and found them dry and scaly. His whole mouth was dry. Opening his other eye, he looked around and tried to speak. "Water?"

"Here." Martin was there. It seemed Martin had been there a lot. He came out of the bathroom carrying a glass of water.

The cool liquid was heavenly in Jason's mouth. It tasted sweeter than any wine. He steadily drank until the glass was empty. "May I have another?"

"Of course." Martin smiled at him and went back to the bathroom.

Jason sat up and looked around. The drapes were open. It looked like early afternoon. But of which day?

"Here you go."

Jason took the glass again, and the water tasted just as good the second time. He drank leisurely, savoring the taste and allowing his mind the time to catch up and try to remember what had happened. It was a futile exercise. The last few days were nothing but a jumble of images, dark and blurry. They could be from a nightmare or reality. Jason had no way to differentiate.

"Are you feeling better?" Martin took the empty glass

from him and set it on the bedside table.

"Yes, I think so. How long has it been?"

"Since it started? This is the sixth day. Midway through the fourth day you turned a corner. Not long after, you fell asleep, and you've been out since then. I opened the drapes hoping that if you were ready to awaken, the light would encourage you."

"That was good. It helped." Jason yawned and looked around again, barely able to believe that it had been so long. "Was I really out of it for five days?"

"I'm afraid so."

"I didn't do anything too terrible, did I? It's just that I have all these images in my head, and I don't know what's real and what was just a dream."

"It was pretty bad for a while, but you didn't do anything to be ashamed of."

That was a relief. Only it wasn't just Martin Jason worried about. He remembered talk of Kale. He saw him. Kale had come in and looked so disappointed in him, as if he could barely contain his disgust at seeing Jason.

"Oh gods. Kale."

"It's fine, I didn't allow him in. He wanted to see you, badly. Once he realized something was going on, he was just as worried as the rest of us, perhaps more. We kept the worst of it from him, but he knows you were sick."

"But I saw him."

"No, it must have been a dream. I promise he didn't see you the entire time."

"It seemed so real."

"I know. He would like to see you now, though. As soon as you feel up to it. He won't take my word that you're fine."

"I'll go see him as soon as I've bathed." Now that the most immediate concerns were out of the way, Jason felt like a mess. His hair was thick with grease, and every now and then he got a whiff of himself. It wasn't pleasant.

"There's no need to leave your room today. I can have

Kale come up here."

"No, that won't be necessary. I want to stretch my legs and get some fresh air."

"Very well. I'll run you a bath."

While Martin was in the bathroom, Jason swung his legs around the bed and stood, only to sit right back down. "Whoa, I didn't expect that." His head was spinning.

Martin came rushing. "What?"

"Nothing, just a little dizziness."

"Give it some time. Go a little slower."

Jason nodded and tried again, moving carefully. This time he made it to his feet without the fear of toppling over.

An hour later, he felt like a new man. Fresh clothes, clean shave, and an appetite for more food than he had ever eaten in his life.

◆ ◆ ◆

Jason caught a glimpse of Kale pacing around the kitchen before Kale was aware he was being watched. He reached for the spot where Jason now knew his lock of hair lay, caught himself, wrung his hands together, and then ran them through his hair. As soon as he saw Jason though, he stiffened, arms falling to his sides. Jason didn't know why he had expected that behavior to change, but he had.

"Look who's decided to rejoin the land of the living. It's good to have you back, sir."

It was easy to focus his attention on Sophie and put his disappointment at Kale's response to the side. "Thank you, Sophie. It's good to be back."

"Well, here, take a seat." Sophie ushered him to the table. Kale's feet stayed planted, but he followed Jason with his eyes, barely even blinking. It was a little disconcerting.

"Let me get you something to eat." Sophie went to the counter and sliced some bread.

"Actually, I came to ask Kale if he would like to go for a walk with me to the park." Jason fixed his eyes on Kale.

Kale's face gave nothing away. Jason wasn't even sure Kale heard him.

"Or we could stay home if you prefer. I just thought you might like to get out. You haven't left the house since you arrived."

"I'll do whatever you like, master."

It would have almost been preferable for Kale to say that he didn't even want to see Jason. At least then Jason would get some type of response from him. Jason didn't know what to do. He wanted to spend time with Kale, but was afraid to push him.

Behind Kale's shoulder, Jason saw Sophie mouthing something. "Make him go." At this point, Sophie knew Kale's mind better than Jason did.

"We'll go to the park then. Sophie, could you pack us a lunch?"

"Certainly, just give me a few minutes, and I'll have a feast for you."

As Sophie prepared their meal, Jason occupied himself by winding his watch to avoid Kale's insistent gaze. The slave remained motionless until Sophie announced that lunch was ready. Both Kale and Jason reached for the basket.

"I'll take that, master."

"No, I can carry it." Jason didn't like Kale waiting on him.

"You're as wobbly as a new colt. I can handle it." Kale's voice was gruff and a little stern.

"You don't have to do that."

"Fine, then let me because I want to. It's heavy. Sophie packed enough food for a small army. I don't want you giving out. You're still weak."

"He's right, sir. Why don't you let Kale take it?" Sophie implored as she placed a blanket on the basket.

"I'm not weak."

"No, I'm sorry, master. I just don't want you to tire out."

Jason recognized that voice. It was the one Kale used to handle Jason. That little bit of familiarity lightened his mood, and Jason realized how silly this conversation was. Were they really arguing over who was going to carry the picnic basket? "Fine." Jason relinquished his hold on the basket and thought he saw Kale push back a satisfied grin.

◆ ◆ ◆

The walk to the park was silent. Jason could navigate his way there with his eyes closed. Before Kale's return, he had tried to spend most nice afternoons there. Kale simply followed behind. This route would be new to him. Jason's townhouse was on the other side of the park from the old one.

Jason automatically went to his usual spot under a giant oak tree and heard a surprised intake of breath from Kale. Of course, this spot would be familiar to him. It was where they had sat together the day Kale had drawn his beautiful—and Jason later thought prophetic—picture of a weed. Over the years, this spot had become such a part of Jason's routine that he had almost forgotten why he had chosen it.

"This is my usual spot." Jason smiled hesitantly at Kale.

Kale nodded and unfolded the blanket. Once he had it arranged, he stood back as Jason sat.

Jason sighed. "Come and sit with me."

Instead of sitting, Kale knelt. This was going to be a long afternoon.

"Relax." Jason tried to sound both commanding and encouraging at the same time. It seemed Kale wasn't going to do much without an order. Other than carry the basket, of course.

"You say that like it's easy."

"There's no reason it shouldn't be." When would Kale understand that? Or were the experiences of the last three years etched too deeply for him to ever trust someone who owned him?

"Reason? You own me. That's reason enough."

"Yes, but I've been more than that to you in the past, and I hope to be more than that again someday." Jason wished he could kick himself. They both knew what he was after, and it was probably a vain hope, but Jason couldn't help himself. "Please, all I mean is that you have nothing to fear from me. I wish you realized that, but if I need to keep reminding you, I'm happy to."

"I thought you might be mad at me." Kale still didn't meet Jason's eyes properly.

"Mad at you? For what?" Of all the things Jason expected Kale to say, this was not one of them.

"For what you went through. It was for me, wasn't it?"

"No, Kale, it wasn't. It was for me. You may have helped me see that it was necessary, that I had let myself get too far out of control, but it was something I needed to do."

"You never drank like that before. I figured it was because of me, of how I left you."

"You made your choices, and I made mine. You're not to blame for what happened after you left. That was all me. I handled it poorly."

Kale snorted. "That's an understatement."

Jason laughed. It felt good, like he was breaking apart the last remnants of the past week and shaking them off. It seemed to startle Kale as much as it did Jason, because Kale finally looked at him—really looked at him—for the first time. The relief on his face was clear. But was it relief over Jason's health or just the more comfortable atmosphere?

"What were you expecting to see?" Jason asked.

Kale shook his head. "I was worried is all. We all were. Martin looked like the god of death my mother used to describe in her stories. I always knew he struck me as familiar, but I didn't know where from until you were sick."

Jason laughed even harder at this. Now that Kale had said

it, Jason couldn't help picturing Martin, somber faced, ushering souls to death. Martin would be thrilled if he knew.

When Jason had sobered, Kale asked, "How bad was it?"

It appeared this wasn't a laughing matter to Kale. "It wasn't good, but my memory is hazy. Martin could do a better job of answering your question. I have flashes. They mix in with my dreams, so I don't know what was real and what wasn't. I'm scared more of it was real than I'd like." It felt so good to freely talk with Kale, to pour out his feelings uncensored. Kale had always been the only person who put him at this kind of ease.

Jason dug into the picnic basket and began to spread out its contents. There were sandwiches, bread, cheese, and fruit. It was more than the two of them could possibly eat. "It looks like Sophie meant for us to be out for quite some time. We'd better get started on this."

Jason handed Kale a sandwich and they both ate. Jason felt as though he hadn't eaten in ages. Everything tasted delicious. The salty ham, fluffy bread, pungent cheese, the sweet grapes and apples—it was all divine. After the first bite, Jason could only think about sating his hunger. Before he knew it, he was leaning back against the trunk of the tree, patting his belly and releasing a rather unattractive burp.

"Excuse me. I knew I was hungry, but I didn't realize the extent of it." Jason looked at Kale. Beyond his first sandwich, Jason hadn't noticed if he'd eaten anything else. "Did you get enough?"

"Yes, master." Kale went about cleaning up the remains.

"Leave the grapes. I wouldn't mind a few more."

A slight smile crested Kale's lips, but he kept silent as he packed away the rest, not that there was much left.

"Are you sure you don't want anything else?"

"I'm sure." Kale settled down next to Jason.

"Eat a few grapes anyway, just to make me feel better." Jason didn't want to be the only one still eating.

Kale obliged and took a few, popping them into his

mouth one at a time. Jason watched him, wondering what to say. There were so many things that needed to be said, but where to start?

"I'm sorry." That seemed like a decent enough place.

"Excuse me?"

"I'm sorry about what happened with Renee."

Kale went rigid.

"Please, talk to me."

"You always did have a knack for uncomfortable conversations."

"I'm mad at myself for believing such a blatant lie." There was no response from Kale. Since Jason expected honesty, it was only fair that he started with himself. "And I'm mad at you for telling it."

"Yeah, well, there's enough anger to go around."

"I don't expect you to forgive me, but I just wanted you to know that I'm sorry."

"I appreciate that."

"Really?"

"No, not really, but I want to. You don't know how badly I want to sometimes."

"Tell me what happened." Jason only had fragments of the story. He wanted the whole thing.

"There's not much to tell."

"What happened after I took you to the dealer?"

Kale shrugged. "I was sold."

"To the labor firm?"

"Yes."

"Were you at the mill this whole time?" There was something devastating about the thought that Kale had been there all along. Surely Jason would have known.

"No, I was laying track for the railroad. A few months ago, that ended and I got transferred to the mill."

"When I first got you back, you told me I had been naïve. Did you know you would be sold to hard labor?"

"Yes, I knew it."

"Then why did you do it?"

Kale shrugged. "It seemed worth it at the time."

"Kale, what could possibly be worth it?"

"You'll never understand because you're not a slave." Kale's speech became more impassioned. "You don't know what it's like to have no control over your life. That was my opportunity to take control. You were going to get rid of me sooner or later, at least this way it was in my hands. Only one of us had a chance of ever being happy, and we both know it was you."

"And I fucked it up."

"Yes."

"I'm sorry." Jason thought his voice sounded as wretched as he felt.

"Not as much as I am."

Kale's words stabbed at Jason. How had he made such a mess of both their lives? It had been bad enough when he only had his own to worry about.

"But, like you said," Kale continued, "we both made our own choices, and we've both lived with the consequences."

"Where do we go from here?" That was what Jason needed to know.

"I don't know."

"How do you feel?"

"I don't know how I feel."

"Do you hate me?"

"I don't know."

That stung, but Jason had asked. At least he was getting honesty. That was a good sign, wasn't it? "Do you like me?"

Kale finally regarded him. "Look, I don't know. Just, stop pushing it. I'm glad you're better. I was scared when you were sick and I couldn't do anything for you. But that doesn't mean anything has changed."

Jason nodded. "Fair enough."

They sat there for a few peaceful moments. Jason knew they were both hurting. They were different men than they'd

171

been three years ago, but he couldn't help thinking that they were also the only people who could understand the other's pain.

"I plan to start coming here regularly again. Would you like to join me?"

"Whatever you want, master." The stiffness returned to Kale's posture.

"I want to know what you want, Kale." Jason ached to reach out and touch him. It had been so long since he had felt Kale's skin beneath his own. Right now, though, it wasn't appropriate.

"Honestly, I don't know." Kale met his eyes, and Jason could see the sincerity in them. Jason could hardly blame him. Moment to moment, Jason didn't know what to do either. Now that he could no longer hide behind his drinking, he was going to have to step up and start taking control.

"Well, then why don't you come? I'm making it an order. But, Kale," Jason paused to make sure he had Kale's full attention, "I'm also ordering you to tell me if you don't want to, and that order supersedes the other one. I don't know what's going to happen between us, and I'm not going to push you into a relationship you don't want, but I think we should spend some time together. Here, we're on neutral ground. Burying and ignoring the problems between us isn't going to fix things. We owe it to ourselves and each other to try to move past this."

Kale nodded and Jason stood, reaching a hand down to help Kale. Kale ignored it, gathered the blanket and basket, and fell in step behind Jason. The day hadn't gone as Jason planned, but he didn't really know what he had expected. It was a start.

CHAPTER THIRTY-TWO

"Go ahead and start reading, Kale." It always took an order. Kale never took initiative.

Jason lay down under the familiar tree and closed his eyes, letting Kale's voice wash over him. With his eyes closed, he could almost imagine all their problems were gone. They came to the park together every day the weather allowed. It was always the same: they ate whatever Sophie had packed them, and then Kale read from whichever book he had brought. To be honest, Jason never paid much attention to the story.

The only thing that stained the perfect picture was the tension buried in Kale's voice. It was never blatant, but it was always there, and it permeated the air between them. Like any stain, the eye eventually glided over it, and Jason learned to ignore it, even though he always knew it was there.

Reading had been Jason's idea. Kale would have never suggested it. After the first conversation they had after Jason's recovery, he figured they needed something to do as an alternative to discussion. His hope had been that Kale would become more comfortable and talk to him. Jason didn't care about what; he just wanted them to talk. The problem was that he had given Kale the control. At the time, it had seemed important, but over the last week Jason had come to realize that Kale was never going to speak first.

Jason didn't know what to do. He didn't want to order Kale to talk, but that seemed to be the only way. Everything with Kale was by order these days. Jason felt like a little kid playing house, ordering the other players into their positions and having them recite lines. The illusion was nice, but reality would be better.

Kale wasn't doing it to annoy him the way he had been prone to do years ago, or at least Jason didn't think so. It was just the state of their new relationship. It was far from ideal, but Jason preferred it to life without Kale, so he persevered.

"It was over before it began," Jason spoke to the sky.

"What?"

Jason grinned. He had surprised Kale, so he had forgotten to tag a "master" onto his sentence. He gathered these little victories. It was petty and probably inconsequential, but Jason relished them—they were all he had.

"My marriage. We only went through with it because of her father."

Jason cracked an eye open when Kale didn't say anything. The tension was thicker than usual. Kale stared at Jason with a look of confusion and discomfort on his face.

"I've been waiting for you to start talking to me, but that's clearly never going to happen. Then I thought about it, and you told me what happened to you when we parted, but I didn't reciprocate. Maybe if you know more, you'll feel more comfortable, loosen up a little bit." Jason sat up so his eyes were level with Kale's.

There was a slight twitch in Kale's eyebrows, and for a moment Jason thought he might get a funny retort. Then Kale pursed his lips and nodded. "Very well, master. Whatever you wish. I'm listening."

Indeed, Kale leaned forward and appeared to be paying as rapt attention as any man was capable of. It was maddening.

"I was devastated the day I sold you. I kept telling myself the pain would dull. Renee tried her best to help me cheer up, but I knew I never would. I damned our relationship the moment I signed your title over."

Kale's face quickly sobered, and he lowered his eyes. If Jason was going to be the one talking, Kale was going to hear the truth. If it was uncomfortable, Kale could steer the conversation any time he wanted.

"At that point, though, her father was gravely ill. The arrangement still had its benefits. Renee would satisfy her father and still have the freedom she craved. I was ruined for anyone else, so I didn't see much downside to going through with it. I felt I owed it to her after everything. I didn't want to see her married to someone who would try to destroy what was good in her. I had already ruined your life by raping you. I didn't want to do the same to her."

Jason saw Kale bristle at the word "rape." Other than that, there was no indication of what he thought. "So we got married. Her father was overjoyed. A few months later, he died. I inherited everything and moved out into the townhouse I'm in now."

Kale's eyes shot to him, but quickly darted away. Jason knew what he wanted. "Do you have a question?"

Jason could see Kale mulling it over, but he eventually shook his head.

"Renee took to traveling—"

"So she never lived in that house? I'm sorry, master, I didn't mean to interrupt."

It was almost painful to see these two warring sides of Kale. On one side was the curious man who had been used to speaking freely with Jason, and on the other was a man who had fear beaten into him from all sides. "No reason to apologize. I'm having a conversation, Kale. Whether you decide to participate is entirely up to you, but I'm not talking to hear myself speak or to dictate to you. To answer your question: no, Renee never lived in that townhouse. I don't think she's ever even stepped inside."

Kale nodded and Jason could see he was relieved. Jason

175

had never even thought Kale might worry about that.

"If you wanted to know, you could have just asked. I didn't even think about it."

"It's not my place, master."

"I'm making it your place, Kale. I want you to talk to me, to ask questions."

There was a pause. Then Kale asked, "So how did it all work?"

"Renee travels mostly. Her mother has a townhouse here. We don't get along, and I try to avoid her at all costs. Whenever Renee is in town, she stays there, and I visit when I'm needed."

Kale's face twisted like he tasted something sour.

"That rarely happens now. Our marriage bed has never been very warm. We tried a few times, hoping for a child so we could be done with it, but it never took. Eventually, trying wasn't worth the effort. We haven't told her mother, though, so she's still hoping for children. But I haven't seen Renee in over a year, so I think even she is losing hope."

Silence.

"This is the part where you ask a question."

"What about the business?"

"Ah, the business. That's really what keeps this whole thing going. As it turns out, I'm pretty good at it."

"That doesn't surprise me." Kale seemed to speak before he thought. It was another slip of the lip and another victory for Jason.

"Well, it surprised me. I was terrified of taking over. I didn't want to, but if I didn't, then Renee's family could have pushed for a divorce. No one else in her family wants to run it, but they are all keen on it continuing to supply the lifestyle they enjoy. Her uncles and cousins keep an eye on me. The secret is that I don't care about the business. Or actually, I don't care about the money. When you look at it objectively like that, it just becomes another puzzle to solve. As long as profits go up, I'm left alone."

"Have you told her about me?" There was an edge to Kale's voice.

"Renee? No, it didn't seem prudent. I think she's been through enough. I'll let her know when there's something to tell. Like I said, I haven't seen her in over a year, so it's not really any of her business. I don't know what she does with her time. We write each other, and we're on friendly terms, but that's it."

Jason's answer didn't appear to do anything to relax Kale. Then it hit him. "My gods, Kale. Have you been worried about Renee all this time? She can't do a thing to you. You don't have to concern yourself with her at all. You'll probably never see her again."

"I wasn't worried." Same old Kale, never wanting his pride touched. Jason was just glad that pride was still intact somewhere. "And when did you start swearing by the gods?"

Jason chuckled. "It's more like I never stopped after you rubbed off on me. I never felt a part of the higher classes once you were gone. Martin cringes every time I use 'gods' instead of 'saints.' Maybe I do it to irritate him."

Jason watched Kale chew his tongue. "Have another question?"

Kale stopped. "You know I do. You're just doing this to torture me."

"I'm improving your conversation skills." The tension was still in Kale, but at least this way Jason had a little fun.

"What about Martin? Where'd he come from?"

"Martin was an unexpected annoyance. Given my lack of experience and unsociable nature, Renee's family insisted on me having a secretary, and they hired Martin. It was made clear to me that I either let them pick my secretary, or they would push for divorce. He's a glorified nanny."

"You need someone, and you don't seem to care to have a staff."

"No, after you I didn't want any slaves. I didn't trust myself. Martin found me Sophie, and it's worked out nicely, just the three of us. If I were to be completely honest, Martin has done well. I just can't help feeling that he looks down his nose at me."

"I think he makes everyone feel that way. I know he respects you."

"Thank you, Kale." Jason squinted at the sun and pulled out his watch. "I've got to head back. There's a meeting for a charity I'm on the board of tonight." Jason was still considering what charities he wanted to devote himself to, but he thought it was important to be active where he could until he came to a decision.

Jason jumped up and reached down for Kale's hand. Kale ignored it, as always. He shied away from any physical closeness. It made Jason crazy. All he wanted was one touch, to feel Kale's hand in his again. To feel that firm strength. But maybe what had made Kale's touch so magnificent before was no longer there. If Kale's hands weren't touching him in love, was it really worth it?

CHAPTER THIRTY-THREE

Kale crumpled the paper between his hands and took a little pleasure at the crisp sound of it wrinkling. The waste paper basket was already overflowing, but Kale tossed the ball of paper anyway. He didn't see where it landed; he was staring at the blank sheet in front of him.

He could do this. It used to be so easy.

Kale closed his eyes and conjured up a picture of Jason. This time, it was Jason at the park. Over the last two weeks, they had begun to talk more, the conversation always guided by Jason. Lately, they discussed neutral topics such as art and literature. Yesterday, Jason had laughed at something Kale said, and it lit Kale up to be the person to bring that expression to Jason's face.

Holding the picture firmly in mind, Kale set his pencil to paper and began to draw. He tried not to think too hard, to just let the image flow through him. When his eyes focused on the page, though, he saw it was no use. This one was just as bad as the others. He took his pencil and scribbled through the image, making a black mess before crumpling it like the dozens before.

No matter what he tried, he couldn't get his hand to draw the lines that should be familiar. Jason as he was years ago, Jason in the park, Jason in his office at the window, Jason happy, Jason sad, an image that made Kale feel joyful, an image that made him furious—nothing worked.

He refused to give up. Drawing had always been a way for Kale to work through his emotions. How could he understand his feelings toward Jason if he couldn't put him on paper?

This time, he kept his eyes open and drew whatever came to him. The curve of the back seemed to be adequate, his hand gliding over the paper easily. Arms formed, a torso, but then it came time for the face.

Rap, rap.

"Come in," Kale called. The light knocking on the door would be Sophie. Kale ignored her as she entered, putting all his attention to forming the eyes and mouth. If only they would cooperate, this one might actually be passable.

"Damn." The face staring back at him was not Jason's. Kale didn't know who it was.

"What are you drawing?" Sophie neared, peeking over his shoulder.

"Nothing." Kale scribbled through it and added it to the pile. "Is there something I can help with?"

"I was just getting ready to make some bread and thought I'd see if you wanted to help. There's lots of dough to be kneaded and pounded."

"I'd love to, Sophie." There was something therapeutic about helping Sophie with the bread, and she knew it. Without any real responsibility, Kale often felt at odds staying in such a nice room. He wanted to be of use, and at least when he was working with the dough, he could take out some of his frustrations on it.

In the kitchen, Sophie tore a large, sticky ball of dough from a giant bowl and slapped it in front of Kale on the floured counter. "Here, get started on this one." There were several bowls full of dough spread throughout the kitchen.

"Dear gods, what do we need all this bread for?"

"It's not for us." Sophie was already busy at work on her ball. "The master is working with a charity that is having a bake sale."

"So he volunteered you to provide the bread?"

Sophie smiled and brushed a golden wisp of hair out of her eyes, spreading flour on her face in the process. "Something like that. Just be glad we didn't get stuck with the cakes. This is relatively easy, if time consuming."

Kale added some more flour to his dough. "Has he always been involved in charity?"

"No, that's a new development. Ever since he gave up alcohol. He's always received a flood of requests from charitable causes according to Martin, but he used to just ignore them or send a check."

"So how did he spend all of his time before?"

"He's always worked himself into the ground. If he's not working directly, he's reading about it. From what I understand, he didn't know anything about steel when he took over the business. There was also a lot of travel involved when he started looking into building a mill near the coast. And he wasn't a complete recluse. If he thought it could benefit the business somehow, he went out to society events. Martin says that's how he's gotten so much business for the mill. In his words, 'It's amazing a man can get the business of so many people he despises.'"

"In some ways he's changed so much, but he's still the same."

"That was him you were drawing earlier, wasn't it?"

"Trying to at least. I used to draw him all the time. Now whenever I try, it just comes out wrong. I can't figure out anything where he's concerned. It's aggravating."

"I don't understand you two. One minute it seems like you love him, and the next like you hate him."

"I don't hate him, that's the problem. I wish I did."

"Like I said, I don't understand."

Kale formed his dough into a nice round loaf and set it aside. Sophie handed him another ball and he dusted his counter again. "At least hating him would make sense to me.

181

Instead, I love him. I've always loved him. But how can you love a man who owns you?"

"We don't get to choose those things. You know that."

"I hate myself for it, Sophie. He can sell me. He did. What kind of relationship is that?"

"Did you always feel that way?"

"It doesn't matter how I used to feel. I don't feel that way anymore. I can't just be around him. It used to be so easy. It came so natural, even before I knew I loved him. Now, though, I can't bring myself to be that way again. Every time I think of relaxing around him, a voice in my head tells me I'm crazy, he owns me and can do whatever he wants."

"Do you trust him?"

"In some ways I do, in others I'll never be able to trust him as long as he's my master. He hurt me, Sophie. More than I knew it was possible to be hurt. I won't give him that power again."

"He doesn't view you as a slave. He hasn't from the moment he brought you home. Slaves don't sleep in the finest room in the house. They don't have leisure time or get to do what they want. You know all that. If he doesn't view you as a slave, why can't you stop viewing him as your master?"

"I want to, Sophie. I just don't know if I can. How is it even possible? When I try to draw him, I picture all the things I love about him, but at the end of the day, he's my owner. Nothing else trumps that."

"Do you want my opinion?"

Kale raised his eyebrows. "You haven't been offering it already?"

"I haven't told you anything you didn't already know. I'm talking about the hard stuff now."

"Go ahead."

"I think you're scared."

Kale bristled inside and suddenly took a keen interest in his dough.

182

"I think you're angry and bitter and scared. I think, deep down, you're miserable, but you're comfortable there. The misery you know is better than the one you don't. So I don't think you've really tried to untangle all that emotion that you work so hard to keep locked away. I think you're just hoping that you can live the rest of your life with it all bottled up and no one will notice. Eventually, you'll die never having to go through the pain of sorting through it all. You'll be unhappy, but there are worse things, you know that, and this way you've picked your poison."

Everything Sophie said dug at Kale's gut. It was hard to hear, but he knew it was true. "I'm a coward."

"You're trying to avoid pain. We all do. You just have to ask yourself if you've finally found something that's worth facing up to all of it. Mr. Wadsworth seems to think he has. Now it's your turn. You'll never be able to figure out things between the two of you until you figure out yourself. And don't think you'll be able to avoid it forever. Eventually, the pressure will kill you, or it will force its way out, and it'll be messy."

The dough beneath his hands was no longer sticky. Kale put it aside and started in on a fresh mound. He couldn't think about this. Right now, he could knead dough. He had kept it all bound up inside this long, so what if he put it off? Besides, even if it did burst out of him one day, that still had to be less painful than actively working through it. Didn't it?

CHAPTER THIRTY-FOUR

Contemporary Masters in Black and White is a special one-week exhibit at the Museum of Art. Up and coming artists from around Arine will be featuring their works composed exclusively of black and white materials.

Perfect. Jason tore the announcement from the paper. This was just the type of event he would like to take Kale to. They hadn't been anywhere together in the last four weeks other than the park, and this was the perfect opportunity to change that. Each day, Jason could see Kale moving closer to him in inches. While his actions were not always consistent, Jason knew Kale still harbored feelings for him. It was just a matter of making him feel safe and secure enough to yield to them.

Jason threw a quick glance at the window. Kale was nowhere in sight. Jason would check his room first and then the kitchen. They used to have such fun looking at art exhibits together; Kale provided enlightening insights from his perspective as an artist, and Jason took pride in knowing that Kale could outshine any artist on display. This could be a positive step toward restoring their friendship.

Jason read the rest of the announcement as he walked. It sounded like it would be a fantastic time, all new artists, and Kale had always favored black and white art. He was so excited about the prospect of going out with Kale that he walked right into Kale's room without knocking.

"Kale—" Jason looked up from the newspaper clipping and stopped cold. Kale had clearly just finished bathing and was getting dressed. Before him was Kale's back, exposed as it had been that day at the mill. It had been so easy to forget what Kale's shirt hid. The scars stood out, livid lines crisscrossing his back. Jason felt acid rise in his throat, but he couldn't tear his eyes away.

Kale startled, snatched his shirt from where it lay on the bed, and shrugged it on, tucking it into his pants as he turned. His face was stricken, and Jason realized he only made the situation worse by staring, but he couldn't help it.

"Master."

Kale's tone demanded that Jason snap out of it, but he couldn't find anything to say.

"Is there something you need, sir?"

Jason remembered the paper in his hand. It seemed silly now to speak of going to an art gallery together, and he shoved the clipping in his pocket. "Did that happen at the mill?"

"No. It was before."

There was some small relief in that. At least the lashes hadn't been applied under Jason's authority. It was hollow solace, though. He was the one who had put Kale in the hands of the men who had done this.

"Do they hurt?"

"After the initial pain you mean? No. They're not easy to see, are they? Think how guilty you felt after what you did to me when Eric broke up with you. Doesn't seem so bad now, does it?"

The real pain was left unspoken. *This is your fault too, and you don't feel a thing.* Except Jason did feel; he felt guilt stab him so hard it took him a minute to get his voice back. "I never wanted that to happen."

"I'm sure you didn't. Just not enough to prevent it."

Jason bridled at Kale's accusations. There was plenty he

was sorry for, but the blame for what happened couldn't be placed solely on his shoulders. "You're the one who told me to sell you. I wanted to keep you."

"Yeah, well, what the fuck did I know? I'm just a slave. I was your responsibility, and you didn't even have the courage to sell me yourself. You didn't care what happened to me as long as you got to rub shoulders with your high society and finally get the approval of your prick of an old man. I got screwed because it meant more to you to have his love, even if it meant hiding who you are. What's that worth, the love of someone who doesn't even know you? They never knew you, not Eric, not Renee, not your old man. None of them knew you like…" Kale's voice caught, and he looked away.

"Like you did." That hitch of Kale's voice caught on Jason's heart. In his mind, he saw this gentle man, beaten and abused, with nobody there to comfort him. What must it have been like, going through all that brutality alone? At that moment, every urge in Jason's body was to comfort. Every impulse was to pull close and hold tight. Only he knew that wouldn't be welcome.

However, standing by and simply watching was not an option. Jason approached Kale and reached up a hand to his face. Kale predictably flinched away at first, but Jason was persistent. It was a token resistance. Kale gave in quickly and allowed Jason to caress his face. Jason suspected Kale was tired of fighting.

"I'm sorry. You should have never had to go through that."

"I don't want your pity." Kale might not have wanted pity, but he was accepting comfort. Jason's hand still traced Kale's face as they talked. The curve of Kale's cheekbone, the smooth feel of his freshly shaved skin, it all felt so good that Jason didn't ever want to stop.

"Good. It's not pity I want to give you."

Kale pulled away and dropped into a chair. His body looked deflated and weary. "You weren't supposed to ever see the scars."

"I saw them back at the mill." Jason occupied the chair next to Kale's.

"Yeah, well, that was different. I couldn't help that."

"You thought you'd be able to hide your back from me forever?"

"Why not?"

"You didn't think we'd ever make love again?" The idea that Kale wanted to hide any part of himself from Jason was disturbing.

"Nothing's changed. It still can't work for the same reason it couldn't before. We're not lovers."

"But you want it. You're not nearly as good at hiding your feelings as you think. At least not from me."

"Not anymore."

"Why?" Jason leaned forward, nearly pleading.

"Too much has happened. I'm not the same person you fell in love with. These scars are the least of it. I'm just as ugly inside. How could you ever love that?"

"Whoever told you you're ugly?" Jason slipped out of his chair and knelt in front of Kale, grasping his head between his hands, forcing Kale to meet his eyes.

"You don't know what's inside me. I'm so bitter. Right now, looking at you, I can't help thinking how mad I am at you for allowing this to happen, for hurting me. It's not fair, and I know it, but I can't let go. I want to."

"I know you do, Kale. I know you. I see you. You'll never be able to hide from me." Jason didn't know if that was the right thing to say. Probably not, it would most likely just scare Kale even further away. "I love you. That love never stopped. I can take your hate right now. I can take the bitterness. Just let me in. Let me help you."

The conflicting emotions in Kale's eyes tore at Jason. There was such uncertainty and fear there. There was only one thing Jason could think to do. Leaning swiftly in, he connected lips with Kale. He felt the surprise behind Kale's mouth, but he wasn't going to back away. In the face of Kale's uncertainty, Jason would be sure. He sucked Kale's bottom lip in between his teeth and slid his tongue along it until Kale surrendered and opened his mouth.

When their tongues touched for the first time, it felt both old and new at the same time. Like coming home after a long absence. This was where Jason belonged. Kale was the man Jason was meant to share his entire being with. Jason explored Kale's mouth, reacquainting himself with this body that had at one time been more familiar to him than his own.

Kale's hands grasped Jason's neck, kneading it as he pulled him closer. Jason hadn't realized he'd been anxious until Kale's hands melted his nerves, and Jason knew that simply kissing was no longer an option. He wanted to taste all of Kale.

"I love you." They were the only words that could have compelled Jason at the moment to break from Kale's lips, and they needed to be said. "I don't need to hear those words from you. I just need to show you. Let me."

Kale nodded breathlessly. There was raw desire in his eyes, but even the passion in his dilated pupils couldn't completely hide the fear. Jason stood, pulling Kale with him and maneuvering them so Kale's back was to the bed. Clothing suddenly seemed a cumbersome thing, thick and heavy between them. Jason wanted to dispose of it as quickly as possible, but there was the risk that removing Kale's shirt would make him self-conscious again. The shirt was going to come off, but some preparation would help matters.

Jason reached for Kale's belt first, hoping to help Kale commit to the idea of sex before tackling the shirt obstacle.

"It's been a long time for you, hasn't it?" Jason had Kale's pants undone, and as his hand wrapped around Kale's balls, his lips latched on to Kale's throat.

"Gods, yes." It came out as part groan. "Too long."

Jason rolled Kale's balls around in his hand. They felt perfect: perfect size, perfect soft skin, and the sounds they elicited from Kale were perfect. He snaked his other hand underneath the front of Kale's shirt until he felt soft chest hair under his fingers. Kale had the best chest hair, not too thick or wiry, just enough to make Jason heady with the masculinity of it.

While one hand was busy playing with Kale's chest hair, Jason moved the other to encircle Kale's cock. It was semi-hard, and Jason lightly ran his fingers up and down its length, his touch feather soft, meant to tease, not satisfy. Kale's head fell back, and he released an agonized moan.

Jason lifted his lips to Kale's ear. "Back up."

Kale did so, moving until he sat on the bed. Jason disposed of Kale's pants and then divested him of his shirt in one swift movement, pushing him down flat on his back. They wouldn't deal with Kale's back today. Jason didn't suspect this would last long enough to broach those issues.

Jason spread his hands against Kale's chest, luxuriating in the feel of Kale's skin under his. No other skin felt like this. Jason knew what it was to be addicted to a chemical. This was an addiction to touch. His hands were drawn to Kale's body as if by an outside force.

Kale's eyes were closed. Jason would have loved to see the pale green that contrasted so nicely with Kale's honey-toned skin, but it didn't matter. Traveling down, his eyes caught on the mark that was turning from red to purple on Kale's neck. He didn't know how Kale would feel about that later, but Jason was satisfied that he had enjoyed the application.

That reminded him, his mouth was unoccupied. He licked his lips and descended on Kale's right nipple, rolling the left between his thumb and forefinger.

"Uhhh."

Jason gripped Kale's cock with his other hand. There was nothing light about his touch now.

"Yessss."

A few tugs and Jason felt droplets of pre-come leaking

from the tip. Kale had waited long enough. Jason was not going to prolong the anticipation any longer. He rolled the little nub of Kale's nipple around in his mouth a few more times and then released it, bestowing a kiss before he left the area entirely.

Before Kale could realize what was happening, Jason knelt on the floor and enveloped Kale's cock with his mouth.

"Ohhhh." Kale's hands came down to Jason's head. Their weight was welcome, not demanding or steering, merely looking for an anchor.

The salty taste of pre-come hit Jason's tongue, and he was surrounded by Kale: Kale's unique scent, his taste, the wiry hairs his cock nestled in. It was Kale, and it was heady.

With one hand he cupped Kale's balls again, but this time he extended his middle finger, stroking the delicate skin right behind the sack.

"Ehhhh." It was a whimper. Kale was on the edge.

The other hand gripped Kale at his base, and Jason began to suck in earnest. It had been years, but Jason still remembered what Kale liked. The right amount of suction, the little flicks of his tongue under the tip interspersed with long, rhythmic licks.

Kale's fingers tightened in Jason's hair, and he thrust frantically into Jason's mouth. Jason relaxed his throat, and when Kale came, he swallowed it all.

"Ahhhh."

Jason released Kale's penis before it became too sensitive and joined Kale on the bed. For a moment, the only sound was Kale's heavy breathing. His forehead was damp, and Jason pushed the matted hair back and then glided his finger over the sweat-slicked skin.

"I never learned to play an instrument. I think you qualify, though. I could spend all day touching you to see what sounds you make."

"I'm not that bad."

"Who said anything about being bad?" Jason leaned

down and gave Kale a soft kiss.

"What about you?" Kale seemed to take in the fact that Jason was completely clothed for the first time. He moved to get up, but Jason firmly pushed him back down.

"Don't worry about me. I can replay that in my head later and take care of myself." Jason stroked Kale's face and watched as his comfortable, sated look was replaced by darkening storm clouds. Jason had expected this. Kale was just realizing what he had done.

"So now what, master?"

There it was. It wouldn't surprise him if Kale tried to put even more distance between them. Now that Kale had let Jason in, he was going to withdraw. It didn't matter; he wouldn't succeed. Jason wasn't backing down, and he could keep pace with Kale as he tried to run the other way.

"May I stay?"

"You can do whatever you want, master."

"I want to do what you want. This isn't about being an owner. It's about being a lover."

"No, it's not." Kale jerked his head out from under Jason's hand. "If it was, you would have respected my privacy and not barged into my room. I wouldn't have the scars on my back."

Kale was right. No matter what Jason did, he would always be Kale's master. Whatever reparations he could make, Kale would always bear those scars. They were a reminder that Jason's decisions had permanent repercussions. That only strengthened his resolve. He wouldn't make the same mistake twice.

"I came in here as your lover."

"But we're not—"

Jason placed a silencing finger over Kale's lips. "Yes, we are. The physical act has little to do with it. I love you, and that's why I was so excited to see you that I forgot to knock. There's an art exhibit I want us to go to." Jason fished the clipping from his pocket and set it on Kale's chest. "I think you'd like it."

"Fetching you drinks?"

"No, I don't want you there as my slave, and you know it. It didn't used to be like that."

"Yes, and look where it got me."

Jason sighed. "When are you going to realize you trust me? I know you do. I just think you hate admitting it as much as you hate admitting you love me."

Kale didn't say anything.

"I am sorry I barged in here. I know you don't like it, and I want to respect your space and privacy. I'll be more careful in the future." Jason gave him one last kiss and then stood. "I love you."

Jason was halfway to the door when Kale's voice stopped him. "Don't think this changes anything. It's just sex. Like you said, it's been a long time."

The words stung, but Jason tried not to let them affect him. He looked over his shoulder at Kale. "It's never been just sex between us."

Back in his room, Jason undid his pants and lay on the bed. Closing his eyes, he relived every moment of their lovemaking as he brought himself to climax. It wasn't as good as the reality, but like Kale said, it had been a long time.

CHAPTER THIRTY-FIVE

Kale fingered the newspaper clipping. He was an ass. The moment Jason had left his room yesterday, he'd felt like a bastard, and the feeling hadn't subsided. The art exhibit was exactly the kind of thing he would enjoy. Jason had taken him to many such events. Why did this have to be any different?

It didn't. There was no reason for Kale not to go, other than his own obstinacy. After the amazing blow job Jason had given him, without asking for or expecting anything in return, Kale felt he owed it to him to attend.

Kale pulled an afternoon suit out of his wardrobe. Jason had provided clothes for any occasion imaginable. The more formal clothes felt stiff and awkward—it had been so long since he'd worn a full suit as Jason's valet. Jason wore them regularly, but he hadn't protested when Kale chose more casual wear. Standing in front of the mirror, he admired himself. It was impossible to tell that he had been shoveling ore in a steel mill less than three months ago.

There was a light knock on the door, and Kale glanced at the clock. Jason was right on time for their regular walk to the park.

"Come in."

"Are you ready—" Jason stopped when he saw Kale. The admiration was apparent in his eyes, and Kale grew more comfortable with his plan. "What are you dressed up for?"

"Contemporary Masters in Black and White." Kale handed him the scrap of newspaper. "I thought we could go if you still wanted to."

"Of course. Should we grab something to eat at a cafe instead of going to the park?"

The thought of sitting and eating with Jason as equals—and that was what Jason had in mind, he was sure—paralyzed him. It was one thing to go to a museum where they would be left alone to wander around, no one paying enough attention to them to tell if Kale was a slave. It was quite another to sit across the table from his owner, acting like a free man. The ambiguity of his station at the art exhibit was the only reason he had even considered it.

"Sophie's already packed us a lunch. I'd hate to spoil it."

Jason peered at him for a moment, and Kale wondered if he saw through him to the real reason he wanted to go to the park. There was no point in dishonesty. Jason was more likely to acquiesce to his desires if he knew Kale was uncomfortable. Something inside him wouldn't allow him to admit that little weakness, though.

"Right." Jason nodded. "I didn't think of that."

Kale smiled. "That's because you're not the one who has to fix it." As soon as he said it, he regretted it. Why did he always have to be an ass when Jason was trying so hard, being so considerate? "I'm sorry, master. I shouldn't have said that."

"No, don't worry about it, Kale. That's the sort of thing you used to say to me all the time. I like it. It's you." Jason's hand was on Kale's shoulder and it sent reassuring warmth through him. There was no need to fear Jason. Kale could say anything, even unleash the full force of his stormy emotions on him, and Jason would stand and bear it. He had. A small voice whispered to Kale that Jason was always going to be standing there, loving him, but the thought was too soft to take hold against years of conditioning.

◆◆◆

"Do you like it?" Jason inquired. They were standing in front of a black and white sculpture. The black crept up the white, flaring out in seemingly random ways, twisting and curling until the white disappeared into the black mass. The placard read: *Inside Out*.

"Yes, I do." They had been casually walking around the exhibit when Kale had stopped in front of this piece and hadn't been able to move on. It spoke to him. The sculpture was very reminiscent of the way Kale often felt. He couldn't tear his eyes from it, and he knew Jason had noticed.

"What is it about this one?"

This outing was supposed to be something fun to make up for the way Kale had been acting toward Jason. Yet here he was, facing down his own internal struggles in the middle of an art museum, all because of one sculpture. He didn't want to explain to Jason the deeply personal and intimate connection he felt to this piece.

Jason had said Kale trusted him, that he just didn't want to admit it to himself. It was true. Kale knew Jason would understand, at least as much as it was possible for another person to understand. He wouldn't mock or ridicule. He would listen, but more than that, he would internalize what Kale said, and they would be closer for it. That was the problem.

Kale tore his eyes from the sculpture long enough to look at Jason. His face was open, welcoming, ready to accept however much Kale was ready to give. In that moment, Kale felt as if it would be a betrayal of Jason and himself not to be honest.

"It's me. That's how I feel. Any time a little light tries to come in or out, it's consumed. I feel like there's this black knot inside of me, and no matter how much I want to, I can't let it go."

"Maybe you don't need to." Kale let his incredulity show on his face. "I'm not saying you should hold onto it either. Maybe you should just stop trying so hard. Let it be." Jason put a comforting hand on his shoulder. Kale was growing fond of that habit of Jason's, though he would never admit it to him. "I can't imagine what the last three years were like for you. All I can tell you is what I've seen. Back at the mill, you were a shell. Everything that was you was locked away deep inside. I assume that's the only way you were able to cope all that time. Anyone would have done the same. And now you're back in a situation that, in some ways, is so familiar. You're trying to be the old Kale, but that person doesn't exist anymore."

"But that's the person you love."

"No, I love you. You've changed, but that doesn't mean I love you any less. The darkness in you has been keeping you safe. It's a survival instinct to hold onto it. The white is trying to get out, but the black is saying, 'It's too dangerous. You don't know how to survive in this world.'"

"I know I'm safe here."

"Bodily, yes. But emotionally, no. That's fine, Kale. It doesn't hurt me that you feel that way."

"But you said I trust you."

"You do, but that doesn't mean all the feelings from the last three years are just going to melt away. I know you trust me. Otherwise, you wouldn't have shared what you just did. But it's going to take time to recondition your reactions and instincts. It'll happen in time. You just need to figure out how to live in this situation without trying to act as though the last three years didn't happen."

"When did you become the wise one of us?"

"I was always wiser than you when it came to yourself. It was all the other stuff where you had me beat."

They stared for a moment longer at the sculpture and then moved on, falling easily into lighthearted conversation. Somehow, Jason made everything seem so simple. It was easy for Kale to be lulled into this comfortable acceptance and forget about his inner turmoil, for an afternoon at least.

CHAPTER THIRTY-SIX

"Thank you for taking me. I really enjoyed it." Kale hoped Jason could sense the sincerity in his thanks.

"You're welcome. Thank you for coming. I know it was hard for you."

It had been at first, but it didn't take long for Kale to realize that no one spared them so much as a glance. They blended right in. At the start, it had felt dangerous. Kale had an irrational fear that someone would jump out, expose him as a fraud, and take him back to the labor firm in chains. Jason had engaged him in conversation immediately, and that had helped. In some ways, it felt the same as it always had when they went to art exhibits together.

"It was, but you made it easy."

Jason brushed Kale's hair back from his face and then leaned in for a kiss. It was soft, but still intense. Kale could literally feel Jason's love in the insistence of his tongue and lips. The taste it left on his mouth was sweet, and there was an undeniable sense of loss when Jason pulled away.

"Why don't you come up to my room?"

They stood in front of Kale's door. During the time Kale had lived with Jason, he had never seen Jason's room. It was an alluring thought, but there was only one reason Jason wanted him to come up. "Because you want to have sex."

"Yes. Is that such a bad thing?" Jason rubbed his thumb

against the back of Kale's hand. It was soft, smooth, and it sent little currents of desire through Kale.

"No, except for the fact that it means more to you than it does to me."

That brought Jason up short. "What do you mean?"

"For me, it's just sex. For you, it means more." Kale didn't want his words to hurt Jason, but all he could think was that it would be far more painful for him to let Jason believe sex meant Kale was in a relationship place that he wasn't.

"I don't care."

"Yes, you do."

"No, Kale, I promise. You don't have to worry about my feelings, although it's sweet of you to be concerned. If it's just sex for you, that's fine. We can just be two people taking pleasure in each other's bodies." Jason slid up against Kale, just enough for him to feel how badly Jason wanted him.

Of course Kale wanted to have sex again. Desire wasn't the issue, doing the right thing by Jason was. No amount of reassurances from Jason could convince him that Jason could separate his emotions from sex. It wasn't in his makeup. But Jason was a man. He could make his own decisions. If he was fine with it, that should be enough for Kale.

Besides, the blood was already flowing south, and his cock stirred. He had been deprived. How could he turn away what was on offer? Especially when he knew how good it would be. "Fine."

As soon as the word left his lips, Jason was running down the hall and up the stairs, dragging Kale along by his hand. Kale thought he might have even heard a giggle. Jason's enthusiasm was flattering.

"Here it is." Jason flung the door open with a flourish, gesturing for Kale to precede him.

Overall, the room was simpler than Kale's. It was larger, but the furnishings were plainer. The wood was a rich brown, the color of Jason's eyes. On the bed was a dark green comforter. Kale had always thought that shade suited Jason's coloring, and he couldn't wait to see the contrast of Jason's pale skin against it.

"What do you think?"

"It's nice. It feels different."

"How so?" Jason tossed his suit coat over the back of a chair and began to unfasten his cufflinks.

"Your room has always been a familiar place to me, and this room isn't." Kale took his cue from Jason and began to get more comfortable. The coat, vest, tie, and cufflinks were gone in a matter of moments, and the first few buttons of his shirt were opened. He felt free.

"That can change." Jason sat on the sofa, looking completely at ease. This was where he had spent the last three years while Kale slept on a dirty pallet in a slave barracks. Kale could feel the bitterness curling up in his stomach and began to push it aside. Then he caught himself. Maybe Jason was right. He couldn't keep trying to stuff his feelings away.

The bitterness opened up, and he let himself simply feel it. He was a grown man. He didn't need to let pain dictate his actions, but simply ignoring the pain and hoping it would go away hadn't worked.

"Tell me what you're feeling." Jason's voice was closer. Kale could feel his breath behind his ear, warm and comforting. He hadn't seen Jason move from the sofa.

"It's not fair. You were here all this time, and I was on a cold floor, surrounded by men like me who were just trying to live one more day. You had the opportunity to be happy, and you weren't."

"I know. It's not fair." Jason remained behind him, and Kale was grateful. It was easier to speak freely when he didn't have to see Jason.

"Did you know that, until last night, I didn't even know if I'd ever be capable of having sex again?"

"That doesn't surprise me. I doubt you had much energy for it."

"No. It seemed a waste of precious sleeping time, even if I could have summoned the desire. I was always with dozens of other slaves, yet I didn't so much as learn another person's name. I'd never felt so alone in my life."

Jason's arms snaked around Kale's waist and up his chest, wrapping him in a warm embrace as he rested his chin on Kale's shoulder. Jason whispered in his ear, "I'm so sorry you had to go through that."

Somehow bitterness couldn't maintain its potency when Jason held him that way. In anyone else, the gesture could be interpreted as foreplay, a segue into the sex they both desired. In Jason, though, it had nothing to do with sex. It was all about making love to Kale, and not in a carnal sense. Jason was going to make love to Kale here in this room, whether they had sex or not.

"I feel lured here." Kale honestly didn't know if the apprehension he felt was from fear or hope.

"Don't. This is my most private place in the house— besides the study—and I wanted to share it with you. We don't have to have sex."

"Oh, we're having sex. If you're going to make me face up to my feelings and all that other shit, I'm sure as fuck getting laid."

Jason guffawed, moving away from Kale to avoid hurting his ear. All Kale could think was that he wanted Jason's body near, preferably without clothes.

"Fair enough. That sounds like the Kale I know." Jason took off his shirt and sat on the bed to remove his shoes.

Seeing Jason's flawless skin, all Kale wanted to do was touch it, knowing from experience it would be as soft and smooth as it looked. All he wanted was to touch with fingers, tongue. Every part of him needed to be touching some part of Jason. However, that flawless skin only served to remind Kale of the marred flesh on his back.

Yesterday, Jason hadn't seen it as he performed fellatio. Kale had spent hours looking at the scarred mess in the mirror. He knew it was enough to turn a man's stomach. Any desire Jason felt was sure to wither when brought face to face with the new reality of Kale's body.

While Jason was occupied undressing, Kale strode to the other side of the bed and hurriedly divested himself of his clothing. Any shyness was overcome by the more pressing need to conceal his scars. It should be easy enough; Jason had always loved taking Kale on his back. By the time Jason stood and turned to the bed, Kale was sprawled on the mattress, hungry eyes roaming over Jason, his cock beginning to harden in anticipation.

Jason spared him a glance before looking down to undo his belt and pants. "Get on your hands and knees."

What? It was said with an odd nonchalance that made it even more confusing. "But this is your favorite position."

"Yes, but it's your least. You prefer it on your front." Jason's pants were cast aside and he crawled onto the bed, his cock bobbing in front of him.

"This is fine. I don't mind." At the sight of Jason's cock, all he wanted was it in him. Gods, he could barely remember what that felt like.

"Tell me why you want it on your back."

He knew. Here Kale thought he had been so clever, but Jason had once again pried his way into his head.

"I want to look at you." Kale couldn't help denying it, even though they both knew it was futile.

The left corner of Jason's mouth twitched up. "As flattering as that is, we both know it's shit, Mr. This-Is-Just-About-Sex. You hate the intimacy of being face to face, so try again."

Jason was straddling him, and all Kale could think about was how perfect he looked. In all honesty, he could see the appeal of facing forward this time. Kale could get lost just watching Jason move, the ripple of long, lean muscles under alabaster skin. "I want it this way."

Jason leaned over him, both hands planted firmly on each

205

side of Kale's head. "Only because you don't want me to see your back." Then, without waiting for Kale's reaction, he dipped down and kissed a spot on Kale's right side. It was a scar from a lash that had wrapped around. "I let it go yesterday. I wanted you to enjoy yourself without any stress, but it's not going to be that way today."

"No." Jason had no right to demand that from him. They both knew there was no way he would still feel any sense of passion when confronted with that disfigured mess. Jason had no intention of having sex with him; this was just another of his therapy exercises. He would look at Kale's back, assure him it didn't change anything, and then blow him to distract from the fact that he couldn't get it up.

"Fine." Jason withdrew to sit on the edge of the bed and reached for his pants.

"What?" Kale shot upright.

"I told you it's not going to be that way today. I know you think I can't stomach it, that somehow it's going to make you less attractive to me, but it's not. I told you, I didn't look at it yesterday out of respect for you, not because of any aversion to it."

"Why can't we just do it this way?" Jason was actually putting his pants back on. Suddenly, that perfectly formed cock was covered, and Kale thought he might do anything to get it back out.

"Because I'm not going to let this fester between us. If we don't deal with it now, it will only become more difficult." Jason shrugged into his shirt and began buttoning it. The man was evil. "I don't need sex. I want you. If that's not on offer, I'll pass."

Kale ran a hand through his hair. How could he make this decision? "I thought you said this was just about sex. That we could just be two people taking pleasure in each other's bodies."

"Yes. I'm not the one reneging on that. I want to take pleasure in your body, Kale. All of it. Not just the parts you're

206

comfortable with me seeing."

"What possible pleasure could you take in my back? It's hideous. You just want to lord yourself over me, to show me that you can make me do this." Kale hadn't planned the viciousness of his voice; it just came out. And it felt good.

"I can't make you do anything, Kale. If I could, I would have made you be honest with me years ago."

"So, what, you're going to try and guilt me into this? I lied to you and ruined your life, so now I owe you?" Kale was getting even more worked up. Somewhere in the back of his mind, a voice told him this was a ridiculous argument. Jason was the one person Kale wanted more than anyone to see him. On one level, Kale felt like it was Jason's right as his lover. That just made him even angrier.

"That's not what I meant at all. But you know that. Who are you so mad at, Kale?"

"You. You're the one who caused this, and now you're the one who leads me to expect sex and then turns the tables."

"No, this isn't about you being mad at me." Fully dressed, Jason sat on the bed face to face with Kale. He reached out a hand, and Kale relished the soft touch to his cheek before he shook it off. He wouldn't be lured in again. "Who are you mad at?"

Kale clenched his jaw and averted his eyes. This was ridiculous. Fine. If Jason wanted him to face up to it, then so be it. "Me. I'm mad at me."

"For what?" There was an infinite gentleness in Jason's voice that Kale couldn't comprehend in his fog of anger.

"For being weak. For not being strong enough to deal with my own problems."

"That's not it either. You're the strongest person I've ever known, Kale. How can you be to blame for this? You didn't put those scars on your back, and I didn't either. So who are you mad at?"

"Them." Kale felt emotion boiling up until it threatened

to spill from his eyes. "The men who did this to me. Gods, there was no pleasing them. The first beating was the day they bought me. Did it just to show they could. Up 'til that point it was the worst beating I'd gotten. They didn't need to do it. I'd chosen that life; I wasn't going to fight. I never did. Gods, I never fought them, but they did this. And now I'm here with you, and it's all ruined. Those bastards ruined me."

The shudders came on quickly, and Jason was there to absorb them. He swooped Kale into his arms and held him tight. With Jason holding him firmly—so tight he knew he was safe and could let go, but not suffocating him—Kale felt the tears pour down his face. It was a relief, like pressure being released. Each wave of moisture that flowed down his face cleansed him.

"They didn't ruin you. These scars are something that was done to you, Kale. You didn't have control over them. You do have control over what's inside. You can deal with that. That's why this is so important. If you keep equating these scars with your other problems, then you'll always believe they can't be fixed. Those scars aren't going away, but they're not you. They have nothing to do with you."

They sat intertwined for as long as it took for Kale's eyes to dry. Once the sobs ceased, the air in the room changed. With the fog of hurt anger gone, sexual tension crackled around them. Jason released Kale long enough to pull off his shirt and then he was back, pressing his skin up against Kale's. The sudden feel of skin on skin exploded in tingling sensations, and Kale was grateful for Jason's attentiveness. He acutely felt every inch of his flesh that touched Jason's, and the rest of his body craved contact.

Jason's hands kneaded into Kale's back as he kissed his shoulder, sucking hard at the flesh as he nipped it with his teeth. It felt heavenly. Tense muscles relaxed; skin burned where Jason's fingers clawed. Kale thought that, if it were possible, Jason would have pulled Kale's body into his, they were so tightly pressed together. Somewhere in Kale's head, he knew Jason's fingers explored the ripples of his scars, but it seemed inconsequential at the moment.

Kale felt himself being pushed backward. Jason's arms placed Kale on his back. It was an unexpected move. Hadn't this all been leading up to Kale being on his stomach? Jason's mouth on his convinced him it wasn't worth thinking about, not when there were more interesting things happening. Inside Kale's mouth, Jason's tongue dove deep in a heated passion that made Kale wonder how long this was going to last.

When Jason broke away, Kale was left gasping for air and loathing the material of Jason's pants that kept them separated. Jason seemed to read his mind. He scrambled out of his remaining clothing as quickly as possible, tangling his foot in one trouser leg in the process. As soon as the pants touched the ground, Jason was back on top of Kale.

Every inch of their bodies touched, lining up beautifully, and Kale surrendered to the blissful sensation. The feel of Jason's cock against his sent pulses of pleasure through him, settling in a knot of barely contained energy in the pit of his gut. Jason was marking Kale all over his chest and shoulders with fierce kisses that resembled bites.

It was all too much. The soft velvety feel of Jason's cock and balls against his, the hair and skin that rested on him like it was meant to be there, the harsh sucking on his flesh, the heady stink of the rapidly forming sheen of sweat that lubricated their bodies—all Kale could do was be still and receive.

When his mind adjusted to the heightened level of sensation, it occurred to Kale to do more than just lay there. What he wanted, more than anything, was to see Jason's face. Both his hands moved to the sides of Jason's head, but a sharp sensation through his left nipple stopped him. Jason's teeth grazed it, rougher and rougher until Jason sucked it into his mouth, flicking and rolling it around with his tongue. Kale arched his back, wanting more, offering himself up for whatever Jason desired.

The pressure on his nipple increased until he thought he would see stars behind his eyes, and then it stopped. As soon as Jason's mouth released his nipple, Kale pulled Jason's head up to look into his face. Rich brown eyes were dilated with passion, but that didn't dampen the warmth of love in them. It took Kale's breath away, and he could no longer stand to look at it. He crashed into Jason's mouth, kissing him with a bruising force that still didn't communicate his desperation to be closer to Jason.

Jason began to ease away, but Kale wouldn't let him. He followed Jason's mouth until he was almost sitting up. Steady hands on his chest applied firm pressure until he surrendered and leaned back on the bed. Jason descended, kissing his way downward from Kale's navel. The light smattering of kisses was a jolting contrast to the fierce desperation of a few moments previous.

"Don't." Kale surprised even himself with his outburst. "Don't get me off with your mouth again. Please. I want to feel you in me." He wanted Jason to satisfy himself as well. He wasn't looking for a repeat of yesterday.

Jason chuckled. "Don't worry. I have no intention of messing with this," he placed a light kiss on the tip of Kale's penis, "at all right now. Just relax and enjoy. I've wanted to do this for a long time."

Jason's warm tongue laved his balls, occasionally sucking one into his mouth. It was thoroughly pleasant, and Kale melted into the mattress. Jason kissed and licked, studiously avoiding Kale's cock. He used his hands to guide Kale's legs to bend and spread, opening him up. Jason's tongue slipped behind Kale's ball sack and massaged the skin there. The sensation felt entirely new, and Kale reveled in it. The warm wetness, the firm pressure of Jason's tongue, and then the chill of air hitting wet skin when Jason moved to a new spot: it all coalesced to form a haze of pure erotic pleasure.

Somewhere through the mist, Kale noticed something

new. The tongue that was so thoroughly pleasuring him was delving further down, further and further until...

"What!" Kale's hands flew to his sides, and he pushed himself back. The feel of a wet, insistent pressure on the sensitive entrance to his ass was foreign and disconcerting. No one had ever wanted to enter him that way, and it felt disturbingly intimate.

"Shh." Jason's face popped up between Kale's legs, his hands running up and down Kale's stomach in a soothing gesture. "I told you, I've wanted to do this for a long time. I would have done it yesterday, but other matters were too pressing." Then he winked—actually winked at him—and lowered his head back to his work. "Just relax. You'll enjoy it."

"How do you know?" Kale settled back down despite his skepticism.

"Didn't we agree when it comes to you, I'm the wise one? Trust me. I want all of you, Kale. I'm not settling for less."

Kale didn't know if there was a threat in there, but he wasn't risking it. Closing his eyes, he concentrated on simply enjoying himself. Jason had gone back to licking his balls and then the skin behind them until Kale relaxed fully. Then he started the slow journey to Kale's asshole.

Everything was more intense on the more sensitive skin of this most intimate place. Once Kale got over the initial strangeness of the new touch, he began to enjoy it. Each move of Jason's tongue sent a current of desire to Kale's cock. The fact that Jason was still ignoring Kale's penis made the desire even more acute, and soon his tip wept, hoping for any kind of attention.

Several minutes later, Kale felt boneless. His cock was a torrent of sexual tension waiting to be relieved, but the rest of him was as sated and pliable as if he had already been brought to climax. It was an odd feeling. He was so relaxed that it took a moment for him to realize that Jason had stopped. He was kissing up the side of Kale's ass and nudging with his nose and hands for Kale to roll over. Relaxed and sleepy, Kale complied.

The full ramifications of what Jason was doing caught up with his brain, and Kale's eyes snapped open as his body stiffened and moved firmly back into place on his back.

Jason propped himself up on one elbow and spoke directly to Kale. "You let me stick my tongue in your ass, but I can't see your back?"

Bastard. This had been his plan all along. He never wanted to rim Kale, he had just wanted to corner him where he knew Kale wouldn't back down.

"I told you this was how it was going to be, Kale. We can stop now if you want, but if we continue, I'm going to look at your back. I've tried relaxing you to make it easier. You trust me. Accept it. Let's eliminate this barrier between us."

Kale tried to ignore the pleas of his stiff cock. It was cheap to make this decision based on sexual gratification. What was he so scared of? As Jason pointed out, he had already done far more intimate acts. And it wasn't just physical intimacy. Kale wouldn't have let anyone else do what Jason had done. The mere fact that he felt so close to Jason right now made this decision harder, not easier. What if Jason pulled away from him? Kale had something very real to lose.

"I'm scared. Are you happy? You've finally gotten me to admit it. I'm not the fearless man you used to admire."

"I do admire you. If you decide to get up and walk out of this room right now, I'll still admire you. But you're only afraid because you don't know what's going to happen. I do. Trust that. I know exactly what's going to happen. We're going to be closer than we've ever been and you'll feel free, more so than you have since you've been back. This isn't something you're doing by yourself. I'm here. There's nothing to fear."

The earnestness in Jason's eyes was convincing. Kale believed him when he said he could walk away. He didn't want to, though. The worst case scenario was that Jason was disgusted. Kale would feel embarrassment and shame. He would leave this room and never come back, ending something that could have never worked out anyway. But if Jason was right, if he really did still love him after, how wonderful would it feel to have that weight lifted from his shoulders? Kale wanted that so badly he didn't even dare hope for it.

Jason seemed convinced it would work. He trusted Jason. It would be a betrayal of both of them for Kale to pretend he didn't. If he went through with this, in a few moments it would all be over or their relationship would have a new beginning.

Kale focused on Jason's eyes, drawing strength from them, and nodded. He didn't trust himself to speak.

Jason nodded back, acknowledging the responsibility he was taking on and reassuring Kale that he would be careful. Everything would be all right. Kale rested his head back, closed his eyes, and let himself be rolled over onto his side. He held his breath, waiting for the horrified gasp, the same as it had been when Jason first saw him at the mill. There was nothing. He strained his ears for any sign of Jason's reaction. When soft lips grazed his back, Kale almost bolted.

Fingertips brushed feather light touches along his back. Kale presumed they were outlining the scars, but he couldn't be sure. Jason's lips danced across Kale's skin. He lingered in one spot and pulled back for a moment before laying down three kisses in a row. Kale kept waiting for Jason to realize that the skin he touched and kissed was disfigured, grotesque. He didn't. Instead, Jason spoke.

"My poor Kale." Another kiss. "Having to endure this all alone." Another trio of kisses. "So beautiful."

"No, it's not." Kale was gruff. He couldn't let the lie stand.

"Yes, it is." Jason's fingers traced a thick scar Kale knew was particularly disturbing. "It's you, and you are beautiful."

"You're the only one who thinks so."

"Good. I get terribly jealous." Instead of kissing, Jason licked a long line down Kale's back, leaving a chill in his spine.

"No one in their right mind would think this is attractive."

"Does it matter what anyone else thinks? Is anyone else ever going to see it?"

"No. I'm not making the mistake of ever letting anyone this close again." Kale's composure was broken by a gasp when Jason lightly blew on the wet trail down his back.

"A mistake, was it?" Jason's voice was amused. Kale felt a hand curl around his half hard penis. "We'll see about that." Jason nudged Kale's ass with his erection. "I love every part of you, Kale."

The hot feel of Jason's arousal surprised Kale. He truly hadn't expected Jason would be capable of maintaining an erection while looking at his back. It was encouraging, and Kale began to shush his brain and concentrate on how he felt.

Loved. Wanted. Attractive. Sexy. That's how he felt.

He didn't know how—it didn't make sense—but it was true. The only man Kale had ever loved had delved into the most private crevices of his life and still wanted him. There was nothing so arousing as knowing the person he wanted found him just as desirable. Kale's cock grew and hardened under Jason's insistent caress.

The warmth of Jason's body retreated, but he maintained his grip on Kale's penis. There was a commotion, and Kale glanced back to see what could possibly be so important.

Jason rummaged around on his nightstand, knocking over a few things in the process, until his hand emerged clasping a canister of grease.

"Nice to see you're prepared. You've been planning this?" Kale was amused.

"I always plan for success." Jason curled his body against Kale's again, removing his hand from Kale's cock in order to

214

open the canister.

Kale was a little surprised that Jason didn't turn him over. He had made his point. Didn't he want Kale on his back now? The thought was banished by a slick, probing finger entering him. "Gods." He moaned.

"Gods is right. It's been too long."

Kale pushed against Jason's finger; the small digit only served to whet his appetite for more. Jason obliged, quickly entering a second finger and then withdrawing his fingers altogether, replacing them with his cock.

The tip sat at Kale's entrance and then carefully nudged its way in. Kale shuddered as something inside him snapped, and a wave of butterflies fluttered in his stomach. Jason paused, giving him time to adjust, but Kale didn't want it.

"No, quicker." Kale couldn't stand the agonizingly slow progress.

"Are you sure?" Jason's grease slicked hand wrapped around Kale's waist, grasped his penis, and began to pump. Kale shivered.

"Yes. Want you. Too long." Desire made him incoherent. All he knew was that it had taken him long enough to reach this point, and he didn't want to waste another moment.

Jason slid home, filling Kale and hitting his sweet spot. Kale began to buck into Jason's hand, wanting more friction. Together, they sank into a rhythm of mutual pleasure.

"Going to come," Kale keened.

Jason picked up his pace, and Kale was able to hold on until he heard Jason's groan of completion behind him. Kale's orgasm exploded through him as Jason held him tight.

When Kale stilled, Jason's voice whispered in his ear, "Good?"

"Fucking amazing." Kale still saw stars. He melted against Jason, thoroughly spent.

Jason's hand idly caressed Kale's stomach. It felt good until Jason grew heavy on his shoulder. He was falling asleep. Jason intended for them to sleep together. In an instant, all feeling of contentment fled. Kale's throat constricted. Each breath was a struggle to fill his lungs. He needed to leave.

Kale rose from the bed and began gathering his clothes.

"Why don't you stay?" Jason was propped up on one elbow, calmly watching.

"I wasn't ordered to, master." If Kale started talking, he would never get out. Jason had developed some strange power over him. Best to keep a distance.

"No, and you won't be. Can you talk to me first, though?"

Kale tried not to look into Jason's eyes, but there was an almost magnetic force pulling him. When he finally gave in, he saw warmth and yearning. There was no fighting against it. "Fine." Kale plopped on the bed, holding his clothes in front of him, trying to show how unhappy he was with this new development.

"Why do you want to leave? We used to enjoy sleeping together afterward." Jason's hand lightly rubbed Kale's back, and Kale felt like that was somehow cheating.

How could he explain what he was feeling? Kale felt he owed it to Jason to at least try to be honest. "I'm the messed up one. You cleaned yourself up; you solved your own problems, and I'm proud of you for it, but I don't know how to do the same for myself. I don't even know how to begin."

"You've already done so much. You're drawing again. You're taking care of the garden. Sophie and Martin love you. It seems the only problem you have is with me."

"And how do I fix that? How do I get over the fact that the person I hate more than anyone else is also the one I want to be with?" Jason tried to hide the hurt in his eyes, but Kale saw it flicker.

"Maybe that's something we need to work on together."

"I don't think there's any fixing this one."

"I'm not demanding your forgiveness, Kale. All I'm asking is that you let me love you. We can work out the rest as we go."

"You do these things to me; you get to a part of me that no one else ever has, and instead of helping, it makes me hate you even more. How come it has to be my damn owner? Why do you have to make me want you so bad?"

Jason smirked. "I'm afraid I can't help that. I love you, and I'm never going to stop showing you."

"See, you say that, and I just want to climb back into this bed with you. But then I remember that you own me, and I feel so manipulated and used. You can throw me away any time you want."

"You want the same power for yourself?"

"I don't know. If you told me that I had to crawl back in this bed with you or you would never touch me again, I probably would."

"I'm not going to do that."

"I know." They sat in silence for a while until Kale remembered he had something to say. "I'm sorry for how I acted yesterday. What I said to you was completely unfair. I understand you don't see things the way I do. How could you? But I just can't separate my master from my lover. You're one and the same."

"You have feelings for me, Kale; I know it. As long as you know it too, I don't understand why we can't work it out. What do you need from me?"

Yes, Kale had feelings for Jason. That was the problem. What kind of person loves the man who owns him? The man who sold him into misery without a backward glance? Kale cracked a mirthless smile. That wasn't quite true. Jason had looked back. Kale had seen the pain in his face, and he'd had his chance to call out. He could have stopped it. He knew. All the time, the power had been in his hands.

"Please, it's not about you. Don't think that. This is my problem." Kale kissed him lightly on the lips. This was all about Kale and his own insecurities. Being able to leave gave him a false sense of control over his feelings. He knew it was false, but that didn't keep him from seeking it. "Just know that being able to walk through that door right now means more to me than you can possibly imagine. That's all I need from you."

Jason nodded, lowering his eyes in resignation.

Kale stood and dressed. "I'll have Sophie bring you up a tray."

"Can you come to my office tomorrow before lunch? I have something I want to discuss with you."

That sounded foreboding, but if Kale was leaving now, he could give Jason this. "Sure. I'll be there." When the door closed behind him, Kale couldn't help standing for a moment with his hand still on the doorknob. He didn't hate Jason more than anyone else. He hated himself for doing this to the man who loved him. If the thought of going back in there and sleeping with Jason, pretending everything was fine, didn't terrify him, he would have. Releasing the doorknob, he made his way to his own empty room.

He was a bastard, and he knew it. The only thing that kept him from complete despair was the hope that someday he'd be able to make it up to Jason.

CHAPTER THIRTY-SEVEN

All things considered, last night had gone better than Jason could have hoped. Kale leaving afterward had been disappointing, but they had overcome a very serious hurdle. Jason worked to adjust to his new perception of Kale. Before, Kale had always been sure and steady. Jason had thought nothing could ever shake him. It was heartbreaking to see how untrue that was and to realize that he had contributed to it. The change didn't decrease his love for Kale. If anything, it strengthened it.

Jason didn't know exactly what time to expect Kale, but he did see when Kale left the garden in the morning. About a half hour later, he heard knocking on his door that sounded too hesitant to be Martin.

"Come in."

Kale entered. Jason couldn't help breaking out in a smile at seeing him. Knowing that those clothes concealed a magnificent body that only he was allowed to see was a turn on, and Jason had to remind himself that he had asked Kale here for business, not pleasure.

"I'm sorry about last night." Kale began apologizing before he had even fully entered the room.

Jason waved it away. "Don't worry about it. Come, take a seat."

When he was situated, Kale started in again. "You were

wonderful, it wasn't that. I just needed to know I had an out."

"I know, Kale." Jason moved the ledger he had been inspecting to the side and placed a clean sheet of paper before him. "I understand you more than you'd care to admit. It was wishful thinking on my part that you'd stay. I didn't really expect it."

"You didn't?" Kale sagged in relief.

"No. We're taking things at your pace, Kale. I'm here for you, and I'll help in any way I can. But enough of that. I asked you here on a business matter." Kale's eyebrow arched. "I wanted to talk to you about the working conditions at the mill."

"What about them?" Kale's tone was uncertain, and he shifted in his seat.

"The welfare of the slaves working for the company has always been of paramount importance to me. However, recently I've come to realize that I have let others convince me that I've done enough, and I don't think that's true. I've wanted to talk to you about this for a while, but I thought we should handle your personal issues first. After last night, I think it's time."

"So, what do you want to know?" Kale's voice was more assured, but Jason could tell he was skeptical. He probably thought this was just another ploy to get him to talk about his feelings.

"Did you get enough to eat?"

Kale snorted. "No. There's no such thing. But I did eat more there than I did working for the railroad. Lunch was nice."

"So quantity wasn't enough. What about quality?"

"The bread was always old. Sometimes it was moldy. I think they got it cheap from bakeries after it had gone past the point of selling. It was served with a broth that tasted more of water than anything. There were a few vegetables, which were nice, but they always tasted like they were turning."

Jason's blood ran hot. What was the point of feeding the slaves more often if it only left them wanting? "I'll have that fixed. I should have inspected the food myself. What about the pace at which you were worked? How did the foremen treat you?"

Kale laughed. The bitter sound cut into Jason. "These questions show that you don't know anything about what it's like to be a slave. The pace? Grueling. All they want is more work out of you faster. You're pushed as hard as you can go and then some. You're not worth the company's investment if you're not working fast."

"But you said those scars didn't come from the mill." The thought of one of his foremen doing that turned Jason's stomach.

"They didn't. The foremen at the mill were better than most. They didn't savagely beat us for no reason, but they would whip you for not keeping up. That's expected."

Jason remembered the crack of the whip, the hot thick air, the acrid smell, and how oppressive it had felt during his inspection. "I don't want my men treating the slaves like animals. I've warned them not to be heavy-handed."

"They're not. You're asking impossible questions. You run a business. You need a certain level of productivity. Slaves aren't people."

"You are a person, Kale." Jason's voice was louder than he intended.

"I know, but what are you going to do? Put all the slaves up in a nice house and let them work when they feel like it? This is the reality we live in, the reality that you refuse to face up to, the same one that keeps us from being what you want us to be."

"I'm not blind to reality, Kale. I can't save all of the slaves, but I can make things better. And this has nothing to do with us. I have you, and you're never going to be treated that way again." Passion rose in Jason's stomach. He had the power to do this, and he would.

221

"I know. Thank you. I'm an ungrateful bastard. I guess I've never gotten used to your unfailing faith that you can do anything."

"I've tried to be a good steward of the people under my care."

"And you've done well. It really was much nicer than I had grown accustomed to. We had mattresses, three meals a day, water breaks, no unnecessary beatings. It was a welcome change."

"That's nice to hear, but what could be improved?" Jason picked up his pen to take notes.

"The bed bugs were a bitch. We were constantly eaten up."

Jason wrote that down. "All right, what else?"

"The water breaks were nice, but we were always required to stay standing. It was all very rushed. All any slave wants is a few minutes off his feet."

"That's more what I had in mind when I instituted water breaks." Jason felt betrayed that his orders hadn't been fully implemented. It was his fault, though. He should have kept a better eye on operations. It was easy enough for them to clean up their act for his scheduled inspections.

"Safety is also a big concern. We weren't given any kind of training. We were just thrown on the line and expected to pick it up as we went. There were countless injuries that could, and should, have been prevented."

"What?" Jason was so stunned he paused his writing. "The slaves aren't trained?"

"No. And since we weren't allowed to talk, we couldn't learn from the older men on the line."

Kale spoke so matter-of-factly. This had been the reality of his life. Bile rose in Jason's throat when he thought that Kale could have been injured or even killed while working at the mill. He would have never known. Jason saw black and dropped his pen. Gods, things could have gone so differently. The thought that Kale could have died in his own mill without him ever knowing about it made Jason sick.

Jason reached for the glass of water on his desk. The cool liquid washed the bitter taste from his mouth. "I had no idea. That will be remedied immediately." He spoke low and through gritted teeth. It was disgusting that he had let such negligence persist.

A strong hand covered his. He looked up into Kale's eyes. "That's the way the world is. It will get better; you're going to make it better. If anyone can, it's you."

Jason placed his other hand on top of Kale's. "Thank you, Kale. You've given me a lot of information."

Kale leaned back in his chair, and Jason missed the feel of his skin. "Is that all you wanted to talk to me about?"

"Yes. I'm going to a dinner and ball tonight. It's a fundraiser for the children's hospital, so we'll have to come back from the park earlier than usual so I can get ready."

"You know, maybe all you rich folk should just send the food and money to the poor. Seems odd to have a party to raise money for sick children. How does a bunch of old bats in jewels and men stuffed into suits getting drunk help the poor?"

It never failed. Kale could always lighten Jason's mood. He let himself laugh at the image Kale painted. "You have a good point. Unfortunately, I don't think these people are nearly as interested in giving to the poor as they are in being seen giving to the poor by other rich snobs."

"That sounds about right. If that's all, should I go help Sophie get lunch ready?"

"Yes, Kale, thank you. I know Sophie likes having your help." Jason stood to walk Kale to the door.

"It's no problem. Got to earn my keep."

Jason pulled Kale to him. "No. Even if all you did was sit in your room and draw all day, you'd still be welcome here. You always have a place wherever I am." Jason peered into Kale's eyes, trying to see if Kale was getting the message.

"I know. I was only joking."

"Good." Jason gave him a quick kiss. Even the light brush of Kale's lips against his made him want more. "I'll see you soon."

When Kale had left, Jason went to his desk to outline his plans for the improvements at the mill. By the time lunch came around, he had all of his ideas down. He dropped them off with Martin on his way to meet Kale for their trip to the park.

CHAPTER THIRTY-EIGHT

"May I help you get ready?" Kale asked as they entered the house.

Jason's eyes widened in surprise while his mouth curved up in pleasure. Kale loved being able to catch him off guard.

"Of course. I'd love you to."

The day had been unexpectedly good. After the talk in Jason's office, Kale had expected to be in a sour mood. As he left, he'd even intended to give Jason some excuse to avoid their regular lunch appointment. However, when Jason came looking for him, Kale not only felt fine about going, he wanted to.

Their walk had been pleasant, and lunch was devoid of any awkwardness. It was a relief to be able to transition so easily between uncomfortable subjects and the thoroughly comfortable chatter he and Jason engaged in at the park.

"What are you thinking about?"

"Huh?" Kale had followed Jason into his room without even thinking.

"You went quiet on me."

"Oh, I was just thinking that today was easier than I had imagined."

Jason began to undress. "It's always been easy between us when we let it. Take a seat." Kale sat on the sofa and watched Jason strip down. The view was enough to make Kale hard.

After doing without for so long, it didn't take much, and the lines of Jason's body bending to remove his shoes and pants was more than enough. When Jason was completely naked, he eyed the tent in Kale's pants. "I'm flattered, but I really don't have the time. Unfortunately."

"I remember a time when you would blow off these things for a good romp." Kale opened his legs a little more, making his erection more visible.

Jason disappeared behind the door of his wardrobe. "The life of a lovesick university student is different than that of a steel magnate."

"Gods, I've never thought of you that way. I mean, I knew you were, but it's…you." Jason was Kale's. He knew everything about Jason—all the foibles—and that image did not match up with the one that others must see when they looked at him.

Jason laughed. "Thanks for the confidence."

"You know what I mean."

"Yeah, I do. It just shows the craziness of the world we live in that I could be put in this position." Jason reached for the formal evening suit he had laid out on the bed and began dressing.

"From what I've heard, you haven't been attending these things regularly. Why now? Need a break from me?" Kale had to bite down on the smile that would give his teasing completely away. It worked. Jason paused and straightened. He came to Kale, stopping only inches in front of him so Kale was face to face with his torso.

"No, never. This is about me getting my life together, being a better person, not least of all for you. There's a lot of good I can do." Jason's hand rested in Kale's hair, fondling it lightly. The little attention gave Kale more pleasure than he thought possible from such a small gesture.

However, there were more important things in front of him. He had succeeded in getting Jason closer. Now Kale reached out and placed his hands on Jason's waist, pulling his stomach to his lips. The brush of skin against Kale's mouth further stoked his desire. "There's a lot of good you can do here." Kale looked up with a wolfish grin.

Understanding dawned in Jason's eyes. "You're a shameless schemer. You were never worried about me leaving tonight."

"Nope."

Jason pulled back and began to dress again. "You're probably the one who's relieved. You can do whatever you want tonight."

"Well, I can think of one thing I won't be able to do."

"Ha. I'm sure if you want to badly enough, you'll be up for it when I get back."

"Really?" For some reason, the thought had never occurred to Kale. He had assumed Jason would want to go to bed after a long and boring evening.

"Really. You can come and go from my room as you please. If you want to spend time with me tonight, be here when I get back."

It was a tempting thought. Jason always looked spectacular when he was dressed up, and it was clear he wasn't going to allow any pleasure before the event. "I'll keep that in mind."

Jason was attempting to arrange his tie and waistcoat. Kale sighed and went to him. "Move." Kale batted Jason's hands away. "You were never good at doing this yourself. How did you manage without me?"

"Not very well, apparently."

"There." Kale straightened Jason's tie and smoothed his shirt under the waistcoat. "Didn't Martin ever help you with this stuff?"

"Oh, he tried, but I usually wouldn't let him."

"Yes, we wouldn't want to betray my memory by actually looking well put together." Kale couldn't help teasing Jason. The boy begged for it.

"Very funny. I just didn't let anyone close enough to do

much of anything."

It hit Kale how lonely they both had been. He shook it off quickly. This wasn't the time. "Do you have cufflinks picked out?"

"Yes, over there." Jason pointed to the dressing table.

Kale picked up the simple onyx links. "No, these aren't nearly fancy enough. You need something with either sparkle or color." Kale rummaged around in the jewelry box. Finding a pair featuring large rubies, he nodded. "These are much better."

When Jason saw which ones Kale held, he protested. "No, those are too much. I only keep them because they were a gift."

"From someone with taste. If you're leaving me and going off to play the part of steel magnate, then you might as well look it." Kale fastened them and stood back. "That's nice. You could do with more color, but now at least you'll stand out."

"I had forgotten how good you were at this." Jason looked at himself in the full length mirror.

Truth be told, Kale had forgotten too. More than that, he was remembering how much he enjoyed being good at this. Being good at something. Useful.

"Gods, I really don't want to go. It's going to be incredibly boring."

"You used to do just fine."

"Yes, but that was only because I had you to look at." Kale felt a warm glow at Jason's words. "You always knew how to make me laugh or snap me out of a bored stupor. And gods know I won't be able to remember anyone's name or anything about anyone but the people I do business with. Somehow, you always kept it straight."

"If you miss it so much, why don't you bring me with you?" Kale found it easy to picture himself in that role again. He would be nervous, but if called on, he would don a formal suit and attend Jason.

"I won't take you as a personal slave. That's not what you are to me." Jason was firm. The set of his eyes and jaw told Kale there would be no swaying him.

"But there is no other way, don't you see that? I am your slave. You can't take me anywhere as anything other than that because it's what I am. It's the same problem we had before." It felt like they had the same argument over and over again. It was exasperating. Kale was finally beginning to come to peace with the way things were; why couldn't Jason just go along?

"I understand the realities, Kale. I know you would be great tonight. I would certainly enjoy not having to leave you here, but nothing good has ever come of me pretending you're only a valet to me. I want you there, but not as a slave. I can't stand it. Unfortunately, this isn't the type of event where we can act casually with each other."

"So, what are your long term plans for us? We fuck, sleep together, and then you go off to work and I hide away here?"

"No, it's not like that, and you know it. There are certain things that I won't be able to bring you to, but that would be true even of a wife. Besides, it's not like you actually want to go."

"I want to be with you."

"And you can, just not at these things. You know I would take you as my free companion if I could. If I thought we could get away with pretending you're free, I would, but there's too great a risk we'd be found out. If you get caught impersonating a free person, I'll lose you forever." Jason's voice was strained.

It was one of the few strict regulations regarding slaves. If an owner let a slave impersonate a free person, that slave became a threat. There was a constant fear in the government that the slaves would one day rebel. Kale never saw much evidence of it ever happening. Even if the slaves could organize, what would they do with freedom? They wouldn't be able to get jobs and feed themselves.

Allowances were made for favored slaves. It wasn't

uncommon for a closeness to develop between a personal slave and master. Privileges were extended and casual relationships established, but there was always a line that couldn't be crossed. The slave always knew he was a slave. Any evidence that the owner had lost sight of that truth and paraded a slave around as a free man would prompt an investigation and seizure of the slave. They played a dangerous game.

"I know. Don't worry about it. I'm not hurt. I just wish you would let me go as your slave. It's not as bad as you think. I've been one all my life."

"I'm glad you want to go, so much so that, if I hadn't committed to this, I would stay home and show you how much." Jason embraced Kale and kissed him tenderly on the lips. Kale didn't want to let the pressure of Jason's body go. "I love you. Now I have to go, or I won't get out of here tonight."

"Fine." Kale stepped back and opened the door for Jason. He followed him downstairs. When they passed the door to the garden, Kale had an idea.

"Wait here, I'll be right back." There was something missing from Jason's outfit, and Kale had figured out what it was. Calla lilies had started to blossom. They weren't blooming yet, but a red lily would add a dash of color that was sorely needed to go with the cufflinks. Kale grabbed the shears and clipped one, returning to Jason in less than five minutes.

"Here." Kale affixed the flower to Jason's lapel. "It's still a little too early, but this one looked like it might do."

Jason smiled down at the flower, then looked at Kale. "Thank you."

"You're welcome. Now, you better go before I strip your clothes off and take the decision out of your hands."

"All right." Jason chuckled and leaned in for one last kiss. "I love you."

The door closed behind him, and all Kale could think of

was how tired he was of seeing Jason walk through that door without him.

CHAPTER THIRTY-NINE

Kale had been in such a playful mood when Jason left, Jason hoped it would continue. He'd hate to think he was missing out on the chance at a good time with Kale just to fulfill his obligation to the children's hospital. It was a worthy cause, but as Kale had said, they didn't benefit much from his presence, just his money.

An odd mix of people attended. Much of the upper class spent the summer in the country. That left people who had business in the city, those who were visiting for a break from country monotony, or the worst of the bunch: those who craved scandal and drama too much to leave the city.

Jason waved away a slave who offered a glass of wine. With relief, he saw that there was a punch bowl off to the side. "You." Jason caught a passing slave's attention. "Fetch me a glass of punch, please." It would have been inappropriate for him to get it himself.

"Yes, sir."

It was odd being served by someone else when Kale sat at home. Kale would have delivered his punch with a quip designed to make him smile. No use thinking of that, though. He wouldn't be able to leave for a few hours. An auction and dinner would require his presence.

Surveying the crowd over his punch glass, Jason didn't see anyone he particularly wanted to talk to. The women were all twittering about, showing more skin than was entirely appropriate, but was tolerated in the lax atmosphere of summer. The air was sweet with their perfume, easily overpowering the men's cologne. It was all a glittering display of decadence. Only a banner on one of the walls reminded them that this was for the good of the children.

"What have we here? The young steel mogul?" Lord Conrad's booming voice turned Jason's head as his heavy hand landed on Jason's arm. "Taking a break from strategizing long enough to join us, huh?" It was a common misconception. Rumor had it that Jason was reclusive because he was a shrewd businessman plotting his next deal.

"Lord Conrad, I wasn't expecting to see you here. I don't believe I've had the pleasure." Jason nodded to the very young lady hanging on Conrad's arm. Her sleeveless, blood-red dress was low-cut and designed from stitch to sequin to draw attention. Her raven hair and milky white skin only emphasized Conrad's graying beard and wrinkles.

"Yes, this is Miss Alisha Pemberton. Darling, this is Mr. Jason Wadsworth, one of the most devious minds in business today."

Ah, mistresses, the other staple of summer life in the city. While all the good wives were back in the country, their men enjoyed a grand time. Jason placed a chaste kiss on her presented hand. "How nice to meet you." He caught her eyes lingering on his ruby cufflinks. Conrad should watch what he said about Jason's wealth. Jason didn't think the diamonds dripping off Miss Alisha Pemberton were her own. If she thought Jason could give her better, she'd take it.

"What about you, Mr. Wadsworth? Don't you have a pretty thing here to decorate your arm?" Conrad asked.

"No, unfortunately. I fear I don't have much time to attract the fairer sex, and my wife is in the country." Jason despised having to play this game, as if he had any real interest in socialites.

"That's the place for wives, Wadsworth. I barely escaped

in time to be here tonight. Nothing drains the life out of a man as quickly as a long summer season."

Jason laughed because it was expected. "Well, let me help you with that. I would love to have you and Miss Pemberton over for dinner." Here was an opportunity. With Conrad in town, Jason could make another bid for his business and secure the contract.

"That sounds wonderful. I'm only in town for another week, though." Conrad looked at Alisha, and she nodded with enthusiasm.

"I'll arrange it then."

"Ladies and gentlemen, the auction will begin shortly." The master of ceremonies banged his gavel against a podium set up at one end of the hall.

"I'll look for your invitation, Mr. Wadsworth." Conrad nodded farewell and escorted Alisha to her seat.

As far as Jason was concerned, the evening was over, but he knew he needed to remain. Scanning the crowd, he looked for anyone else who might interest him and found his old roommate, Carl Bonham. He was the only person with whom Jason kept in touch from his short time at university. He rarely ran into anyone else, including Eric Vanderhoff. It was amazing that Jason had once thought Eric the center of the world, but now that he was one of the wealthiest men in the country, he realized how little Eric was. The Vanderhoff heir was still partying, chasing after boys and girls alike.

Carl caught his eye and smiled. Jason made his way over to him. "How good to see you here, Carl."

"I was thinking the same thing, Jason. It's been a while."

"It has."

"You're doing well, I hope?"

"Better than ever, and yourself?"

"Marvelous. I'm going to be a father." Carl beamed.

"Well, that's something worth toasting." Jason raised his refreshed punch glass. "Congratulations."

"Thank you."

Jason eyed a familiar slave hovering behind Carl. "I see you have the same slave with you."

"Oh, Charlie? Yes, he's a good boy. Don't see the point in making a change if it's not necessary. Are you still without one? I know someone who's selling an excellent valet if you're interested."

"No, thank you." Jason recalled that, of all the slaves back in college, Kale had been closest to Charlie. He projected his voice a little louder, clearly signaling that this was for Charlie's ears. "In fact, I recently purchased back my old slave, Kale."

Charlie visibly startled and even met Jason's eyes briefly. Charlie's face was riddled with questions.

"Really? Well, good. That was a nasty business. Glad to see it's worked out. How is he?" Carl glanced back at Charlie. Apparently, he knew of their friendship.

"He's doing well. The problems that caused him to be sold in the first place have been resolved. We've come to an understanding." Charlie seemed to breathe easier and a small, knowing smile formed on his lips. Apparently, Jason had been the only one to believe Kale's lie.

"Good to hear. Would you like to sit with me?"

"I'd be delighted." Jason followed Carl to some chairs near the back row. The rapping of the gavel on the podium echoed through the hall, and everyone settled down. Jason glanced back to where Charlie stood against the wall. The slave nodded his thanks, and Jason grinned. It felt surprisingly satisfying to be able to share their good news.

◆ ◆ ◆

Outside his bedroom door that night, Jason wondered what he would find when he opened it. As soon as he was able, he had left, aware of who waited for him at home. When he had come through the front door, he had almost expected Kale to come meet him. Now at his room, he envisioned opening the door to see Kale lounging on the bed, maybe even already naked.

When he turned on the light, though, no one was there. Jason sighed. He had wanted to unwind with Kale tonight, but if Kale wasn't up to it, then Jason would respect his wishes. He was so disappointed he almost missed the letter resting in the center of his bed.

I'm helping Sophie with the cleaning. Find me when you're ready. And don't undress. I want to do that myself.

Kale

Jason laughed. Leave it to Kale to surprise him. This worked out well. Jason wanted to talk to Martin about his conversation with Conrad. A lot of preparation would be necessary if they were going to be able to entertain on such short notice. He would need the head start.

◆ ◆ ◆

"Martin?" Jason was outside his secretary's open office door. It was rare for Jason to come down here, but it was late and he didn't want to ring for him.

"Sir?" Martin glanced up from a book, the surprise in his voice mirrored on his face. "Did you enjoy your evening?"

Jason waved a dismissive hand. "It was fine. I actually had something to discuss with you."

"Yes?" Martin stood and gestured for Jason to sit.

Jason seated himself as Martin warily lowered to his own chair. It felt odd to be on this side of the desk. "I ran into Lord Conrad tonight. He's in town for a week visiting with his mistress. I've invited the both of them over for a little soiree. It's an excellent opportunity to solidify this deal. I'm going to need you and Sophie to put it together for three days from now."

Martin's eyes widened. "Sir, that's not nearly enough notice."

"I have every confidence you can do it. I want you to send out invitations tomorrow. We'll be inviting him and Miss Pemberton, Carl Bonham and his wife, Hector Isaishin and his wife, and Lord Rockford along with his mistress, Amelia Bancroft. It doesn't need to be anything too fancy, just passable. I'm counting on you, Martin."

"Yes, sir. Would you like me to invite your wife, sir? I'm sure we could get her here in time."

"No."

"If everyone else has a date, it would appear strange for you not to."

"I won't have her in the same house as Kale. A wife won't impress Conrad, not when he's bringing his mistress." He wouldn't subject Kale to her presence.

"Very well."

"Whatever you need, ask. It's important this goes well."

"I understand, sir. Thank you for telling me tonight."

Jason chuckled. "I thought you'd appreciate it. Do you know where Sophie is?"

"Yes, I believe she and Kale are scrubbing the kitchen."

"I'm going down there. I'll tell Sophie to come talk to you." Jason rose, and Martin mirrored him. "Thank you, Martin."

"My pleasure, sir."

◆◆◆

Boisterous singing floated on the air outside the kitchen. No wonder Kale hadn't greeted him when he came home: he wouldn't have been able to hear him arrive. Jason was loathe to stop the merriment, but Martin would need Sophie as soon as possible, and Jason needed Kale. He walked in to see the two on their hands and knees, up to their elbows in suds.

The singing didn't stop. They just looked up at his entrance and continued. Kale broke into a grin when he saw

Jason and rose up on his knees, warbling with gusto.

"—*and we'll drink under the maple tree coming morning!*" Kale spread his arms wide at the end of the song.

Jason burst out in laughter and applause. Kale scrambled to his feet, almost losing his balance on the slick floor, and came over. Jason marveled that they had come this far. Not so long ago, Kale had tensed whenever Jason had entered a room. He was glad the fun no longer had to end with him.

"Welcome home, master. Did you have a good time?" Kale wiped his hands on a dishcloth.

"Good enough, though apparently not as much fun as I could have had if I'd stayed."

"We all ate sandwiches for dinner, and since Sophie didn't need the kitchen for cooking tonight, we thought we'd get a good scrub in."

"Well, don't let me disturb you. I'll just go upstairs." Jason tried to contain his smile as Kale looked at Sophie with a miserable expression on his face. Jason knew he didn't want to leave Sophie to finish alone.

"Go on, I'll not be the one to ruin your night. Have fun." Sophie shooed Kale and gave him a knowing wink.

"Actually, Sophie, Martin needs you. He's in his office. I told him I'd send you up."

"Oh, well then." Sophie stood and cleaned off the suds. "This will have to wait. Welcome home, sir. I'm glad you had a pleasant evening."

"It's getting better by the minute, Sophie." Jason grabbed Kale's arm and dragged him up to his room. Sophie's laughter trailed after them.

◆ ◆ ◆

"I ran into an old friend tonight." Jason was lying in bed with Kale. They hadn't lasted very long once the door had shut behind them. The clothes had flown as they tumbled into

239

bed. Sated, they were covered in sweat and still panting. "Carl Bonham from the old house. He had Charlie with him."

Kale perked up. "Really?"

"Yeah. You were friends with Charlie, weren't you?"

"We got along." Kale shrugged.

"More than that. Weren't you fucking before we started?" Jason smiled at Kale, letting him know he didn't mind.

Kale rolled his eyes. "Yeah. He was a good man. How is he?"

"Good. He was very interested in you." Jason looked pointedly at Kale. Would Kale realize he had figured out that even Charlie had known what was really going on?

"You told him you had bought me again?" Kale sat up.

"Yes." Jason didn't give him anything else, wondering if Kale would divulge more about how Charlie had known he was lying when Jason didn't.

"You didn't tell him what I've been doing all this time, did you?" The anxiety in Kale's face was worrisome, and Jason sobered.

He reached out a hand to Kale's face, as if he could smooth away the worry lines. "No, I figured it's no one's business."

Kale exhaled, his body relaxing back down onto the bed. "Thank you."

"You shouldn't be embarrassed about it. It's not like it was your fault. It's not you who should feel shame."

Kale snorted and looked at the ceiling. "It's not exactly something you like having people know. I don't want pity. Of all people, Charlie especially doesn't need to know. He'd disagree with you about it being my fault."

"Really?" Jason tried not to show too much interest.

"Yes. He told me I was a fool. Thought I should tell you the truth. He kept trying to convince me that we'd be happy together and you'd do fine without Renee. I was hardheaded. I hadn't even fully admitted to myself that I loved you."

Jason's heart skipped a beat. That was the closest Kale

had ever come to saying he loved him. Jason was sure of Kale's feelings for him, but to hear him so casually reference them in those terms left him a little giddy.

Kale turned to Jason when he remained silent. Seeing the look on Jason's face, he rolled his eyes and shook his head. "Don't act like you don't know it. We both do. After all this, I think it's become glaringly obvious."

"Yes. Still, you don't talk about it much."

"I'm just trying to be careful until we know how this is going to play out."

Jason could give him that. He hadn't expected declarations of love any time soon. "I made it clear to Charlie that the misunderstanding that had led to you being sold has been cleared up. He appeared to be very happy for you. I think he wanted me to let you know that."

Kale smiled, and his eyes got a faraway look in them, as if lost in memory. "Thanks."

"You can see him if you want."

"What? Are you setting up play dates between slaves now?"

Jason chuckled. "No. I'm throwing a very important dinner party to try to secure Lord Conrad's business. Carl and his wife are on the guest list. I can ask them to bring Charlie to help." Jason had thought about surprising Kale with Charlie the night of the dinner, but thought better of it. Kale might not be up to it, and he didn't want to force anything.

"I'd like that. Thank you."

"You're welcome."

"When's the dinner?"

"Three days. Lord Conrad isn't in Perdana for very long. If I want a chance to nail this down, it has to be now."

"What? That's not nearly enough time. This place isn't ready for entertaining. Sophie and Martin are going to be drowning in work." Kale got up and started collecting his clothes. Jason felt bereft without Kale's weight by his side. "I might as well go to bed now. I'm going to have to work

241

around the clock to pull this off."

"You'll help?" Jason was pleased Kale was taking so well to the idea.

"Of course. What else would I do?"

"I appreciate it." Jason had hoped Kale would sleep with him, but at least they were separating on a good note.

"I wouldn't let you do this on your own. You say this is important to you. Then it's important to me too." The words warmed Jason, and he marveled that such a fine man was his.

Dressed, Kale came over and gave him a quick peck on the lips. "Don't worry. I'll see you at lunch tomorrow. Good night."

"Night, Kale. I love you."

Kale gave him an exasperated look, and Jason chuckled, throwing a pillow at him. "You don't have to say it. Go. Get your beauty sleep."

Kale went to the door. "Sweet dreams." Then he was gone.

With Kale's kiss lingering on his lips and the picture of his naked form fresh in his mind, Jason had sweet dreams indeed.

CHAPTER FORTY

"Thank the gods you're up. I need an extra pair of hands. I take it the master told you about his wonderful idea to have a little party?" It was far too early in the morning for Sophie to be this stressed. Already her hair was coming loose from its knot, and her eyes were wide as she ran around taking stock of what they had in the kitchen.

"Yes, he told me. Calm down, Sophie. It will all be fine."

"That's easy for you to say. You're not the one doing all the work."

"Oh, I'm not, am I? I guess I'll go back to bed then." Kale made an exaggerated turn and started out of the kitchen.

"Get back in here, Kale. I'm sorry. I didn't mean it. But what is he thinking?"

"I know. His enthusiasm tends to outrun his common sense."

"You could say that."

"Calm down. Let's get a menu decided on, and then we can go from there." Kale placed the paper and pencil that he had brought with him on the table and sat.

"I don't even know where to start. It's been so long since I've cooked for anyone but the four of us."

"Sit, Sophie." Sophie seemed so startled at being ordered by Kale to do anything that she complied. "Now, what meat do we want to serve?"

"How about veal?"

"No, Mr. Isaishin is coming, and he doesn't eat veal, or at least he didn't used to." Sophie sat back, her face screwed up in an odd glance. "What?"

"It's just hard to remember that you've done all this before. You know these people."

Kale shrugged. "It's not a big deal. Duck would be a safe choice. You make that great duck with berry sauce. Why don't we go with that?"

Sophie considered. "I could do that."

"I have vegetables from the garden that we can use as sides. If we make a cake for dessert, we can prepare it the night before so we're not so rushed on the day. Your strawberry soup would be excellent for the soup course and will go nicely with the duck. For the other appetizer, we could do a nice cheese tartlet. Yours are delicious. And there you have it, a full menu that will please everyone. We can do this, Sophie."

"If you say so. The menu sounds excellent. Let me make up a list of all the ingredients, and I'll need you to let me know how many and what kind of vegetables will be ready."

"Your wish is my command." Kale gave a grand bow, keeping his head lowered until he got the desired laugh out of Sophie.

◆ ◆ ◆

Lunch with Jason was cut short. There was too much to do for Kale to justify spending his usual leisurely afternoon in the park. Jason had picked up on Kale's preoccupation—he hadn't done a very good job of covering up the fact that his head was anywhere but on their discussion—and told him not to worry about it. They would go back to their normal routine after the dinner party.

Back at the house, Kale sought out Martin in his office.

"Martin? I was wondering if I could talk to you."

"Yes, Kale. Certainly. Have a seat." Martin was at his desk glancing between two papers. He would write on one, consider it, then cross it out and write something else.

Once Kale was seated, Martin looked at him. "What can I do for you?"

"Actually, I was wondering what I could do for you. I know this dinner party has been sprung on you, and I want to help out any way I can."

"I'm sure Sophie can use you."

"Oh, I'm already helping her. I just know that a lot goes into these things, and I figured you could use some help yourself."

"I don't know how you could help, Kale." Martin shook his head and shrugged.

Kale tried not to bristle too much at Martin's dismissive attitude. After all, the man had no reason to believe Kale was capable in this area. "What are you doing now?"

"This? It's the seating chart. I can't figure out how to arrange everyone. I wanted Lord Conrad at one end of the table and Mr. Wadsworth at the other, but he doesn't like that. He wants to be able to talk more comfortably. So that leaves the question of who should be at the other end."

"The hostess." If Martin didn't know that, then he was in desperate need of help.

"We haven't one."

"What?" Kale had assumed that for such an important business occasion, Jason would have Renee come. It seemed that Jason always put business and the welfare of the company first.

"He doesn't want to bring Mrs. Wadsworth to town for this, and he hasn't given me the name of anyone else."

There was only one reason Kale could think of for Jason's dismissal of Renee. He would have to talk to him about it. "Well, leave it blank for now. I'll ask him about his date later." Kale craned his neck to see the names written around the rectangle that was meant to be the table. "Oh no, you can't put Miss Bancroft next to Mr. Bonham. They don't care for each other. You'd be asking for trouble."

Martin scratched out the names. "How do you know that?"

"Back when I was a valet, I had to know about most of the upper class in Perdana. I know almost everyone who's been invited." Kale pointed at the diagram. "Move Mr. Isaishin next to Mr. Bonham. They're old friends from university."

Martin made the necessary changes and then turned a grateful glance to Kale. "I'd be much obliged if you could help me organize everything. I didn't realize this was something you knew how to do."

Martin never quite got over the fact that Kale had been a labor slave. He was aware of Kale's past service as a valet, but it seemed Martin could never reconcile that with the broken man he'd seen at the mill. Kale liked Martin, and they got along well, but he didn't think they'd ever share the type of friendship he had with Sophie. For some people, the divide between slave and free was too much to overcome.

"I'm happy to help. We should also have fresh centerpieces for the table. There are some flowers in the garden that should be ready. I'll have Sophie help me come up with an arrangement."

"We'll need to spend all of tomorrow cleaning and making this place presentable."

"Don't worry. We'll get it all done." Kale rose and started to the door. "I'll go talk to him now about his date and get an answer to you for the seating chart."

"Thank you, Kale. I appreciate it."

"You're welcome."

◆ ◆ ◆

"There, I think that should do it." Kale stood back to admire the outfit he had laid out on the bed. His eyes scanned over every detail, making sure there wasn't a thread out of place or a spot that needed laundering.

"I can't believe you're already picking out what I'm going to wear." Jason had been visibly excited when Kale showed up at his door, but as soon as Kale made it clear that he was there to work, he had deflated. It was flattering, but Kale knew there would be plenty of time for fun later.

"We're not leaving anything to chance. I'm going to have Sophie press everything tomorrow and hang it in the wardrobe. As long as you don't mess with it, it should be fine. I'll polish your shoes the morning of the dinner."

"Bless the saints, because I was scared I'd lose sleep over that tonight." There was a playful glint in Jason's eye.

Kale pointed a baleful stare at Jason. "Stop it. I couldn't care less about any of this, but it's important to you." Kale folded the clothes to take down to Sophie. He tried not to pay Jason any mind, but he could feel the other man watching him. Watching turned to stalking until Kale felt Jason's arms wrap around his waist. Immediately, Kale's skin began to tingle, aware of what was on offer. Kale was having none of it.

"Martin tells me Renee isn't coming." Kale resumed folding, and Jason whipped his arms away.

"No, I don't need her here for this." Kale watched as Jason plopped down on the sofa and tightened his lower lip. It was going to be a battle.

"You need a date. You're going to stand out if you don't have one. You don't want the absence of your wife distracting from the business at hand or dampening the mood."

"It's no secret that we're estranged. I daresay it would cause more of a stir if she came."

"Fine. Get someone else or hire a whore. I don't care, but you must have someone there."

Jason's eyes fixed on Kale with an almost feral desire, and Kale knew what was coming. "I want you there."

"I will be. Serving. Just the way it used to be. You need a date."

"That's not what I mean. I want you there as my date."

"I know, but it's not going to happen. We can either go round on this and come to the same conclusion, or you can just give in now."

"You don't always win."

"Yes, I do. The fact that you're married is evidence of it."

"Oh yes, I forgot. You're the reason we're in this mess to begin with." Jason's tone was mild and his lip had relaxed some. Kale thought he might just have a chance of talking some reason into him. "The only way I'll have a date is if you don't serve."

Then again, reason never was Jason's strong suit if his heart was involved. "I have to serve. We don't have enough hands as it is."

"We can hire help."

"That still doesn't make it appropriate." Jason scowled and opened his mouth to say something, but Kale put a finger to his lips. "I would love to go as your date. You have to know that. But it's too risky. Mr. Bonham, for one, knows that I'm a slave. It's impractical. If he hinted at what I am and Lord Conrad picked up on it, it could be catastrophic. I can't go as your date. You know it, so stop this silly fighting, and let me be there to serve. At least that way I'll get to see you. I'll even be closer to you than if I was sitting at the other end of the table."

When Kale saw the fight leave Jason's eyes, he removed his finger from Jason's lips. "Fine," Jason muttered.

"So, who should I have Martin place at the other end of the table?"

Jason sighed, as if he had the most vexing problems in the world. "Have him sit there."

"It'd be better to have a date. Martin being there will

make it seem too much like a business dinner."

"It is a business dinner. It's either him or you. That's the last I'm saying on the matter."

"I'll let Martin know." Kale gathered the clothes he was taking with him and headed for the door.

"Don't I at least get a kiss?" Jason's bottom lip jutted out in a pout.

It was irresistible. Kale feigned exasperation and went to him, sucking that perfect lip into his mouth. "If this goes off well, we can celebrate later. If you don't let me leave now, though, you're only going to be stressed tomorrow and the next day."

"Fine. I'll be reviewing my notes on Lord Conrad's operations in my office if anyone needs me."

As Kale walked down to the laundry room with Jason's clothes, his whole body relaxed. There was plenty of work to do, but it was calming being able to help and be of use. A sense of belonging and satisfaction came with serving Jason this way. If only he could make Jason understand that this wasn't something he was doing out of obligation or because he was a slave. He was doing it as Jason's lover. Of course, explaining that to Jason would also be admitting he viewed him as a lover, and he wasn't quite sure he was ready to take that step. One thing at a time.

CHAPTER FORTY-ONE

How everything came together so well, Martin would never know. The past few days he, Sophie, and Kale had worked together as a seamless team. If they could only get through the next hour before the guests arrived, they would be fine.

"Martin, get these people under control. They're running around like they don't know which way is up." Jason walked into the chaos of the dining room and surveyed the scene with dark eyes. They had hired help for the evening, and Jason bristled each time one of them tried to make his way past him. There was last minute dusting, arranging of furniture, and placing of silverware. It was chaos, but it was organized chaos. In fact, Martin really wasn't needed at all.

"They're fine; they know their work. Leave them to it, and it will all get done." Martin tried to use a soothing tone. He wasn't worried about the hired help. Jason was more likely to cause problems at this point.

Jason fidgeted, loosening his cuffs and collar. It made Martin a little nervous to see his employer this way. Normally, Jason was very calm and collected when it came to business matters. This was more than just business, though. In all the years Martin had worked for Jason, other people had never been allowed into his home.

"Where is Kale? He's the only one who knows what he's doing!" Jason bellowed.

It stung that Jason didn't seem to appreciate Martin's contributions. After all this time, he should have been used to it, but he wasn't. The sting was more acute because, over the last few days, he had conceded much of the planning to Kale. Martin wasn't one to turn away help, but how was it that a slave knew more of these matters than he did? The whole planning process had left him feeling decidedly inadequate. "I believe he's in the garden—"

"What is he doing out there? This isn't the time for him to be tinkering with those blasted plants." Jason's face twisted into an ugly picture of disgust and incredulity.

At that moment, Kale carefully walked in, carrying an intricate centerpiece. A hush fell over the dining room as the help moved back from the table, clearing the way for Kale. Kale approached the table and gently arranged the piece. A few tweaks to make sure it was centered, and Kale stepped back. It was lovely, a concoction of flowers, fruit, and crystals. How Kale and Sophie had come up with it was a mystery to Martin.

As soon as Kale was done, the other young men descended on the table using measuring sticks to make sure each place was properly set, and the dining room was abuzz with activity once again.

"Where were you? I need you here." The harsh tone of Jason's voice swept away the pleased look that had graced Kale's face at the placement of his creation.

"I'm sorry. I'm here now. What do you need?" Kale slightly lowered his head and spoke softly. It cooled some of Jason's heat.

"This suit. It's uncomfortable. I feel like I'm suffocating." Jason hooked his finger under his collar and extended his neck.

"Here, let me see." Kale stepped forward and took over, lightly readjusting Jason's tie and collar. Then he moved to Jason's wrists, touching the skin with one hand and adjusting the cuff with the other. The result was instantaneous. The tension visibly melted from Jason's body at Kale's touch. Martin had been jealous of Kale's abilities, but now he just wished Kale would never leave Jason's side.

The calm didn't last long. "Hold on." Jason jerked his wrist free from Kale's grasp and strode to the serving table where the drinks were already waiting. "What is this?" Jason held up a bottle of wine. "This is swill. We should have one of the wines from Lord Conrad's vineyards. Why don't we have one of the bottles he gave me?"

"You're not drinking, sir."

"I know that, but that doesn't mean my guests should be subjected to subpar fare when they are in my home."

"We threw everything out when you ordered us to. We couldn't find any of Lord Conrad's wine in town on such short notice."

Kale was behind Jason, straightening his suit and brushing off specks of lint. "I'm not interested in your excuses." Jason whirled on Kale, hitting his hands away. "Will you stop? Go do something productive. Gods, leave me alone!"

Martin had never seen Jason lose his temper with Kale. Martin knew Jason worried about the way Kale had stiffened around him when he first came, but Jason had been engaging in his own version of that behavior. In the beginning, he had tiptoed around Kale, being careful to never do anything that might disturb him. It appeared he had moved past that stage.

The reaction in Kale was almost painful to watch. Immediately he retreated. Martin could see a flash of fear in his eyes before he bowed his head. Kale, the confident valet, the man Martin had come to think of as a friend, was gone, and in his place was the image of a brow-beaten slave. "I'm sorry, master."

Jason seemed to notice the change as well. The stress lines in his face turned to worry, and he stepped forward, reaching out toward Kale and then letting his hand drop, as if he didn't know the right thing to do. "I'm sorry, Kale. I just…I'm stressed. I can't think with all this damn activity. Tonight has to go perfectly."

Jason was working himself up and getting more frustrated as Kale stayed resolutely still. Martin could feel the nervous energy coming off Kale in waves and could see him shrinking as Jason's tone rose. "It will go perfectly, sir. Kale, why don't you go to the kitchen and help Sophie?"

Kale looked to Jason for confirmation of the order. Jason nodded, and Kale hastily retreated.

"Martin, I didn't mean that." Jason looked wretched.

"I know, sir. He knows it too."

"He didn't look like it."

Martin guided Jason out of the dining room and into the parlor where he would greet his guests and wait for dinner. "It's a reflex, sir. A survival instinct, I'm sure. You can talk to him afterward. You need to focus on tonight."

"I just need this to go well, Martin. A lot is riding on this evening."

The change was remarkable. Jason had always been coolly detached from his work. Martin had never understood how he could appear to care so little and yet perform so well. This was about more than a business deal. Martin had a feeling that Jason was trying to prove something to himself and impress Kale. It was as if Jason had something to live for now. All that time Martin had spent trying to help Jason had been in vain. The cure had never been with him.

CHAPTER FORTY-TWO

Kale despised himself for his reaction. The fear had been a reflex, but once it gripped him, he found it nearly impossible to shake. He was so caught in the feeling that he didn't even notice Charlie waiting for him when he made it to the kitchen.

"What's wrong?" Charlie's voice was familiar, and Kale struggled to snap himself out of his shock.

"It's nothing." Kale ventured further into the room, still feeling dazed.

Sophie took one look at him and came over. "Don't lie. It was something."

"The master got mad at me. It's nothing. Really. Just the stress of the evening." Kale used his eyes to plead with Sophie, but she didn't back down. So instead, he turned his attention to Charlie and was all smiles. "Hey, I haven't seen you in a while. How are you doing?"

Charlie didn't look like he was ready to believe Kale's protests, but he was agreeable enough to brush it aside and hug Kale. It was comforting. They had a long history together as roommates, lovers, and friends. "I'm good. I would have been here earlier to help, but my master needed me."

"Don't worry about it. You're here now."

"I was thrilled when I heard Mr. Wadsworth had purchased you again. I'm so happy for you. It's about damn time. Only you two could make the obvious take this long. So, are you willing to admit you were wrong?" The grin on Charlie's face was infectious.

"It all would have been fine if he had just done his part and been happy. I didn't ask him to come nosing into my life."

"Ah, you were doing just fine without him, huh? That why he can make you walk in here looking as fearful as a broken man? Where were you the last three years?"

This had been a bad idea. Kale didn't want Charlie's pity. It was humiliating having been sold into hard labor. He should have known it would show, especially to Charlie who knew him so well. "Fine, Charlie. You were right. If only I had bowed to your superior intellect years ago, I'd be wining and dining right now."

Charlie laughed, even though it didn't reach his eyes. That was the friend he had known. Only pushing as much as was necessary to make a point, but never wanting to cause harm.

"So long as you know it." Charlie's cheerful voice and quick grin made it seem as if he hadn't aged a day.

"Now why don't you tell me about what's been going on since I left while we help Sophie plate? You don't look like you've changed a bit."

"Same old, same old. I missed you. It wasn't the same in the house after you left." On and on they talked, and Kale was surprised at how nice it was to have Charlie there. The camaraderie was pleasant, and he liked having someone around who knew him from before and could see him as he was without judging him. He had missed their friendship.

Together they served throughout dinner. Charlie's whispered jokes and comical glances as they worked kept Kale from locking up again. In some ways it was just like the old days, except back then Kale had been sure of his place. He wouldn't have been scared of Jason, and he would have ended the night in Jason's bed. Charlie's presence was the only thing that made the night feel somewhat normal. If only he didn't have to leave.

CHAPTER FORTY-THREE

The click of the door closing behind the last of the hired help broke the tension in Martin, and he sagged against the door, breathing a sigh of relief. They had done it. Once the evening had commenced, Jason had been in proper form. The transformation to consummate businessman had happened, and Martin was, as always, impressed.

With all the stress and anxiety finally alleviated, Martin was also exhausted. It took more effort than it should have to heave himself away from the door and make his way to the parlor where Jason waited.

"Thank you, Martin. Tonight was a success. All we need to do is sign the papers, and the deal's sealed. I couldn't have done it without you." Jason lounged on a chair, his tie open and coat flung across the back of the sofa.

The gratitude was unexpected. It wasn't Jason's custom to be so free with appreciation toward his secretary. As much as Martin had yearned for those words all these years, he couldn't let them stand as they were. "I'm afraid it had very little to do with me. Kale's the one responsible for tonight."

A smile spread across Jason's face. "It's good of you to say so. It was supremely awkward being complimented tonight and knowing that it was all you and Kale."

"That's the way it is." Martin shrugged and sat himself down across from Jason.

"And don't discount your own role tonight. You were superb at dinner. Your conversation was engaging, and you balanced the entertainment of the night with the business very well. I always struggle with that. I just want to get the business done and leave."

"Thank you, sir." Martin couldn't remember ever being complimented by Jason before this night.

Jason nodded and sipped from a glass of water. Martin had been impressed by his refusal to drink alcohol. If there was ever a night to break that resolve, it had been tonight.

"Where is Kale? I thought he would join us as soon as everything was cleared away and in order." Jason looked around as if Kale might appear.

"I don't think he's coming. It's late, and I doubt he feels comfortable." It had been unsettling seeing Kale retreat into himself the way he had. It was so easy to forget he was a slave. He and Jason usually moved in sync, responding to each other in a way that only two people who were intimately familiar could. It had been interesting, to say the least, watching them dance around each other the past several weeks.

Jason's jaw tightened. "Things have to change. It was humiliating being served by Kale. The way he reacted to me earlier was horrible. Doesn't he know that it was just the stress of the evening? It was nothing more than a lover's spat. I tried to apologize."

"That's the problem. You're not lovers. Kale's your slave and that was abundantly clear tonight." It was painful to watch these two—who were so obviously besotted with each other—keep running up against the same barriers.

Jason slammed his glass down on the table next to him so hard Martin thought it might crack. "I don't like it, Martin. It's wrong. Unnatural. I want to free him."

"Free him? You know there's no way to do that. A slave is a slave."

"What then? Should I sell him? Keep him? Things can't

stay the way they are. It's just going to get worse. This is unacceptable."

"I don't know, sir." Martin couldn't claim to understand Jason and Kale's relationship. A man of Jason's station having these types of feelings for a slave was disconcerting to Martin's sense of the world. But he knew one thing: it was good for Jason. The changes he had observed in his boss were inspiring. Jason had finally come alive, and Martin couldn't bear to think that he might revert to the way he was. There was no mistaking that the key was Kale. If Kale was gone, or if this rift did not resolve, Martin feared for Jason.

They sat together in a tense silence, Jason brooding over his glass of water. Martin wouldn't leave until Jason did. There was still alcohol in the parlor, and Martin didn't want to leave Jason alone with it in his somber mood.

Finally Jason swallowed the last of his water and stood. "Here are some notes I wrote while you were cleaning up." Jason handed him a few sheets of paper. "If you could take care of them?"

"Of course."

"Good night, Martin."

"Good night, sir." Martin followed Jason and headed to his office with the notes. He set them down on his desk and then headed back downstairs to clear out the alcohol. Before he reached the stairs, he caught sight of Jason down the hall, a hand on Kale's door and a sad look of longing on his face.

Saints help them if Jason lost Kale again.

CHAPTER FORTY-FOUR

Rain pitter-pattered against Jason's office window. Still, he gazed out, hoping for a glimpse of Kale that he knew he wouldn't get. No one in their right mind would be outside in this weather. This was ridiculous. He was a grown man. If he wanted to see Kale, he should just go find him. The only problem was he didn't know what he would say. What was the point in apologizing when he couldn't fix the problem?

This morning, he had woken up to the hard realization that Kale was right. All this time, Jason had tried to deny it. He had tried to pretend they could live in their own little cocoon where they created their own reality. There was no escaping it: they couldn't work like this. A man didn't own his lover, it was that simple. On some level, Jason had been trying to forgive himself for the mistakes of the past by making things right with Kale. Things weren't right, and forgiveness was out of his reach.

It was easy for Jason to curse the day he had been given Kale. But the minute he did so, every inch of his body recoiled. Blasphemy. Even with the pain he was in now—the pain he had been in for three years and from which he had only been granted a brief respite—he still couldn't regret a second of the time he had spent with Kale. A world without Kale was unimaginable.

Which left him with the question of what to do. Jason

rested his forehead against the cool glass of the window and closed his eyes. This wasn't his decision to make. It was Kale's future too. They would have to talk soon. Jason needed to settle this matter within himself, and he would need Kale's input to do that.

Jason moved to go find Kale, but was stopped by the sight of his desk. It was littered with mail. Jason and Martin had both let it slip lately with everything else going on. The pile would have to be sorted, and he might as well do it now. Even as he sat at his desk, he knew it was an avoidance tactic. So? He was giving up his dreams for the second time in his life. He was entitled to delay it a few hours.

The amount of correspondence he received had recently increased. Now that he was doing more charitable work and getting out more, the invitations poured in faster than ever. With the preparations he had undertaken for the possibility of working with Conrad, he had been getting more frequent reports from the mill and from contractors working on the expansion.

Only one letter in the bunch was personal in nature. *Renee Wadsworth*, the name in the return address jumped out at him. Surprisingly, he didn't feel the urge to drink. Maybe that improvement would stick, no matter what happened with Kale. A pang in his heart tried to convince him otherwise, but Jason ignored it. He would have to become good at that.

He tore open the letter and read it. As always, Renee was polite and enthusiastic. He actually enjoyed it.

I spent some time in Naiara. Amy Carrison invited me to her family's house. She's an old friend from the time I spent studying in Calea. I didn't realize her family's country home was so close to Timar.

We had a lovely visit. It's amazing how a country so near could be so different. I've always loved Naiara, and their culture fascinates me. I'm thinking of planning a more extended visit later. For now, though, Amy is coming for a visit next week. I can't wait to show her the house here. It's always been my favorite. Let me know if you want to come before summer is over.

Something about that part of the letter niggled at him. There was something there. What was it? His heart was screaming that there was something right in front of him of vital importance, but his mind wasn't catching it.

Naiara. Calea, the capital. Culture. Different. Close.

Slaves.

There were no slaves in Naiara. It was the fundamental cultural difference between their two countries. People crossed the border every day. If he and Kale moved there, Kale would be free. It would be against the law for Jason to keep him as a slave.

An old fear crept up Jason's spine, insecurities that pre-dated the time he had sold Kale. If Kale had a choice, he most certainly would not choose to remain with Jason. Jason wasn't naïve. He knew Kale's feelings for him, but he also knew that he was merely the best option Kale had been offered thus far. There was no way Kale would stay with him if he were free, not after everything. The scars were too deep.

This was no longer about their relationship, though. There was no relationship, at least not a workable one. However, getting Kale to freedom was the only way to set things right. If Jason could make this happen, then he could forgive himself and move on with his life. A little voice deep in his chest whispered that he might even get everything he'd ever wanted. There was a chance Kale would stay with him, and they could build a life together in Naiara. The sheer magnitude of the joy that filled him at that thought was overwhelming. It grew from deep inside him and filled him with a dizzying light that threatened to carry him away.

Jason bolted to his feet and strode downstairs. He needed to find Kale.

CHAPTER FORTY-FIVE

Jason burst through the kitchen door, startling Sophie and Kale. The short walk from his office had only added fuel to his air of excitement.

"Kale, will you join me in the parlor, please?"

Kale looked momentarily confused, and Jason had to hold in his laughter. He knew he must make an interesting sight with his collar unbuttoned and Renee's letter clutched in his hand.

"Yes, master."

Jason didn't bristle at the use of the honorific; if anything, it made him smile wider. If things went as planned, Kale wouldn't be calling him that much longer.

In the parlor, Jason motioned to the sofa. "Go ahead and sit, Kale." Jason had intended to join him, but after he set Renee's letter on the side table, his nervous energy wouldn't allow him to stay still long enough. "Last night, I was frustrated. I was nervous and stressed, and I took it out on you. I didn't mean to, and I'm sorry. Seeing you recoil from me like that was heartbreaking."

"I'm sorry—" Kale began.

"No, don't. You don't have anything to be sorry for, and that's not why I came here. It just made me realize that you've been right this entire time. We can never work as master and slave, not when we want to be so much more to each other. It may have worked at one time, but we've been through so much, and it just isn't possible." Kale's pale green eyes darkened in sadness, and a shadow of concern crossed his face. Jason needed to hurry up and get to the point. "So why don't we change our circumstances? We could move to Naiara. Slavery is outlawed there. You'd be free. I don't know why I didn't think of it before." Having presented his plan, Jason sat next to Kale and took his hands in his, gazing at him expectantly. His eyes darted eagerly along Kale's face, searching for a hint of Kale's thoughts.

"How will I live? I've been a slave my whole life."

"I'll support you. You don't need to worry about anything." Where was the excitement in Kale's eyes? Didn't he understand what this meant?

Kale pulled his hands free of Jason's. "How is that different than slavery?"

Jason was at a loss. This was not the reaction he had expected. "You could sell your art to make money."

"And how are you going to run the business here in Arine?"

"I can work it out, Kale. These are little details that we can figure out later." Jason had absolute faith that everything would come together. All he needed was Kale's support.

"There's no guarantee that we'll even work after we move. Relationships fall apart every day. Is it really worth uprooting your entire life for something that isn't a sure thing?"

"Yes." It came out quick and vehement. Jason snatched Kale's hands. "You don't think I'm scared of that? Ever since I first realized I loved you, I knew that the only reason I had a chance with you was because of your lack of options."

"That's not what I meant."

"No, I understand. What I need you to understand is that I'm in a place in my life where I'd rather you be free, even if you leave me, than live in this world where I own you in every way except the one that matters."

Kale looked as exasperated as Jason felt. "It's a lovely idea. I just don't see how it will work. I won't be free as long as I have to rely on you. I don't want you to think that I'm with you because I don't have a way to support myself."

"Why can't you just let me love you? Why does everything have to be so difficult? Just say yes, Kale. Gods, this is our chance. We have to take it. Let me do this for you."

"Because you have the luxury of dreaming. I don't. I want to believe, but I can't. The first thing my mother taught me was not to dream of freedom. It never leads to a good place, and it's the quickest way for a slave to end up dead. So go ahead and dream, you were always good at it. It's one of the things I love about you. But I can't join you in it." Kale shook his head.

"Fine," Jason spat as he stood. He whirled on Kale, pointing at him. "But I'm going to do this. Mark my words, Kale. I will make this happen." Without another look at Kale, he turned and stormed out of the room.

The walk did nothing to cool Jason's fire. Once in his office, he slammed the door behind him. The sound and vibration of the doorframe didn't give him satisfaction. He tried to burn off his anger and frustration by pacing, but that only stoked the flames. Why couldn't Kale just let them be happy? Most frustrating of all was the knowledge that he was well within his rights to force Kale to make the move. It was tempting. But how could they build any kind of lasting relationship on top of such a shaken foundation? It wouldn't work. Jason dismissed the idea and promised himself he wouldn't consider it again.

There would be no forcing Kale, but Jason felt sure he could persuade him. His pacing slowed as he made an effort to see the situation from Kale's perspective. It wasn't fair for Jason to expect Kale to react the way he would. Jason had been free his entire life, had taken it for granted. For Kale, the opposite was true. When viewed from that angle, naturally the thought of freedom would be scary. It was a large unknown. The last several years of Kale's life had been tumultuous, and now Jason was aiming to upturn his life once again.

Jason would do whatever was needed to reassure Kale. Words, however, would not be enough. Kale knew him too well. Jason was honest enough with himself to admit that he was apt to dive head first into an endeavor without fully thinking through the consequences. Throughout his life, this strategy had worked well enough. Only now, the stakes were higher than they'd ever been. It wasn't his life at risk: it was Kale's.

The thick carpet under his feet muffled the sound of his footsteps, allowing him to think in near silence. Pacing methodically, each step measured and sure, Jason calmed his thoughts to a more rational pace. This was just one more problem that needed a solution. If it was the unknown that Kale feared, then Jason would have to take away the element of uncertainty. The only way to do that was to move forward. He wouldn't force Kale, but he would make the necessary preparations so the road would be clear should Kale choose to take it.

The first step to moving forward would have to be writing Renee. She had more contacts in Naiara than he did. Besides, she would need to know. The changes on the horizon were too momentous to keep from her. Through everything, they had always maintained their respect for each other. Jason was sure she would be happy for him and encourage him in this endeavor. Kale was wary of her, but he hadn't seen the aftermath of Jason's decision to sell him.

Besides, Renee was the only friend Jason had who would understand what he was trying to do. Right now, he needed a friend. Sitting at his desk, he pulled out a piece a paper and began to write, unleashing all of his hopes, fears, and dreams onto the page, trusting that she wouldn't ridicule him. They had loved each other once. There was still love, albeit a different kind. Jason counted on that love to help him.

CHAPTER FORTY-SIX

The air in the parlor was still abuzz with the fervor of Jason's impassioned speech. This was just another of Jason's childish ideas. The boy had no grasp on reality. It was endearing, but Kale couldn't afford to let himself get sucked into hoping it could happen.

After a few moments, he couldn't stand it any longer. The optimism and resolve in the air was becoming oppressive. Kale stood and walked to the kitchen, feeling oddly detached from his body. As soon as he stepped into Sophie's domain, she broke into his abstraction.

"What's wrong with you?"

"Nothing." Kale didn't spare her a glance. He simply sat at the table in a daze.

"Then what's going on? You're different." Sophie eyed him suspiciously and joined him at the table.

"You'll never believe the conversation I just had."

"With whom?"

"The master. He has come up with a brilliant plan. Since I am clearly never going to be able to have a normal relationship with him as a slave, he wants to move us to Naiara so I'll be free."

"He what?"

The surprise in Sophie's voice was enough to snap Kale out of his daze. "Yep. Turns out geography has been our

273

problem all along."

"Why aren't you happy? This is marvelous news. You should be celebrating with him." Sophie shook his arm, as if trying to will her excitement into him.

Kale made no effort to suppress the incredulity of his expression. "You're not serious."

"Why not?"

"How would it even work? I can't support myself."

"I'm sure Mr. Wadsworth will take care of you. He loves you."

"How will that be different than being his slave, Sophie? How would I be free if I depended on him for everything?"

"Part of being lovers is taking care of each other and letting yourself be taken care of. That's how it is being free."

"I can't just leech off of him."

"I'm sure you could find your own way to contribute."

Kale was accustomed to feeling like the only sane one when he was with Jason, but he'd thought Sophie was more pragmatic. "It's crazy, Sophie. I can't leave Arine."

"You've never wanted to travel?"

There had been a time when Kale had dreamed of it, when the books he read did more than just pass the time; they actually inspired him. It all felt like a lifetime ago. Besides, what did that have to do with anything?

"Arine has always been home." His words triggered a memory of a carriage ride from Jason's childhood home to Perdana. Sitting across from Jason, he had come to the determination that Jason was home to him. When had that changed? What did this country hold for him? This country that enslaved him? Suddenly his argument seemed empty, even to him.

"Boy, you are crazy. I won't stand here and bite my tongue any longer." Sophie leaned forward across the table. "This is the answer to all your problems. Happiness is within your grasp. Reach out and take it. The only thing holding you back is fear, and that's a piss poor reason to accept the life others have dictated for you. If you're not going to do this because you're too scared, then you don't deserve him."

"It's not that simple," Kale moaned. Why was this so hard to understand?

Sophie leaned back in her chair. "Do you love him?"

It was blunt, to the point. Kale was done lying to himself on this point, and even if he wasn't, he couldn't lie to Sophie. "Yes."

"Do you want to be with him?"

"Yes." Even now, part of his body yearned to be in Jason's presence, to be having this discussion with him.

"Do you want to be free?"

He wasn't as sure as he would have liked to be on this question. He knew what he wanted when the fear was stripped away. "Yes."

"Do you trust him?"

"Yes." The answer was out of his mouth before he could censor it.

"Then what's complicated about it? Seems like the simplest thing in the world to me."

It was. It was so simple Kale couldn't trust it. Nothing could be that easy. "I'm afraid."

"Of what?" Sophie's face was full of the same open innocence as Jason's.

"The unknown. What if we don't last? I don't want him to remain with me because he feels some sort of obligation. What will I do? How will I live? I mean the practical stuff. All my life, when I haven't known what to do, it's always come down to obedience. Just obey. The rest is out of my hands. I wouldn't even have that anymore."

"And what if it all works out, and you get everything you've ever wanted? If you're scared, if you have fears, then you should be talking to Mr. Wadsworth about them. That man loves you. If you love him and trust him like you say you do, then you should trust him with your worries. To hide away from him is a slap in the face."

"I won't be enough for him, Sophie. He told me he's scared I would leave him, that the only reason I'm with him is a lack of options. The reality of the situation is that if he freed me, he'd realize there's no more to me. He thinks I'm this great person who has been oppressed by my condition, but I'm not going to transform into some incredible man the minute we step over the border. I'm still just going to be me."

Sophie chuckled.

"What's so funny?"

"You. You are exactly what he wants."

"He thinks so now, but he just doesn't know any better."

"How did it make you feel when he said he thought you'd leave him?" Sophie's question was unexpected.

"It crushed me." It still devastated Kale that he had allowed such an idea to grow in Jason's mind.

"Don't you think he should know that? Don't you think he might feel the same way?"

Kale hadn't thought of it. It was too out of the realm of possibility that everything could work out. He despised himself for his fear. Would the old Kale have been this scared, or would he have jumped at the opportunity? That was the Kale Jason had fallen in love with. He wished he could be that man again. "I've always had to take care of him, Sophie. Part of that is knowing what's best for him. He may be willing to stay with me, but it's not in his best interest. I know him better than you do. Once he realizes that I'm not the man he thought I was, he's going to stay with me out of obligation, and I don't want that."

"You need to realize that he's not the same boy he was when you knew him. He's grown up, and he can make his own decisions. Give him some credit. You want him to believe that you wouldn't leave him, but you're not willing to pay him the same courtesy."

"Because I understand that loving him means doing what's best for him, not what seems good in the moment."

"And how did that work last time?" Sophie gave him a

stare that was as much responsible for knocking the wind out of him as her words were. She patted his hand and then stood, leaving him with his thoughts.

She was right. Still, the fear remained. At this moment, it felt like fear would always be there. Right now, his relationship with Jason didn't work because of slavery. Once the slavery was stripped away, any shortcomings would be his own. He would have to take personal responsibility for his relationship with Jason, and as Sophie said, the last time he tried that, the results were disastrous.

Chapter Forty-Seven

As soon as Kale took their picnic basket to the kitchen, Jason sought refuge in his office. The last several days had been tense. Jason had made a real effort to keep his relationship with Kale normal. They did the same things as always, but there was an underlying strain. Jason was preoccupied with thoughts of how their life could be, and Kale could clearly sense his restlessness.

It was easy enough to come up with legitimate reasons to escape the awkwardness. Jason had plenty of work to do. He sat at his desk, ready to tackle the latest correspondence, when a thrill shot through him. Martin had delivered the post while they were out, and on top of the pile was a letter from Renee. He tore into it, his heart beating heavily in his chest. If he had been wrong about her, she could make his life difficult. It didn't matter. He would move forward even without her support, but he desperately needed someone to understand.

Holding his breath, he read.

My dearest Jason,

I am so happy for you. I wish you had told me sooner of Kale's return so I could have sent you both my best wishes. However, I can understand wanting to let things settle before writing. I only hope that's the real reason you kept it a secret and not for any fear of my reaction. I knew it was a mistake to sell him, even back then. I only tried to convince myself otherwise. For years, I've regretted the role I played in both your unhappiness and Kale's. I'm sorry. I knew he must have been lying to you, but I ignored it for my own selfish reasons. I can't express the joy it gives me to know that he is back in your life and that you have a chance at happiness. The world is at rights again. Although you don't need it, you have my blessing.

The idea to move to Naiara is a brilliant one. From my experiences in the country, I can say with some confidence that both you and Kale will be happy there. Their culture and society is very welcoming. It's the perfect place to make a fresh start. As for contacts, I would recommend you get in touch with Mr. Smoot, a lawyer in Calea. He should be able to assist you with the legalities involved in the move. I've met him on a few occasions, and he comes highly recommended.

Don't worry, I won't tell the rest of the family of your plans. You'll need to be prepared to show them that the company will continue to flourish. Do your best to take any legal precautions possible to prevent this causing a problem. My family would be foolish to question you after all this time, but mama isn't above pettiness.

All my love,

Renee

Jason leaned back and laughed. The relief of having her encouragement was stupendous. It would be easier to move forward knowing he wasn't facing an entirely uphill battle. He was so happy that he couldn't even find it in himself to be upset with Renee for not speaking up sooner about Kale. The fact that she was open and honest with her apology touched him. There was no point dwelling on the past, not when the future held such promise.

With the letter in hand, he made his way to the side table where the telephone was kept. There was no reason not to call Mr. Smoot and begin preparations immediately. Jason was sure of his plan, and he was certain Kale would follow once he had done all the legwork. He had to believe it. There was no way his life could continue on its present course.

CHAPTER FORTY-EIGHT

A stream bubbled through rolling hills lush with vegetation on the page in front him. Kale could almost smell the fresh air and hear the birds in the trees. Ever since he had decided to stay in Arine, he had been drawing landscapes from his childhood, almost reaffirming his decision, as if drawing the country would provide proof that it was his home. He kept to his room, avoiding Sophie and her disapproving glances. Any time he read, his mind wandered to what it would be like to experience life as a free character in one of his novels. Drawing at his table had proved better for his resolve.

A light rap sounded on the door. "Kale?"

"Yes?" Kale flipped over his sketch when Jason popped his head inside.

"I was wondering if you could join me in the parlor. I have something I'd like to talk to you about."

"Of course." Kale pushed aside the nervousness in his stomach as he rose.

Inside the parlor, Kale was surprised to see both Martin and Sophie there as well. The nervousness that had abated came forward with full force.

"Please, everyone, have a seat." Jason stood at the fireplace, facing them. Kale sat next to Sophie on the sofa and looked to her for any hint as to what was coming. She met his eyes with a confused, expectant look, clearly wondering the same thing as Kale. A quick look at Martin, sitting opposite him on an armchair, revealed nothing. Martin looked as composed as ever, watching Jason with polite attention. Kale followed his gaze to Jason, and Sophie followed suit.

"I have an announcement. I've decided to take a business trip. Martin and I will be leaving tonight." Kale whipped his head around to Martin and thought he saw surprise before Martin covered it. "I don't know when I'll be back."

What was happening? Was it something Kale had done? He wanted to ask, but in private. A week ago this man had been talking about moving to a different country and living their lives together. Now, he was just going to up and leave? Had the idea to move to Naiara really been an ultimatum on Jason's part? If so, could Kale jump up now and change his mind, prevent Jason from leaving? No. It was too sudden. Kale couldn't make this decision. Not like this. Jason would be back.

"Sir, where are you going?" Kale silently thanked Sophie for asking. He didn't think he could trust his voice.

"Just away on business. It doesn't matter."

Nothing about Jason's voice or expression gave Kale any hint as to what was going on. Why was he telling him in front of Sophie and Martin? Since he hadn't accepted Jason's invitation to move, was he now relegated to the same status as the rest of the household? It felt almost like he was in a dream. His right hand pinched his leg, just in case. Nope, this was definitely real.

"Well, I wish you a safe journey."

"Thank you, Sophie."

Sophie and Jason both looked at Kale. What was he supposed to say? Yes, he had been giving Jason a hard time about their relationship, but surely he merited a private goodbye. If he opened his mouth now, he knew that he would not be able to control what came out. It could be sad, angry, mean, or begging. He felt the eyes in the room boring into him, and the silence stretched out, seeming longer than was possible. Without meaning to, he started to fidget, the nerves finding their long-accustomed outlet in his right hand.

This was too much. The news. The eyes. The expectation. He shot to his feet and fled. It was the only thing he could do. On the way to his room, he heard voices behind him, too distant for him to make out the words. As he closed the door to his room, he gulped in air. He hadn't realized his lungs were burning.

Sitting at his table, he saw the sketch he had been working on when Jason fetched him. He turned it over and saw the familiar countryside. It all seemed so trivial. Jason was leaving, and it was his fault, he was sure of it. For the second time in his life, he had screwed up the best thing that had ever happened to him. He didn't try to fight it anymore. He let the darkness inside take over and consume him until the ache in his chest was so strong that the only way to relieve the pain was to give in to the tears.

CHAPTER FORTY-NINE

Jason waited until he could no longer see the house from the carriage window before he turned to Martin. The man looked absolutely befuddled. Jason had kept him in the dark about his plan. He couldn't risk Kale finding out about it.

"Can I know where we're going now?" The exasperation in Martin's voice made Jason smile.

"Why yes, you can. We're going to Calea."

"Calea? Whatever for?" Jason didn't think he had ever seen Martin's face in such a state of shock.

"Kale and I are going to be moving there, and I'm going ahead to arrange matters."

"But I thought Kale was against the idea."

"Oh, he is. But that's only because he doesn't know how it will work. Once I get everything settled, he'll see that there's nothing to it. That's the whole point of this trip."

Jason could tell Martin thought he was crazy. That was fine. Everyone had thought he was crazy when he took over the mill and made such drastic changes. That had turned out all right, and he knew this would as well.

"Are you sure you can convince him, sir? I'd hate for you to get your hopes up."

Not too long ago, Jason would have been upset by Martin's lack of confidence. Now he was able to see that these were the sincere words of someone who was concerned for him. He had always been unfair to Martin; the man had only ever tried to help. Jason had never fully appreciated that Martin had been thrust into an awkward situation. For a long time, Jason had been too wrapped up in himself and his own problems to care about anyone else. He hoped to change that.

"I appreciate your concern, Martin. I know how this must appear to you, but I have to take drastic measures. Kale's scared because this is all one big unknown for him. I'm going to try to alleviate those fears as best I can."

"And how are you going to do that, sir?"

"I have an appointment with a lawyer in Calea who is going to help me arrange everything. Once it's all mapped out, I will come home and present it to Kale."

"But how will you run the business from Calea?"

"I can come back for inspections, meetings, and such. I'll be relying on you more. That's why I want you in on my meetings with the lawyer. You're going to be shouldering more responsibility if everything goes as planned. I trust that you'll keep everything that happens on this trip to yourself until I feel ready to reveal it to Kale."

"Of course, sir. I would never break your confidence."

"I know. That's why I brought you. You've been a great help to me all these years, Martin. I know it hasn't always been easy. Most men would have given up on me, but you didn't. Thank you."

Martin's eyes shone. Jason had put this man through a horrible time, but now he was turning a new corner. "It's been my pleasure, sir."

CHAPTER FIFTY

"Would you like me to get us a cab, sir?"

"No, Martin, that's all right. After being cooped up in that train, I'd like to stretch my legs. Arrange for our luggage to be dropped off at the hotel, with the exception of my briefcase." The bustling of the train station fed the buzz of excitement that stirred in Jason. This was going to be his new home. He was eager to get outside and look around.

"Very well, sir." Martin talked to a porter and made the necessary arrangements. When he was finished, he came to stand next to Jason. "Where to now?"

"Mr. Smoot's office is nearby, but our appointment isn't until three o'clock. I thought we could look around." Jason reached for his briefcase, but Martin held onto it and moved it out of his reach.

"I'll carry it, sir."

"That's all right, Martin, there's no need. I can manage."

"It's my job, sir."

Jason was about to protest, but thought better of it. If he was serious about improving relations with Martin, then he needed to let the man take pride in his work. "Thank you."

"Not at all, sir. Lead the way."

Finally, they were on their way out of the train station. This was his first time in the city, and Jason was curious about how different it would be from Perdana. Jostling through the throngs of people, he finally made his way to the entrance. Walking through the front doors, his eyes were immediately assaulted by the bright sun, such a stark difference to the dim lighting of the station. As soon as his eyes adjusted, he was amazed at what he saw and heard.

Instead of carriages, automobiles filled the streets. In Perdana, automobiles were rare, and Jason had always preferred to take a horse and carriage. Automobiles were too loud and cumbersome. It looked like he would have to get used to them, though. All around him were the sounds of motors, horns, and people calling to one another. Rather than be annoyed at the noise, Jason viewed it as a herald of opportunity and change. It was refreshing.

"Where are we headed, sir?" Martin's voice brought him back to the moment, and he realized he was blocking the entrance to the station.

"Left. Mr. Smoot's secretary was kind enough to give me directions over the telephone. We'll head in that general direction until it's time for us to be there." Martin fell in step next to Jason.

Walking around the city, Jason had to be careful to remember to watch where he was going. Every few minutes, he was craning his head to see a new building or look in the shop windows. The architecture here was different. The buildings were topped with pitched roofs instead of rounded. Every surface was awash with color.

"Oh look, that must be the opera house or library." Jason pointed to a tall structure peeking over the nearby roofs. Not much could be seen other than a glimpse of a dome and tall spires pointing toward the sky. It was amazing.

"Very impressive."

"And look at the styles they sell." Jason peered into a clothing shop. "They're not nearly as stiff as what the women back home wear."

"I bet the women themselves aren't much different, though."

"No, I suppose not. People are pretty much the same everywhere, aren't they, Martin? Except something has to be different because they don't have slavery. Why do you think that is?" Jason stopped walking and faced Martin head on.

Martin seemed surprised to be addressed so directly. Jason should have expected that. He didn't exactly solicit Martin's opinion on trivial matters much. "I don't know. I suppose, given a different history than our own, their worldview would be altered."

Jason chuckled and resumed walking. "So, slavery is the correct worldview, and theirs has been altered?"

"That's not what I meant, sir."

"I know, but you don't seem to think slavery is wrong. Do you think I'm making the wrong choice trying to free Kale?"

"No, sir, I think it's the best thing for you and Kale. However, I'm not sure that your situation means that as a country, Arine should give up slavery. It works for us. I will admit that my experience with Kale has made me question some things I'd assumed about slaves, but I'm not sure how I feel about the institution as a whole."

"Fair enough. You've been a good friend to Kale, and that's all I could have asked."

"He's an easy man to like."

"That he is." Jason didn't need any reminding.

"How exactly is this all going to work? I don't understand. Will Kale just automatically be a free citizen by virtue of crossing the border?"

"That's what we're here for, Martin. I'm going to make sure every possible contingency is covered. I'm not going to risk this falling through. I've exchanged a few calls with Mr. Smoot's assistant discussing some ideas I've had, and he assures me that his employer can take care of everything."

"Should we start toward his office? Your appointment is soon."

"Yes, it's on Third Street. His assistant said we should

stay on this road until we get to Third, and then we turn left. It will be right there."

They spent the rest of the walk in silence. With every step Jason took, his anticipation grew. He was laying the foundation for a new life. Nothing was certain from this point forward, but he felt sure of his course.

They didn't have to wait long at the attorney's office. A few minutes after they were seated in a plush waiting room, Mr. Smoot stepped out of his office. It was the first time Jason had seen him. He was short and round, and he would have looked too cheery for an attorney if it weren't for the immaculately groomed silver beard and the spectacles perched on his nose.

"Mr. Wadsworth, I presume?"

Jason rose and shook his outstretched hand. "Yes. And you must be Mr. Smoot. It's a pleasure to meet you."

"Likewise, sir. If you'd like to step into my office, I believe we have much to discuss."

Jason and Martin started toward the office, but were stopped by Mr. Smoot. "Given the delicate nature of the matters we will be discussing, I can make your secretary quite comfortable here in the waiting room."

"No, thank you. Mr. Grimlock is my most trusted associate. I'd like him present. Anything you can say to me, you may say to him. I value his opinion."

Mr. Smoot appeared surprised, but was no doubt used to accommodating the high-class clientele he served. "Of course, sir. Right this way then."

The office was absurdly large. It felt like walking down the aisle of a library to reach the desk situated at the end in front of a large window. The walls were lined with a plethora of books, most looking like they were seldom touched. Jason didn't require these embellishments like some of Mr. Smoot's other clients surely did. What Jason required were the attorney's connections, and if that meant tolerating a bit of pretension, then so be it.

"Now, I understand your aim is to move yourself and your slave to Naiara to effectively free him."

They were all seated comfortably around the desk. Martin, as always, had paper and pen ready to take notes. Good. Jason would need them. "Yes, that's correct. I want to make sure that every possibility has been covered. Legally, this must be as air tight as we can make it. I won't risk any negative consequences to Kale."

"Well, the law here is pretty cut and dry. As soon as he crosses the border, he'll be free. The only way that could be challenged is if you pursued his extradition as a runaway slave."

"That won't happen."

"I thought not." Mr. Smoot smirked, and a wave of uneasiness hit Jason. He was entrusting this man with his future and the future of his lover. He trusted him because Renee did, but was that wise? It was Renee, after all, who had caused Kale's sale. No, Jason would not entertain such thoughts. He had to trust someone, and he had forgiven Renee. It wasn't fair to be suspicious of her intentions.

Jason brushed aside his worry and focused on the conversation at hand. "Will he be able to pursue full citizenship, though? I don't want him to be a second class citizen here."

"Yes. He can petition for refugee status, in which case, if granted, he will be put on a fast track toward citizenship."

"I've been led to believe that you have contacts in the government who could help expedite the process."

"I do. I haven't been able to confirm anything in the short time since we began communicating, but I should have something firm for you in a few days. Are you going straight back to Perdana, or are you staying in town for a while?"

"I'm going to be here for a few days. I have some matters I'd like you to handle for me, and I'll be staying until they're done."

"Then I should have some more information for you

before you leave. What else can I do for you?"

"I want a bank account opened in Kale's name. I have a check for the opening balance. I want Kale to be as independent as possible." There was a familiar tightness in his chest. He hoped independence didn't translate into Kale leaving him, but that was a risk he had to take. "Martin, if you'd hand me my briefcase, I have the check in there."

Martin handed over the briefcase, and Jason extracted the check and handed it to Mr. Smoot. When the lawyer's eyes lighted on the sum, his eyebrows shot high above his wire rims. "This is very generous."

"No, it's not, actually. I'd like to put more in there, but I know he'll protest as it is. All that is included in that sum is how much he would have earned had he been paid a wage since he came into my service."

"Well, this will certainly give him plenty of independence. Now, what last name shall I put on the bank account?"

"Mine. Slaves don't have last names. It's the best I can do right now." Jason couldn't help hoping that Kale would choose to keep his last name. It was just the sort of sappy thing Kale would roll his eyes at, but Jason didn't care.

"That should be fine, given the circumstances."

"I also want you to form a company for me. It needs to have offices both here and in Perdana. You can coordinate with my lawyer, Mr. Winslow, in Perdana if need be."

"Very well. I assume it is to protect your assets." Jason nodded an affirmative. "What assets would you like in it?"

"Only one. This." Jason pulled out a piece of paper from his briefcase and handed it over to Mr. Smoot, who examined the document carefully.

"I see."

That piece of paper was the only thing that tied Kale to Jason. It was Kale's title, and before Jason left Calea, it would no longer be in his name. It was a scary thought, but necessary in Jason's view. This was the irrevocable step. In some ways it was a relief to not have Kale's title anymore, but at the same time, he was giving up the most precious thing he had ever owned.

"I'll have the company formed and the bank account opened in the next couple of days. I'll also talk to my contacts in the prime minister's office about your citizenship questions. I'll send word to your hotel when it's done. Should only be two or three days."

"Thank you, Mr. Smoot." Jason stood to conclude their business.

"Before you leave, I have some property listings here, sir. I thought you could take a look at some of them, and if you'd like to start purchase paperwork before you leave town, I can handle that for you as well." Mr. Smoot handed a sheaf of papers and newspaper clippings to Martin.

"No, thank you. I don't want to pick out a place without Kale. We may not even settle in the city. It's up to him."

"Very well. I hope you enjoy your stay in Calea. I'll be in touch."

◆ ◆ ◆

Three days later, Jason received a note from Mr. Smoot's assistant stating that everything was ready. Jason and Martin had spent much of their time exploring the city, trying to get a feel for the culture and societal norms. On the second day, Jason had lunch at a prominent gentleman's club to meet some of the men he would be doing business with in the future. Regardless of what happened, it would be beneficial to have contacts in Naiara.

When Jason and Martin arrived at the lawyer's office, Mr. Smoot delved right into the business at hand.

"Here is the paperwork on the bank account, as well as a checkbook for it. You'll see that the current balance is the same as the amount of the check you gave me."

Jason glanced over everything and then handed it all to

Martin. "Thank you."

Mr. Smoot didn't acknowledge the thanks. "Here is all the paperwork for the business Mr. Winslow and I established for you."

"Excellent." Jason held onto the business papers. He wasn't finished with them.

"Now, as far as citizenship goes, I have some good news and some bad, I'm afraid. The good news is that the prime minister's government is prepared to offer Kale full citizenship as a refugee as soon as he crosses the border."

Jason released the breath he had subconsciously been holding. "That's wonderful! I don't want him wandering around stateless."

As before, Mr. Smoot simply continued. "Unfortunately, you may not be able to get citizenship for yourself right away."

Jason waved away his concerns. "It's of no consequence. I can go through the proper channels."

"I'm glad you won't be inconvenienced. Just remember to have Kale come to our office as soon as possible when he gets here. The likelihood of there being a problem is small, but better to be safe."

"Of course."

"Is there anything else I can help you with before you return to Perdana?"

"Yes, actually, there is." Jason lifted the business documents from his lap and placed them on the desk. This was it. Taking a deep breath, he continued. "This entity owns Kale's title, correct?"

"Yes, sir. Exactly as you requested." A bit of confusion entered Mr. Smoot's eyes.

"I would like to transfer this company into the ownership of Kale Wadsworth." It was the first time Jason had said Kale's name appended with his own last name. It felt good, but gave him a sense of hope that he knew might prove false.

The confusion now showed openly on Mr. Smoot's face.

"May I ask why, sir?"

"It's simple. I don't want to own Kale anymore. As long as I own this company, I, by extension, own Kale. Furthermore, this is the closest to freedom that I can give him in Arine. He's still a slave there, but he's a slave who owns his own title." Mr. Smoot began to object, and Jason held up his hand. "No, I know that it won't hold up under scrutiny in court, but it's enough that he can stay in Arine or visit, and if someone who knows he's a slave sees him, he can claim to be owned by this company. It will never warrant a second look. However, I will not own him, even as a technicality."

"Very well, Mr. Wadsworth. I'll coordinate with Mr. Winslow. It will take some time to finish the paperwork, but I can send it on to you in Perdana when it's done. I'll go have my assistant draw up the proper forms for your signature, and then you can be on your way."

As soon as the door closed behind Mr. Smoot, Martin turned to Jason. During these meetings, he had been so quiet that it was difficult to remember he was present.

"This isn't exactly orthodox."

It would have been easy to be offended by Martin's statement, but Jason reminded himself that Martin was on his team. "No, it isn't. There's no guarantee that Kale will want to move here with me. I'm not going to have that decision swayed by his slavery. This way, he is as free as he can possibly be, given the circumstances. He'll be able to do what he wants. If he decides to come here with me, I need to know that he came to that decision free of any duress."

Martin chuckled.

"What?"

"You. And Kale. The two of you. The only people who seem to be in any doubt that the both of you are going to work are you two. It makes for an amusing show for the rest of us. As long as you don't mess it up, if you don't mind me saying."

Jason smiled and tried to laugh, but he couldn't muster it. "I'm glad you have so much faith in us, but I suppose it's different when it's your heart involved. I'm not taking anything for granted."

"A good policy. I think, though, that you'll be pleasantly surprised when all is said and done."

"I hope so, Martin. I hope so."

They settled into a comfortable silence until Mr. Smoot returned, carrying a few pieces of paper. "Here are the forms for you to sign, transferring ownership of the company to Kale Wadsworth." It was even more thrilling to hear someone else append his last name to Kale's. Mr. Smoot placed the papers on his desk and then held out a pen to Jason.

This was it. Jason reached for the pen. It was heavy in his hand. All he had to do was place his signature on this form, and Kale would no longer be his. Any bond between them would have to be formed freely by mutual feeling. He put the tip of the pen to the page and paused. Was this really what he wanted? He wouldn't be able to protect Kale anymore. From what, he didn't know. The pause was only momentary. With a flourish, his signature was complete. There was an emptiness in Jason's chest. Hopefully Kale would fill it soon.

"There's still some paperwork that needs to be done, but I won't need your signature on anything else. If you like, you can go back home, and I'll forward these to Mr. Winslow so he can finalize everything on his end."

"Of course. Thank you for your time, Mr. Smoot. Your expertise is much appreciated." Jason stood, and Martin followed suit. Before Jason began the long walk out of the office, Mr. Smoot held out his hand.

"It's really admirable, what you're doing, Mr. Wadsworth." Mr. Smoot's voice was more sincere than at any point thus far. The change was so marked that Jason suspected Mr. Smoot didn't really like any of the pretension of his practice. Apparently, it was all part of the façade he put up for his clients.

Jason shook his hand and stared into his eyes. The earnestness he saw warmed him. "Thank you."

An hour later, he and Martin were on the train headed back to Perdana.

CHAPTER FIFTY-ONE

Kale looked up from his sketch when Sophie entered the kitchen. They had been using the time while Jason and Martin were away to catch up on housework. Any time Kale wasn't working with Sophie, he was with her in the kitchen. The house felt too empty, and he liked to feel her presence.

"What's that you're drawing?" Sophie carried several parcels. She had invited Kale to join her at the market, but he'd wanted to stay behind and draw today.

Kale left the table and helped Sophie put everything away. "Go take a look. Tell me what you think."

Sophie walked to the table and gazed at the sketch. Kale couldn't help stilling as she looked at it. "It's wonderful. It looks exactly like Mr. Wadsworth."

Kale released his breath. "I'm glad you think so." He put the last of the groceries away and stood behind Sophie. "I know he's been wanting a portrait. I thought this would make a nice welcome home gift. If he ever comes back."

Sophie laughed and smacked Kale over the head good-naturedly. "It's only been five days. Of course he's coming back."

Kale smiled at her as they both settled down at the table with some green beans and two bowls. He knew he was being silly, but there was a part of him, deep down, that feared Jason would despair of him and stay away. "I just miss him. It doesn't help that I feel like a complete ass."

Sophie quirked an eyebrow at him. "Finally coming to your senses, are you?" They both picked up some beans and snapped off their ends.

Sophie had a way of making him feel comfortable, even when discussing difficult subjects. "Yeah, I think so. It was a nice idea, taking me to Naiara. The kid's too sweet for his own good, willing to uproot his whole life just to try to make me happy. How did I ever deserve to belong to him?" Kale tossed his completed beans into one of the bowls and grabbed some more.

"I don't know. What do any of us do to deserve the people who love us?"

Kale grunted. "Nothing. I can't believe how I acted. It's not his fault his plan won't work."

"See, that's where you lose me, Kale. Why won't it work?"

Kale paused in his work and mirrored Sophie's exasperation. "Because. It won't. He's always been an idealistic kid who comes up with these pie-in-the-sky dreams, and it's always been my job to either make them happen or steer him in a different direction."

"You call him a kid, but he's a grown man who runs the biggest steel company in the country."

Kale looked at the beans. "Nah, he'll always be a kid to me."

"Still, the man knows his own mind—better than you know yours, I think."

Kale could concede that. However, in the last few days, he had come to understand one thing: he was already lost to Jason. "I've tried, Sophie. I really have. While he's been gone, I've let the idea of freedom roll around in my head, but every time I start to get comfortable with it, warning bells sound. I can't pretend that I'm anything other than I am. Even if his plan did work, I can't comprehend being free without looking over my shoulder every day, wondering when it was all going to come to an end. I could barely fathom going to the art gallery with him."

"Didn't you used to do that sort of thing all the time?"

"Yes, but it was different back then. I was different. That was before I knew how bad life could get. I was naïve." Kale finished off the last of the beans.

"And now you're bitter. When are you going to let go of it? It's all in your head, and you have complete control over it. You just have to choose to let go of the past, and allow yourself to love and be loved."

"I'm trying." Kale let the desperation he felt show in his voice. Did she really think he enjoyed feeling this way?

"Not hard enough." With that, Sophie rose from the table, taking the bowl of beans with her, and began fixing supper. She was never one to let Kale get away with anything. This was his problem to solve. She would be there to support him, but ultimately he was the one who had to do the work.

The truth was, Kale was ready to release it all. The bitterness, the hurt, the pain, everything. The hardest part had been admitting that he loved Jason and that Jason loved him in return. Why then was he holding on to the last remnants of the darkness he had let consume him for so long?

It was easy. It was comfortable. That's why. Logically he knew it was holding him back from happiness. He had fooled himself into thinking that he didn't control the darkness, that it was everyone else's fault. They did this to him.

Except that had never been true. He had done this. He had let those around him turn him into a person who was willing to condemn himself and the man he loved to a lifetime of unhappiness because it was easier than taking responsibility. That ended now. Kale was no coward. He once was a man who Jason Wadsworth had looked up to. It wouldn't be easy, and it wouldn't happen overnight, but he was at least going to act the part well enough and long enough that he eventually forgot to be scared, bitter, angry, and all those other emotions that constantly battled for his soul. If only Jason would come home, Kale could be the man Jason needed him to be.

Kale stood, threw the discarded ends in the bin, and went to stand by Sophie. "I'll try, Sophie, I really will. And I'll play along with his plan. If you catch me being such an ass again, please do us all a favor and wallop me."

"No problem, dear. I'll wallop you right now if you think it will help." The smirk on Sophie's face prompted Kale's laughter.

"That's all right. I think I'm good." Kale reached for a knife and one of the carrots Sophie had finished washing. With every chop of his knife, he buried his negativity deeper. He could pretend he was the happy, healthy man Jason deserved. He could pretend for as long as it took.

CHAPTER FIFTY-TWO

The familiar buildings of Perdana were heartening in a way Martin hadn't anticipated. The clip-clop of horse's hooves was a nice change from the puttering of automobiles. He'd never thought he would have been so happy to be going home. The trip to Calea had been pleasant enough, but it wasn't home. Plus, he admitted to a childish anticipation about how Kale would react to what had transpired on their trip.

Pride filled Martin when he thought about the fact that he was the only person privy to Jason's plans. Sitting at home right now, Kale had no idea the lengths Jason had gone to to ensure his future. Like a child, he simultaneously felt pride at his secret knowledge and couldn't wait to see the secret divulged.

"I shouldn't be long with Mr. Winslow. There are just a few things I have to sign to finalize the deal with Conrad. We'll go straight home afterward."

Martin could handle one more meeting with an attorney. Looking across the carriage at Jason, Martin saw his employer with new eyes. Jason radiated a calm that Martin supposed came from doing something so altruistic. There was a confidence about him that ran deeper than the confidence that had always possessed him in business matters. Still, when Martin held Jason's eyes for any length of time, he saw uncertainty there. That was one more reason to get home as quickly as possible: Jason needed to hear Kale's answer to his proposal. Martin was certain what his answer would be—as long as Kale could get his head out of his ass long enough to give it.

When the carriage pulled up to Mr. Winslow's office, Martin prepared to suffer through one last meeting. At this point, it was just a barrier to getting back to his family. That's what Sophie and Kale had become to him.

Walking toward the door, Martin had to catch himself when Jason suddenly stopped in front of him and turned. "Why don't you grab a bite to eat at that cafe? The food on the train was horrid. Get a pastry or something. I won't be long."

Martin's face dropped, but he worked to quickly compose it again. By the time his "Yes, sir," left his lips, it was to Jason's back as he continued on to the office.

He tried not to think until he was seated at a small outside table. What had happened? Had he erred somewhere? He thought Jason trusted him now.

Martin shook his head. Of course Jason trusted him. That didn't mean Martin had to be privy to all the man's business. Besides, hadn't he said he was just going to be signing some papers to finalize the Conrad deal? He probably thought Martin would rather be outside. After all the time they had spent in stuffy offices and on the train, who wouldn't rather relax at a cafe instead of going into yet another attorney's office? This didn't mean anything. The man was entitled to his secrets.

By the time Jason came out, Martin hadn't been able to convince himself that his exclusion was for his benefit. Jason knew Martin was all business. The only explanation was that there was something Jason didn't want him knowing about. What could it be? Martin knew everything about their business dealings. The only parts of Jason's life that had ever been secret to Martin were the personal bits. What personal business could take him to Mr. Winslow's office?

"Did you enjoy yourself?"

It was impossible to tell from the smile on Jason's face that he was hiding something. The polite lie slid from Martin's lips. "Yes, thank you, sir."

"Let's get going then. Home beckons!" Jason patted him on the back as he hailed a cab. He was as cheery as Martin had ever seen him. That would fit the story of him finalizing the Conrad deal, except Jason never got emotional about business, one way or the other. It was all a game to him. If anything, Jason's demeanor was proof that something else had happened in that office.

It was a short ride to the house. Jason began to fidget, and his body strained toward the window, as if willing the carriage to move faster. Martin tried to focus on his own excitement and thought ahead to the homecoming and the news that would soon be shared. "I can't wait to get there either."

Jason smiled at him. "I never took you for the type to get homesick."

"Usually I'm not. In light of recent events, though, I find I want to see Kale and Sophie. It feels like more of a home than it used to."

"I'm glad. Needless to say, I'd appreciate it if you wouldn't say a word about anything to Kale or Sophie."

"Of course not, sir. It's not my news to tell."

"Yes, well, it's not mine to tell yet either. I'm not going to say anything until I get all the official paperwork back. This is too important to get Kale's hopes up only to find out there was a kink somewhere along the line, and it doesn't work."

Martin's stomach dropped. He would never dream of divulging a confidence, especially when he had worked so hard to finally be allowed into Jason's. However, he did not look forward to the coming days. How long would it take for the paperwork to come through? It didn't matter. He would have to remain silent. "That's wise." It was. He just didn't like having their roles switched. He was used to being the responsible one.

CHAPTER FIFTY-THREE

"Will you stop? Looking isn't going to make them get here any quicker." They were in the front sitting room, which was hardly ever used. Sophie had some mending on her lap that was keeping her busy, and Kale had his sketchpad, which gave him the illusion of doing something other than obsessing over when he would see Jason.

Kale let the sheer curtain drop. "They should be here by now."

"Martin said on the phone that the train was getting in at one, and there were some stops they had to make before coming home." Kale glanced at the clock. It was two-fifty-two. Sophie caught his look. "It takes time. Between getting their luggage, the usual delays, and navigating the crowds, it was probably a good thirty minutes before they even left the station. Don't worry, you'll see your lover boy soon enough."

Even though Kale was beyond fooling himself on this count, he still bristled at the outward acknowledgement of any romantic intentions. "I'm just worried is all. I hope there wasn't any trouble."

"I'm sure there wasn't." Sophie joined Kale in the window seat and pulled the heavy drapes closed. "Draw or read or something." She went back to her mending, and Kale's hand moved to the familiar spot over the lock of hair in his pocket while he tried to picture Jason. He wanted to pull it out and look at it, but doing so in front of Sophie was out of the question. When it seemed Sophie had forgotten about him and was absorbed in her work, Kale pushed the edge of the velvet drape just a few inches to peek outside.

"Oww!" Kale snatched his hand back. Sophie glared at him, her arm still midair from slapping his hand away. He hadn't even seen it coming. "That's hardly fair."

Sophie pointed a stern finger at him. "Fair? I've been dealing with this all morning. Don't make me drag you by your ear to the kitchen. There's plenty of work to be done down there."

Kale laughed, but quickly composed himself when he saw Sophie's baleful stare. "Sorry, ma'am. I'll be good, I swear."

Her hand struck like lightning, hitting the back of his head this time. "Oww. What was that for?" Kale rubbed the stinging spot.

"Calling me ma'am."

Kale smiled, and Sophie settled back into her work. He didn't try to move the curtain again, but he stared at the window, trying not to think about anything at all.

The clip of horses' hooves and the clatter of carriage wheels slowed and then stopped in front of the house.

Not caring what Sophie thought, Kale pushed aside the curtain. "It's them, Sophie!" Butterflies fluttered in his stomach as he saw Jason emerge from the cab. All he wanted was to run out and meet him, but nerves stopped him. What would he say? He was left standing uncomfortably in the entryway, waiting for Jason to step through the door.

As soon as the door began to open, Kale rocked onto the balls of his feet. His stomach felt like it had completely turned over when he saw Jason standing in front of him, close enough to touch. The relief that poured through him when he saw that Jason was smiling at him stilled the butterflies. He took a step forward and then stopped. He wanted to crush Jason to him, to feel his lips on his and his skin beneath his hands, but he was suddenly keenly aware of

Martin and Sophie standing nearby.

"Welcome home, master."

Before Jason could respond, Kale felt Martin's hand on his shoulder, diverting his attention. "It's good to see you, Kale."

That was odd. Martin looked merrier than usual. It almost looked like he had something else to say. "You too, Martin."

"Sophie!" Martin went and hugged Sophie, leaving Kale and Jason to stand awkwardly with each other.

"Why don't we leave these two alone?" Kale would have looked back to mouth his thanks to Sophie, but the slightest hint of a blush rose in Jason's cheeks at Sophie's tone, and Kale couldn't look away. It was the first time Jason had blushed since Kale had returned.

As soon as they were alone, Kale could see the desire in Jason's eyes, but he wasn't acting on it. Kale wanted Jason to make the first move, but perhaps it was time to take the initiative himself. After all, they hadn't been on the best of terms when Jason left. For all Jason knew, Kale was still upset with him.

Stepping forward, Kale wrapped his arms around Jason and kissed him. Jason's lips were hesitant under Kale's, no doubt surprised by the sudden move. Then his arms came up and twined around Kale. Being enveloped by Jason this way made Kale wonder how he had survived without him. Jason's lips relaxed, and he welcomed Kale into his mouth. The familiar touch of his tongue felt new again after their time apart.

Kale was the first to break away. "I have something for you." He wanted to clear away any tension between them before they went further.

"Oh?" Jason sounded bemused at the sudden change.

Jason followed Kale to the sitting room, and Kale wiped his suddenly sweaty palms on his pants before he reached for his sketchpad. Kale pulled out the drawing he had done of Jason. He had put the finishing touches on it just the night before. It was a relief to be able to finally draw the most important person in his world. As soon as he had decided not to fight his feelings anymore, his hands had suddenly started to cooperate. He had feared that fully putting himself into the drawing would produce hideous results, given the internal battle he had been fighting. The opposite had been true. When he poured himself out on the page, the image of Jason had formed effortlessly through the charcoal lines.

After glancing over it one last time to make sure it was presentable, he handed it to Jason. "I wanted to give you a gift to apologize for my behavior. I'm sorry for being such an ass lately."

Jason held the paper almost reverently. The silence grew as Jason's head remained lowered over the drawing. Kale began to shift his weight between his feet, waiting for any response.

"Thank you, Kale. This means the world to me." Jason looked up, and Kale could see the tears pooling in his eyes.

Kale's heart melted. This had been a good move. But he felt uncomfortable under the weight of Jason's scrutiny and tears. He huffed an exasperated sigh and grabbed Jason's hand. "Come on. Let's get up to your room before you start crying."

Jason laughed as Kale led the way upstairs. Once they reached Jason's room, Kale opened the door and shoved Jason inside, resolutely closing the door behind them.

"It feels so good to be home." Jason carefully placed the drawing on his dressing table before throwing his hat and gloves on the sofa.

"It's good to have you home." Kale leaned against the door and simply watched Jason. If possible, he felt he missed Jason even more now that he was home. It had been easy to forget the nuances of Jason's movements. He wanted to watch him all day, almost as much as he wanted to touch him.

Once Jason had removed his suit coat, cufflinks, and tie and generally made himself more comfortable, he turned and saw Kale watching him. "What are you doing?"

Kale smiled. "Just watching you. Gods, you're beautiful." There was that blush again. Kale would do anything to keep seeing it. It made Jason seem more innocent, more full of hope, like he had been before. Kale had thought Jason had grown out of blushing, and he was nearly giddy to find that he hadn't.

Jason walked to him and pulled him away from the door, lifting Kale's shirt as he did.

Kale stilled Jason's hands with his own. "Wait." This was it. He had to do this now before he lost his nerve. "Before we go any further, I want to say something, and I want you to know that I'm not just saying it because of the sex." Kale led Jason to sit chastely on the bed. "The truth is, I should have said it ages ago. I've made you wait far too long. You have the patience of a saint." He smirked and brushed Jason's hair back from his face. The love that shone back at him made his offering seem inadequate. Still, it was all he could give. That had to count for something. Taking a breath, he delved into the abyss. "I love you."

The pure joy radiating from Jason's face stole the air from Kale's lungs. It was like staring into the sun. Every part of Jason's face lit up. His hand went to the nape of Kale's neck and began to massage as his eyes bore into Kale's. Those eyes seemed to tell Kale that he knew how hard this had been for him, and they offered him comfort that his trust was well placed. Then, almost as if Jason knew his message had been received, his lips crashed into Kale's.

When they finally separated, Kale caught his breath. "I didn't think this would come as a surprise to you."

"The sentiment isn't, but the words are. I never thought I'd live to see the day you'd say them. I had resigned myself to never hear them from you."

"And you were fine with that? I didn't know you thought I was that much of an ass."

"You were worth it. I could hardly blame you. I

311

understood your reasons for never saying it before now, but gods am I happy you finally said it." Jason's smile threatened to break his face, so Kale occupied his mouth with another kiss.

Unwilling to leave Jason's mouth, Kale's hands fumbled with the buttons on Jason's shirt, sliding it off his shoulders. Kale's hands caressed Jason's chest and back, reveling in the feel of smooth skin under his rough hands. Jason broke free of Kale's mouth and sucked on the side of his neck, right at his pulse point. The intensity made Kale's eyes roll back. Each second, the suction increased until the pleasure mixed with an edge of pain that made it even more powerful. When Kale didn't think he could take anymore, Jason released him.

Kale scrambled to remove his shirt in the brief separation. Raising the fabric above his head, a cool touch on his side sent a tiny shiver through him which was soon chased away by the friction of Jason's hands against his skin.

"You've filled out since you came here. I can't count your ribs anymore."

Kale grunted, discarding his shirt. "Good. I feel like a man again, instead of the scared animal you found." He didn't want to talk anymore. There had been enough words today. He wrapped Jason in his arms and set upon his lips.

Kale's tongue explored Jason's mouth, staking its claim. This was the man he loved. His body crushed against Jason. There was no such thing as close enough. Kale had never wanted anything as badly as he wanted to be with Jason. While they couldn't have Jason's ideal relationship, Kale could show him the depth and power of his feelings.

Keeping his arms firmly around Jason, Kale maneuvered them onto the bed, facing each other. His hands flew to Jason's pants. At the same time, Jason fiddled just as frantically with Kale's. They succeeded at the same time and their cocks sprung free. Separation had taken its toll—neither one wanted much foreplay. They threw their pants off the bed, and Jason reached for the tin of grease on the bedside table.

Kale's hand encircled Jason's wrist, halting his movement. There was something he wanted, and he hoped Jason would want it too. His lover looked at him, eyebrows raised in question. "I was wondering if I could top?" It felt strange making the request, but Jason wanted Kale to behave like they were equals in the relationship. This wasn't perfect. If they were equals, Kale wouldn't have asked, he would have just taken the lead the way he'd done years ago with other slaves.

A delighted glimmer entered Jason's eyes. "Of course." He withdrew his hand, and Kale retrieved the tin. When he knelt up and gazed down at Jason, a surge of protectiveness flowed through him. The man below him—the center of Kale's world—looked up at him with an expression that was part affection, part adoration, and part desire. It was enough to make Kale gasp.

"What is it?"

"You."

A red flush crept up Jason's face. Dear gods, was it possible to love someone more than this? It didn't matter. Kale would only ever be Jason's. After taking a healthy bit of grease, Kale replaced the tin and began to prepare Jason. The fierce urgency was gone. In its place was gentle care. Jason was his, and Kale was going to ensure his enjoyment.

Jason's movement against Kale's fingers betrayed his eagerness, but the little grimaces of his face told Kale to take it slow. Once he was satisfied that he wouldn't hurt Jason, he placed his cock at Jason's entrance and tenderly pushed, keeping a close eye on his lover's expressions. The ring of muscle gave way, and another flood of emotion washed over him as he was encased in heat.

Part of Kale had always known he loved Jason. They both had known. The feeling had initially been scary; love had never had a place in Kale's adult life. The certainty of the sentiment—when he knew certainty was foolish in a slave's life—had been intimidating. And while he loved Jason as much as he ever had, the emotion had finally been unleashed, and Kale experienced the full magnitude of it for the first time. A great weight had been released, and he felt he could fly. If he had known how liberating, how light it would feel to finally say the words, to express his love freely, he would have done so long ago.

But he hadn't known. He had been bridled by fear. There were still legitimate fears to be had, precautions to take, but Kale was no longer scared of loving. That was an immeasurable feat.

His eyes focused on Jason beneath him. It had been easy to see on Jason's face when Kale had found his sweet spot. Now his long thrusts brushed it consistently. Jason's eyes were closed, and Kale was tempted to tell Jason to open them. He knew Jason would obey, but he thought better of it. Better to let Jason experience his pleasure. Besides, there was something enticing about watching without him staring back, seeing the way his moans coincided with his facial movements.

A light sheen coated Jason's skin, and beads of sweat pooled on his upper lip. Kale dipped down and took that lip into his mouth. The salty taste on his tongue mixed with the sweet taste of Jason's skin. "I love you." The words came easier the second time. He doubted he'd ever be the type of man to say them often, but he wasn't going to hold them back when he was moved, either.

"Kale, please." The high pitched whine was not what Kale had expected. He pulled back and saw Jason's teeth clench behind his parted lips, the tendons of his neck raised. Glancing down, he saw that Jason's cock wept a steady stream of fluid. Kale's eyes darted back up, and realization dawned. Was it possible? Jason was holding back his orgasm. Kale knew what he was waiting for, and the knowledge that this boy—his boy—was going to come from the penetration alone toppled him over the edge with Jason following soon after.

◆ ◆ ◆

Lying in the calm that followed their lovemaking—gods, when did it go from fucking to lovemaking?—Kale couldn't deny that Jason looked happier than he had ever seen him.

"Will you stay here tonight?" Jason peered up from the crook of Kale's arm, and he was overwhelmed by the unguarded hope and unabashed love he saw in his eyes.

There was still a darkness in the depths of Kale that knew he could obliterate that hope with just one word. A part of him still wanted to exercise that power, to hurt Jason in order to protect and guard himself. What was surprising was how easy it was for Kale to push those feelings aside. "Yes."

Jason's face relaxed into the contented expression of a man who was right where he wanted to be. There was nothing wrong in the world at this moment. How could there be? Kale had Jason in his arms, the only man he had ever loved. This was one of those perfect moments that made it possible to go about the rest of life, knowing you had tasted this deep sense of rightness.

"What are you thinking about?" Jason's voice pierced his thoughts.

"How perfect I feel right now. How I almost ruined it all with my hardheadedness. How I hope this moment never ends."

"It doesn't have to, you know."

"I wish it didn't." Kale squeezed Jason's shoulder. "The reality is, you have work to do, a world to conquer where I can't follow."

"Have you given any more thought to what I told you before I left?"

Kale considered feigning ignorance. In the end, it wouldn't help anything. They needed to talk about this. "I have. I want to apologize again for the way I reacted. I still don't see how it could work. The sentiment means something to me, though. I want you to know that. It means more than I think you could possibly understand." A part of him knew he should share his deeper concerns with Jason. It didn't seem right that he could talk about his fears with Sophie, but not with him. The truth was, he knew Jason would try to dispel his fears, and he would most likely succeed—which scared Kale in its own way.

Jason's giggling drew his attention away from his thoughts. "What?"

"Nothing. I just think you're wrong. Give me time, and I'll show you."

"Why can't we just be content with this? I'm happier now than I've ever been in my life. Why can't this be enough?"

Jason sat up, and Kale felt empty without his weight beside him. "Because, Kale, as long as you're a slave, you'll never feel comfortable enough to make any kind of real relationship work. We'll have these glimpses of what it could be like, but they'll never be more than that. I'm not willing to settle; I want the whole deal."

"I can try. It worked once."

"You can try, but it won't work. It didn't work before. It ended in disaster, and it's only by the most magnificent streak of luck that we're here together. I'm not going to sit still and wait to see how it's going to end this time. Can you even call me by my name? You told me you love me today. I know what a big step that was for you, and I'll treasure it forever, even if you never say it again. But can you call me by my name?"

Kale tried. His lips parted, and he willed his mouth to form the word. It was simple. Except the word caught somewhere in his throat. Every instinct, every danger signal, fired in his brain. This was wrong. Except it wasn't. His lover deserved to hear his name on Kale's lips. But that was something Kale couldn't give him, because it was a lie. Jason couldn't be Jason to him, he was his master. He always had been and always would be. Calling him by his given name was the first step toward pretending he was free. It was the first step to catastrophe.

He was left gaping like a fish out of water.

"I don't blame you, Kale. I understand. I really do. But I want a lover who can call me by something other than *master.*" Jason sneered the last word with such vehemence that Kale didn't think he could ever use it again. On Jason's lips it sounded vulgar, almost more of a lie than Jason's name. Almost.

"Is that why you left? Because I couldn't give you the answer you wanted?"

Jason's face twisted in upset confusion. "Is that what you thought?"

"We weren't on the best terms when you left. I thought maybe you wanted to get away from me."

Jason was on top of him, hand in his hair, before Kale could even register that he'd moved. The intensity of his face, so close to Kale's, held him captive. "That's absurd, Kale. I never want to be away from you. Don't you understand that's why I want you free? Because I want to be with all of you always?"

"Then why did you leave?" Kale felt himself growing vulnerable. Jason's departure had hurt, and it took strength for Kale to let Jason see it.

"I had business to attend to. It's nothing you need to worry about."

Kale thought he saw something in Jason's eyes, something he held back, but before he could examine it further, Jason turned around and laid back in the crook of Kale's arm, face casually—but not, Kale thought, incidentally —turned away.

317

CHAPTER FIFTY-FOUR

"Mail's come."

Jason looked up from his newspaper at Martin's jovial tone. One look at his face trying to suppress a rather undignified grin told Jason all he needed to know. "It's here, isn't it?"

"Take a look." Martin tossed the pile of mail on Jason's desk.

The thick envelope stood out among the thin letters. Jason snatched it and tore it open. The first thing that fell out was Kale's official title. It was amazing how much one document could affect him. His name was nowhere on it. Kale was legally no one to him now. Familiar fears crept up, but he pushed them aside. This was right. Getting rid of this piece of paper drew them closer. The legal separation was only an illusion.

After the title came the corporate documents. Everything was in order. It was done. Jason took in a deep breath, letting the relief wash over him. More than once over the last two weeks, he had worried that something would go wrong.

"Excuse me, sir, but are you going to tell him now?"

There was excitement in Martin's eyes that sparked nerves in Jason's stomach. "Gods, I have to tell him."

"Yes, sir. I believe that's the point."

Jason released a nervous laugh. "I suppose so. Would you

mind leaving me, Martin? I need a moment."

"Of course, sir." Jason gazed back at the title, but instead of hearing Martin's steps retreating, they came closer until he felt a hand on his shoulder. "Don't worry. He's stubborn, but he's not stupid. It'll be all right."

Jason looked up into the face of the man who had gone from secretary to friend. "Thank you."

Martin nodded and left. Silence weighed heavy on Jason. It would prevent him from moving if he let it. Jason reached down and pulled the bank documents out of the bottom drawer of his desk. He would have liked to put more money in the account. Initially, he had planned to put an amount equal to a living wage for each year of Kale's life spent in slavery. However, he knew Kale would never tolerate that. It was a long shot convincing him to accept the money for the last four years. Sighing, he gathered everything together into the envelope and stood. "This is it."

On his way down to the kitchen to find Kale, he tried to convince himself that Kale would be happy. Things had gotten better. Kale had stopped calling him master, which was a relief, even if he still wasn't using Jason's name. It was odd to think that Kale was sitting in the kitchen right now, preparing for their daily jaunt to the park, not knowing that Jason held in his hands documents that would change his life forever.

Jason stopped. It all seemed so very arrogant all of a sudden. Jason had gone and permanently altered Kale's life without even consulting him. Shit, he was going to be livid. What had Jason been thinking?

No, it would be fine. Jason started walking again. He did what he had to for Kale to be happy and for them to have a chance. Kale would see that. He had to.

As soon as Jason walked into the kitchen, Kale looked up from where he was helping Sophie can vegetables. "Are you ready for lunch already? It's a little early."

Kale's voice was warm and welcoming. Jason wondered

how it would sound in a few minutes. "No. Actually, I have some news to tell you. Would you join me in the garden?"

Kale must have taken in Jason's expression and the undercurrent of tension in his voice, because he sobered and stood, peering at Jason with concern in his eyes. "Of course. Is everything all right?"

"Yes, everything's fine. Just some news to share." Jason tried to comfort him with a smile, but it was a token gesture. They walked outside in silence.

Jason ushered them to a bench overlooking the vegetable patch. He sat with the envelope balanced on his legs and appraised Kale's handiwork. The garden had come to life; vibrant colors were all around them. This was what Kale had done. It was beautiful.

"You're starting to worry me." Kale reached out and placed a hand over one of Jason's. The warmth and weight were comforting. They gave Jason the courage to face Kale.

The face that looked back at him had aged since Jason had first seen it. Countless hours had been spent tracing every contour of that face, yet he'd never acknowledged how much it had changed. Sun and stress had aged it. In some places, the pigment had been permanently altered by his years laying railroad track. The pale green eyes had an ever-present shadow behind them, as if Kale were so used to worry and fear that his eyes were irreversibly wary. Still, Jason liked it better than any face in the world.

Those eyes peered at him with concern, wrinkles forming at the edges in heightened anticipation. It was time for Jason to face up to what he had done.

"You wanted to know where I went on my business trip. I was in Naiara. In Calea, to be precise."

"You what?" Kale withdrew his hand, and Jason missed it fiercely. He needed the anchor.

"Please, just listen." While Jason pulled the new title from the envelope, Kale rose and walked, as if trying to release some of his frustration. "Here." Jason stood and held out the title. "I solved our problem." Kale took the document. "You're no longer my slave. Look."

All the color drained from Kale's face. The sheer terror Jason saw was too reminiscent of the Kale he had found at the mill. Kale's eyes scanned the document. "You sold me? How could you? How is it better if I belong to," Kale squinted at the title, "P and C Enterprises?" His chest heaved with his labored breathing, causing his next words to come out in a whisper. "You've taken the only thing that mattered to me." He fell to his knees, looking like he was about to retch.

This was not going well at all. How could Jason mess this up so spectacularly? "No, no, no. Kale, listen." Jason hurried and knelt in front of Kale, dumping the contents of the envelope on the ground. "Here, these are the articles of incorporation." Jason thrust the papers toward Kale, but he was too shocked to take them. Jason scrambled to Kale's side and held the relevant page in front of him, pointing so Kale would see. "You're the sole owner of P and C. It's you. You own your own title."

Kale's face slowly turned to look at Jason, features twisted in confusion. "What? How? I don't understand."

"You're free. Or at least as free as I can make you while you're still in Arine. I had my attorneys establish a company with offices both here and in Calea. It's a dummy corporation really, just paper, but it has assets. I signed your title over to P and C and then signed the company over to you. If you want, you can go to Naiara. The prime minister is prepared to grant you citizenship. You'll be free there. But even if you don't go, the company that owns you is owned by you. You own yourself. It probably wouldn't hold up in court, but there's no reason for anyone to challenge it. And here." Jason picked up the bank book and handed it to him. Kale accepted it in a daze. "It's a bank account with all the money you would have earned since you were given to me, if you had been paid a wage. It's all there. You're free, Kale."

"I'm free?"

Poor Kale looked so confused, Jason couldn't help laughing. He took hold of Kale's head between his hands and gave him a fierce kiss. "Yes, you're free. You can do whatever you want. It's your choice. But, if you'll have me, I'll follow you wherever you want to go. This was the only way I could come to you and ask forgiveness for the way I wronged you."

Kale's eyes finally met his, and it seemed Jason's happiness poured into him. "You have it. You've had it for a while now. Do I have yours? I've done so much to hurt you, even after you've tried so hard. It was all my fault to begin with. Do I have your forgiveness?"

"Yes. Of course. Always."

Kale looked down and read the name on the bank book. "Kale Wadsworth?"

Jason gave a sheepish grin. "You needed a name, and I wanted to give you mine. You can change it if you want."

"No, Wadsworth is good. I'm honored." Kale looked back up, and his eyes were full of such sincere gratitude that it humbled Jason. "And I'm really free?"

"Yes." The reality was sinking in, and Jason loved seeing it.

"Gods." Kale launched himself at Jason, taking him in such a hard embrace that Jason had to catch himself. "I can't believe you did this for me. You gave me my freedom. And your name."

"Anything for you," Jason whispered. His voice began to catch, and hot tears drifted down his cheeks. He felt as if the sun was rising inside of him. Words couldn't describe what it felt like to do this for the man he loved. Now he would have to wait and see what Kale decided. Jason loved him with every fiber of his being. He was sure Kale would make him proud. He only hoped he would be permitted to be part of his life after Kale had established himself. He wanted more than anything to see Kale as a free man.

"Why are you crying?" Kale pulled away and wiped a tear

323

from Jason's face.

Jason mustered a smile. "Just thinking about the life you have ahead of you."

"Well, there's no sense wasting time dreaming about it. If you're still all right with moving, I think I'd like to see Naiara. Seems I should at least have the gratitude to accept their offer of citizenship."

"You don't have to have me there, Kale. You can do it on your own." Jason didn't want Kale under any illusions that his freedom was contingent on their relationship.

"I know. But what fucking good would freedom do me without you?" Kale paused, as if waiting for an answer. When Jason didn't give one, he continued. "I love you, you idiot. So much that I'm willing to admit that maybe you were right, and your plan wasn't so bad after all. But I want you with me to find out, if you think you can still tolerate me."

"Of course. It would be my pleasure." Jason couldn't remember life ever being more perfect. He wrapped his arms around Kale and kissed him again. This time, though, he went slow. He wanted to savor the taste of his free lover.

CHAPTER FIFTY-FIVE

Martin thought Jason might just burst. He looked like he had swallowed the sun, and the man beside him seemed to be soaking up the rays in awe. Kale was barely recognizable. It wasn't difficult to guess what this was all about. Jason had asked Martin and Sophie to join them for dinner in the dining room, and now they sat around the table as Jason and Kale stood flushed and bright-eyed before them with an announcement to make.

"I am happy to report that Kale has agreed to move to Naiara with me." Jason met Kale's eyes, and the two looked as if they were the only people in the room.

"Praise the gods. Of course he has!" Sophie vaulted up to embrace both men in a hug.

Martin kept decorum and stood to shake hands once Sophie had released them. "Congratulations, sir. And you too, Kale."

"Thank you." As Martin shook Kale's hand, he couldn't suppress the grin that broke out on his face. It was impossible not to get swept up in their happiness.

"And for the other bit of news." Jason cleared his throat, and Martin and Sophie took their seats. "Martin, when I went to Mr. Winslow's office on our way home from Calea, it was to have these finalized." Jason picked up a stack of papers from a side table and handed them to Martin. Martin didn't bother looking at them. He figured Jason would tell him what he needed to know. "I have instated you as president of Arlington Steel. I will retain my position as chief executive, but with me being out of the country, I need someone here who I can trust to run the company."

Martin's mouth hung open. It was entirely undignified, but he didn't know how to care. "What?"

"I've been getting that a lot lately." Jason and Kale shared a smile. "Well, what did you think was going to happen?"

Martin felt foolish. "I thought I would come with you and work for you there." Who would take care of Mr. Wadsworth? Looking at the beaming man with his arm around Jason, Martin knew Kale would do a better job than he ever had. Still, it had been Martin's job for almost three years. It wasn't easy to abandon it.

"Martin." Jason fixed him with a stern stare. "Your value extends far beyond scheduling appointments, writing correspondence, and generally keeping me out of trouble. This has been a long time coming. I'm not going to let you hide behind me any longer. You're going to step forward and show the world what I already know: you're as valuable a part of this business as I am."

Martin cleared his throat to compose himself. It was horrifying enough having already betrayed such a level of emotion at Jason and Kale's announcement. He would be mortified if he actually allowed a tear to pass. "But what about the Arlingtons?"

"They'll go along with it, or I'll resign."

"No!" Martin was stricken. He didn't want Jason making any ultimatums that he might have to follow through with.

"Don't worry, Martin. I had a little forethought on this. The contract with Conrad stipulates that I must stay at the head of the company. Otherwise he takes his business elsewhere. The Arlingtons won't be happy about this change in leadership, but they'll tolerate it for Conrad's money."

"I don't know what to say, sir. Thank you. I appreciate

your vote of confidence." All this time, he had assumed Jason didn't recognize what he was capable of. To be given this kind of trust, for Jason to put his reputation on the line for him—it was overwhelming. He was the president of Arlington Steel. Him. The secretary. It was a break in the social hierarchy he was willing to embrace.

"It's well earned." Jason patted Martin on the shoulder and took a seat at the table. Martin was relieved. He didn't think he could rely on his legs to support his weight. "You might as well stay here. I'll continue to employee Sophie. There's no point in this house sitting empty. That is, if you agree, Sophie."

"Of course, sir. I wouldn't dream of having it any other way." Sophie began to dish out the food that had been forgotten in the excitement.

Martin looked around him and knew that he would miss Kale and Jason terribly. This was his home, and they were his family. Instead of dwelling on thoughts that threatened tears, he raised his glass and toasted the brilliant future that lay ahead.

CHAPTER FIFTY-SIX

A lonely traveling bag sat in the middle of the blood red comforter. Kale surveyed the room. The wardrobe was empty of his clothes. The table was cleared of any personal effects. There was no evidence he had ever lived here. Every personal item he owned was in that bag. It only amounted to some clothes, his sketchpad and supplies, and a few books. And, of course, the documents giving him his freedom. He picked up the bag and headed to Jason's room.

He still couldn't believe he was going through with this. Life had been surreal ever since Jason had told him what his business in Calea had been. When Jason had told him, Kale thought he felt every emotion imaginable. Elation, fear, anger, hope. Given how much turmoil he had dealt with over the issue, it should have taken some time for him to come to a decision. But when he had looked into Jason's face, there was no controlling it. He couldn't say no.

"Do you need any help?" Kale stood in Jason's doorway, watching him pack a valise.

"Sure. Are you ready to go?" Jason glanced over his shoulder and spotted the one bag. "That's all you have?"

"Well, what else did you expect? I'm leaving all but a few of the books." They had decided that Jason would send for most of his belongings after they were settled, and the rest of Kale's books could wait until then.

"It's just a small bag is all. I feel like I'm over-packing now." Jason had his valise stuffed to the brim, and another suitcase leaned on the sofa.

"That's because you are. You can't take all that on horseback." Jason was paranoid about taking the train over the border now that he didn't have proof of ownership of Kale if something should happen. Kale knew it was paranoia —nothing would happen—but he shared enough of Jason's nerves that he hadn't protested when Jason insisted they take the train to a border town and then cross on horseback.

"Good point. I can leave the suitcase then. I'll just take the valise. All I need are clothes, toiletries, and my documents, right?"

"And this." Kale reached over Jason for the tin of grease on the nightstand and handed it to him.

Jason blushed as Kale knew he would. "Thanks." He packed it away and closed up the valise. "I guess we're ready."

They had said their goodbyes to Sophie and Martin the night before. There had been too many tears for Kale's comfort, so it was decided that Sophie and Martin would be out when they left. Kale was glad. He found it difficult just making his way downstairs and to the front door for the last time.

When the door closed behind him, he turned to take one last look at the townhouse. This was where he had been reunited with Jason, where he had healed, where he had learned to be free.

"You ready?" Jason laid a hand on his shoulder. Kale could see that he didn't want to rush him, but they needed to catch their train. Besides, the future waited for them, and this was their past.

"Yeah, I'm ready." The smile that greeted his answer made Kale think for the hundredth time that day that he was the luckiest man alive.

Jason hailed a cab. When it stopped, the cabbie jumped down and put their bags in the luggage compartment. "We're headed for the train station," Jason directed.

"Yes, sir."

Jason didn't wait for the cabbie to open the door. He did it himself and climbed in. The sight of that open door waiting for Kale stirred a fresh batch of nerves, and his right hand reached automatically for its familiar place on his pant leg. He caught himself. Instead, he reached into his pocket. It was time to end the nervous tic.

He looked down at the lock of hair as it emerged in his hand. He had put it in his pocket out of force of habit that morning. Closing his eyes, he still remembered the night he had clipped it. He could never have imagined then that he would be standing here, under these circumstances. Freedom hadn't even been within his realm of imagination. There was no way a slave could ever be this happy. But he wasn't a slave anymore. He was free. He had traveled so far from that sad night.

Opening his eyes, he saw that Jason watched him from the carriage. Their eyes met, and Kale knew that they never needed to be apart again. With one last glance at the lock of hair, he untied the string that bound it and released it. The breeze played with the hairs as it blew them down the street. Kale watched their journey for a few seconds before he climbed into the cab beside Jason.

"Why'd you do that?" Jason held his hand.

Kale thought a moment. "I don't need it anymore. That lock of hair was about hope and a dream. Now I have the real thing, and I'm never letting it go again."

Jason blushed, and Kale wondered how many times a day he could get Jason to do that. It would be fun to find out. He let himself submerge in the happiness he felt and surrendered to a grin that made his cheeks ache. He signaled the cabbie, and the carriage lurched forward. They had a train to catch.

CHAPTER FIFTY-SEVEN

Jason barely noticed the heat of the sun that bore down on them. The only indication of it was the annoying sweat dripping into his eyes. They were almost there.

The train ride had been pleasant enough, but he and Kale hadn't talked much. It was too big of an occasion, too much loomed in the future, and there was still the fear that something could go wrong. Those fears wouldn't be settled until they were safely across the border.

"There it is."

Jason looked to where Kale pointed. In the distance, there was a splash of blue in the sea of green. The river. All they had to do was cross it, and they would be in Naiara. Kale would truly and forever be free. On the other side of that river was a new start for both of them. Without meaning to, he broke his horse into a gallop. Naiara was calling to him with her promise of a future for him and Kale together.

When he pulled his horse up at the bank of the river, Kale was right beside him. "Do you think this is a good place to cross?" Jason deferred to Kale. Nothing but his concern for safety could have stopped him from plunging ahead.

"Yes, it'll do. Just take it slow. Trust your horse. She knows what she's doing."

Jason nodded and nudged his mare into the water. He was surprised at how calm Kale appeared. Of course, he rarely got ruffled. Ever since he had recovered from his experiences at the labor firm, he had gone back to his calm self. Recovered might be too strong a term. There were still nightmares Kale denied remembering and the occasional irrational flash of fear, but those were lessening.

They surpassed the halfway point, and Kale bolted ahead. The look on his face was wild. By the time Jason's horse was out of the river, Kale was jumping off his. He ran forward a few steps and then stopped, arms outstretched, breathing deeply. Jason tied the reins of both horses to a tree branch and went to stand next to Kale.

"I'm a free man. This is what it feels like to be free." Kale's voice was rich and solid. It was the voice Jason had fallen in love with. Except, instead of the undercurrent of tension that had been omnipresent since Kale had returned to him, there was joy. Pure joy. Jason had never heard that before, and he was immediately addicted to the sound.

Jason couldn't say a thing. All he could do was take in the scene before him. There was nothing more beautiful than the sight of Kale happy.

Suddenly, Kale turned to him and lifted him up in a crushing hug. Jason was aware of the world spinning as Kale's lips connected with his. It was the most joyful kiss he had ever experienced. The feel of Kale's tongue, confidently exploring his mouth like he was meant to be there, stamped out the remaining fears Jason harbored about the possibility of Kale's affections drifting.

Jason felt Kale's lips flatten into a smile against his and then slowly succumb to laughter. Jason joined him, and Kale stopped spinning. They stood entwined, laughing and drinking up the cheer between them. Jason thought it wasn't possible to be happier than he was at that moment. He was wrong.

"I love you, Jason."

Jason sobered. Was it possible? To hear that sweet voice say his name sent Jason to levels of elation he had never before known. He had given up on ever hearing his name on Kale's lips. He figured if he was going to say it, he would have already, after Jason had given him his title. To hear him say it now, though, Jason understood. Kale had needed to wait until he was truly a free man. It was worth the wait.

"I love you, too, Kale."

Kale caressed his face and then kissed him again. "Jason. Gods, it feels so good on my lips. Jason, thank you."

"My pleasure." They stood in silence for a moment. Then Jason said all he could think to say. "Where to?" Jason stepped back so Kale was free to move. He watched Kale's back as he surveyed the horizon. Appearing to come to a decision, Kale took the reins and began to walk his horse away from the river. Jason marveled at his confidence. He remembered years ago watching Kale sleep in a carriage on the way to his father's house and thinking about what kind of man Kale would be if he were free. He had imagined him as a leader of men, confident and sure. Before him stood that man, and he was in awe of him.

They would have to go to Calea soon to get everything squared away with Kale's citizenship, but they didn't have to stay there. They could take their time and explore, see where life took them. Jason was no fool. He suspected they would have problems along the way. Kale was bound to have some issues adjusting. But they would tackle them one at a time. And if the time ever came when Kale didn't want him anymore, he would deal with it then. For now, he was grateful for the privilege of spending his life with this man.

Jason was so caught up in his thoughts that he just stood holding his horse's reins, not even following Kale. The figure walking away stopped and came back to him, holding out his hand. Jason looked into Kale's face, so sure and steady, and took his hand. Together they walked forward into their new life. No matter what lay ahead, right now Jason had everything he had ever wanted.

Thank you for reading *Measure of Strength*.

If you liked *Measure of Strength*, please consider telling your friends about it or leaving a review.

To learn more about the author and sign up to be notified of new releases, visit CaethesFaron.com/Newsletter.